The Ghosts of Tupelo Landing

★ "This sequel shines."
—*Kirkus Reviews*, starred review

★ "The perspicacious Mo LoBeau is at it again!"
—*School Library Journal*, starred review

★ "Turnage's ability to create convincing characters
and her colorful use of language combine to make
this a fresh, droll, rewarding trip to Tupelo Landing."
—*Booklist*, starred review

★ "The budding detective has clearly taken to heart
something her foster mother always emphasizes:
'All the world's a stage, sugar, so hop on up there.'"
—*Publishers Weekly*, starred review

★ "We certainly hope there is more to
come from the Desperado Detectives."
—*BCCB*, starred review

"A rollicking sequel."
—*The Wall Street Journal*

A JUNIOR LIBRARY GUILD SELECTION
A SIBA "OKRA PICK" FOR BEST SOUTHERN-FLAVORED LITERATURE
A *BOOKPAGE* MOST ANTICIPATED CHILDREN'S AND TEENS BOOKS OF 2014

An infinite number of things can always go wrong.

"What do you think will happen tomorrow?" I asked the Colonel.

"I think we'll be good friends to Dale," he said. "It can't be easy to send your father to jail, even if he's Macon Johnson. And I think we'll tell the truth. Beyond that, it's a crap shoot. But *if* everything goes as expected, we all testify, the judge rules, and Macon goes to prison for a very long time."

Of course, nothing went as expected.

By sundown the next day, Dale and his mama needed a bodyguard, Lavender's life hung in the balance, and the Desperado Detective Agency had a case we'd never want in a million years.

It's hard to say when things started going sideways.

Other Books You May Enjoy

The Odds of Getting Even

by Sheila Turnage

PUFFIN BOOKS

PUFFIN BOOKS
An imprint of Penguin Random House LLC
375 Hudson Street
New York, New York 10014

First published in the United States of America by Kathy Dawson Books,
an imprint of Penguin Group (USA) LLC, 2015
Published by Puffin Books, an imprint of Penguin Random House LLC, 2016

THE LIBRARY OF CONGRESS HAS CATALOGED THE KATHY DAWSON BOOKS EDITION AS FOLLOWS:
Turnage, Sheila.
The odds of getting even / by Sheila Turnage.
p. cm.
Companion to: Three times lucky and The ghosts of Tupelo Landing.
Summary: "Desperado Detectives—aka Mo Lo Beau and her best friend Dale,
along with newly appointed intern, Harm Crenshaw—must take on a new case when
Dale's daddy goes on the lam just before his trial is about to start" —Provided by publisher.
ISBN 978-0-8037-3961-1 (hardback)
[1. Mystery and detective stories. 2. Fathers—Fiction. 3. Crime—Fiction.
4. Community life—North Carolina—Fiction. 5. North Carolina—Fiction.]
I. Title.
PZ7.T8488Od 2015
[Fic]—dc23
2015008293

Puffin Books ISBN 9780142426166

Printed in the United States of America

5 7 9 10 8 6 4

Designed by Jasmin Rubero

For Rodney, of course

Contents

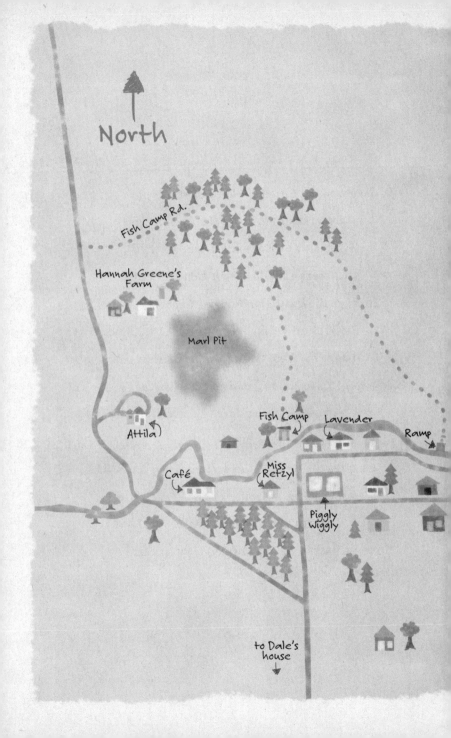

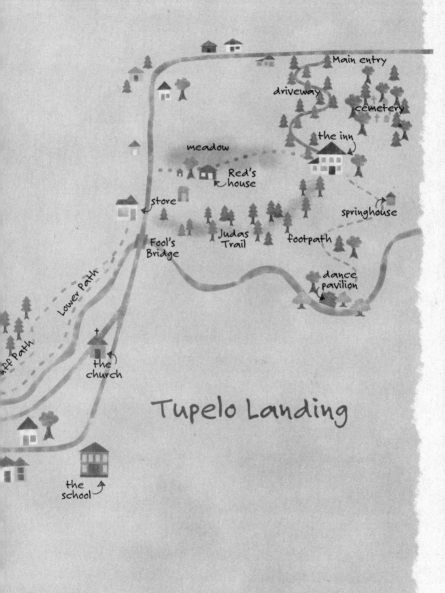

Main entry

driveway

cemetery

the inn

meadow

Red's house

store

springhouse

Judas Trail

footpath

Fool's Bridge

dance pavilion

Lower Path

ff Path

the church

Tupelo Landing

the school

Chapter 1
Tupelo Landing Inside Out

Mr. Macon Johnson's kidnapping trial snatched Tupelo Landing inside out sharp as Miss Rose snaps a pillowcase before she pins it to her wash line. It gave my best friend Dale Earnhardt Johnson III a triple shot of worry before the courthouse even opened its doors.

In the first place, Mr. Macon Johnson is Dale's daddy.

In the second place, Dale and me—cofounders of Desperado Detective Agency—helped put Mr. Macon behind bars last summer, making us top witnesses against him.

And in the third place, Dale's the first in his family ever to testify on the side of the law.

The idea of his daddy's trial twisted Dale so hard, he forgot how to sleep.

As for me—Miss Moses LoBeau, a sixth grader in her prime—I looked forward to sending Mr. Macon to the slammer where he belongs. Nobody hurts Dale without hearing from me. Nobody kidnaps the Colonel and Miss Lana without answering to me, either. The Colonel and

Miss Lana are my family-of-choice, and I am theirs. As best friend, Dale is family too.

Besides, a conviction would look good for Desperado Detective Agency.

"This case is a slam dunk," I reminded the Colonel the day before the trial. "Dale and me *heard* Mr. Macon confess." He closed the trunk of our vintage Underbird (which used to be a Thunderbird until the *T* and *H* fell off) and sent the Piggly Wiggly grocery cart careening across the parking lot.

"A slam dunk?" The Colonel snorted. "There's no such thing, Mo. An infinite number of things can always go wrong."

The Colonel's handsome in a rugged, don't-mess-with-me way. He wears his hair short and bristly and his muscles strong and lean. "Fasten your seat belt, Soldier. And don't get your hopes up over this trial."

We zipped through Tupelo Landing, NC—population 148—and headed for the café we run with Miss Lana, at the edge of town.

"Cat," I said, reaching across the Colonel's arm and hitting the horn. An orange cat shot to the sidewalk. The Colonel likes to pretend he wouldn't have swerved.

I know better.

I waved at Dale's brother, Lavender, the dashing racecar driver I will go out with in just seven more years, as he tooled by in his blue 1955 GMC pickup truck. Miss Lana says nobody's perfect. I say Lavender proves her wrong.

"What do you think will happen tomorrow?" I asked the Colonel.

"I think we'll be good friends to Dale," he said. "It can't be easy to send your father to jail, even if he's Macon Johnson. And I think we'll tell the truth. Beyond that, it's a crap shoot. But *if* everything goes as expected, we all testify, the judge rules, and Macon goes to prison for a very long time."

Of course, nothing went as expected.

By sundown the next day, Dale and his mama needed a bodyguard, Lavender's life hung in the balance, and the Desperado Detective Agency had a case we'd never want in a million years.

It's hard to say when things started going sideways.

Life still felt on track as the Colonel and me lugged our groceries around the side of the café and into our home in the back half of our building. We seemed on track an hour later when Miss Lana peeked in the door to my flat—which my enemies say is nothing but a closed-in side porch opening off our living room.

"Do you have your courtroom outfit ready, sugar?"

Miss Lana asked, smoothing her Marilyn Monroe wig. Costuming counts with Miss Lana, a former child star of the Charleston community theater. So do staging and dramatic pauses.

"Yes ma'am," I said, nodding to my rocking chair. I'd laid out my new blue jeans and my clean-enough red sweater. "I'm going as a normal sixth grader," I added as my phone jangled.

She sashayed off as I scooped up the receiver. "Desperado Detective Agency. Felonies are our delight, lost pets our duty. How may we assist you?"

"Mo, it's me. Dale." Like I wouldn't recognize my best friend's voice. "Meet me outside. Daddy's invited us over, but we ain't got much time."

Over would be to the county jail.

"Harm's going too," he said. Harm, who's new in town, is my best friend next to Dale.

I hesitated. Miss Lana says be sensitive and the Colonel says tell the truth. It can be a mind-pretzeling combination. "No thank you to visiting your mean-as-a-snake daddy, but I appreciate the invitation. And I can't believe Miss Rose is taking you to county lockup," I added.

"Mama's not taking me," Dale said. "Lavender is."

Lavender?

"I'll get my jacket," I replied, and hung up the phone.

˙˙*˙*

Five minutes later Lavender wheeled his graceful old pickup truck into our parking lot. Lanky Harm Crenshaw, who has manners, hopped out and held the door for me. "Afternoon, LoBeau," he said, swinging his tattered gray scarf over his shoulder.

Harm's tall for a sixth grader. Lately he's been too fashionable to wear a coat, preferring to go scarf-and-sweater for a manly look. If Harm was old enough to shave, he wouldn't. Ever since him and Dale formed a singing group, he's trying to be popular with girls older than him.

He's already popular with me. "Hey yourself, Harm Crenshaw."

I peered inside the cab. "Excuse me, Dale. You're in my seat." Dale rolled his eyes, which are as blue as Lavender's, and slid out. Even his freckles looked peeved.

I slipped in next to Lavender, who smelled like motor oil. Lavender will one day be NASCAR famous. Until then, he fixes things. Dale and Harm crowded in and slammed the door. If we fit any tighter, we'd have to alternate breathing.

"What's Mr. Macon want?" I asked.

"Nothing good," Lavender said, heading through town. "I wish you'd change your mind about visiting him, little brother."

Dale shook his head. "I got things to ask. Some I can ask you and the Colonel, but some just Daddy knows. This is my last chance." He peeked at Lavender. "I wish you'd come. It's mostly you he wants to see. He says it's important."

Lavender took the truck through her gears smooth as water. "Sorry, Dale. Whatever Macon wants, I don't have it anymore." He poked at a newspaper on the dash. "You Desperados made the paper again."

Harm read the story out loud:

MACON JOHNSON TRIAL OPENS TOMORROW

Small-time crook Macon Johnson goes to trial tomorrow. He's accused of helping Robert Slate and Deputy Marla Everette kidnap two of Tupelo Landing's citizens—Miss Lana and the Colonel, of café fame.

Eleven-year-olds Mo LoBeau and Dale Earnhardt Johnson III of Desperado Detective Agency helped capture Macon Johnson, and are top witnesses against him.

"Daddy's mean to me and Mama, and people say we're better off with him in jail. But don't write that down," Dale told reporters at the time of the arrest. "I only turned Daddy in because he confessed to the kidnapping."

Mo had a different take: "I can't wait to testify. I'll get even with Mr. Macon if it's the last thing I do."

The Desperados also captured Deputy Marla Everette and Robert Slate, who will stand trial next year. Their list of alleged crimes includes breaking and entering, bank robbery, kidnapping, and murder.

Dale slumped. "It sounds bad when you read it in that newspaper voice."

We wheeled into the jail's parking lot.

"Dale, if you're determined to do this, I'll wait right here for you," Lavender said, cutting the ignition. "I know I've said it before, but I wish you wouldn't go in there. Not this time, little brother."

"I got to," Dale said. Dale can be stubborn. He looked at Harm and me. "Daddy got this set up special for us. Visiting hours are almost over. Let's roll."

Mr. Macon sat in the cafeteria-style visiting room, tense as a snarl of wire. Dale took a seat across from him. Harm and me sat, flanking Dale like bodyguards.

"Thanks for calling," Dale said. "I been wanting to talk. I guess my messages didn't get through." He slipped a paper from his pocket.

I peeked over. At the top it said, Things to Ask. Underneath lay a haphazard spatter of words and squiggles.

Dale ain't a linear thinker.

? Things to Ask

by Dale

#1 House!
Keeping safe
$$$ → ~~Security system~~
guineas!

Fast, loud, best *Watch dog that is not a Watch dog #3

Watch out Macon's enemies ??. WHO?!

? ? Build them a house or fence?
Coyotes/bobcats?
What else?? ★
? ? repairs? Who?
WHAT ELSE?

QUEEN ELIZABETH

special foods? YOGA
vet if needed? Who?
coyotes? Danger?

scarecrows (but mostly $) for trade) $

IDEAS FOR MONEY?
xx No child support? xx
my music — on the verge
♪♫♩ = $$$ (Parties?$)
mama's tours of farm
winter produce — collards
sweet potatoes

*Uncle Austin?? safe?

The Colonel Mr. Red
Lavender.

Pinto = Lazarus.
Lavender.
Nevermind.

★ Newton!! Depressed?!
How to help?!! (Cold-blooded)

Court. Testify.
Pre-forgive. It would mean a lot

Mam
Bill Glas
Where do I
Politeness?

Mr. Macon shot a look at the door. "Where's Lavender? It's Lavender I need to talk to, not you."

Miss Lana says never plunge into business without exchanging pleasantries.

I smiled at Mr. Macon, who pretty much hates me. "I love what you've done with the place," I said. "Is that new paint? Because the gray tones really make your orange jumpsuit pop. As for Lavender, he can't make it due to the fact that he's not coming. Dale showed up for you."

"Tell Lavender to get in here. It's important."

"Why?"

"Because I said so."

We didn't move. I watched Mr. Macon's face—all angles and planes, like clay cut with a knife.

His eyes glittered. "Dale, how's your mama?"

"She's good," Dale said, studying his note. "It's just me and her now. I'm man of the house, and I got questions."

Dale? The second-smallest kid in sixth grade? The man of the house?

Dale looked into his father's eyes. "If you go away, Mama and me won't have your get-even reputation to keep us safe anymore. I thought about getting a security system, but they cost, so I traded for guinea fowl instead. Guineas shriek every time anything moves. *You* know birds: We got coyotes running at night, do I need to—"

"Stupid plan," Mr. Macon said, his voice razor-quick. He leaned forward. "I hear Lavender has a new racecar. Tell him to come talk to me about it."

He's going away for fifteen years and he wants to talk racecars?

"Time's running out, Dale," Harm whispered, glancing at the clock.

Dale sighed and skipped to the last item on his list. "Good luck in court tomorrow, Daddy," he said. "I hope they don't call my name to testify, but if they do, I came here to ask you to pre-forgive me. It would mean a lot."

Mr. Macon took a cigarette from behind his ear and tapped the filter on the table. "Life's about getting, and then about keeping. I take care of what's mine. I hoped you'd be man enough to do the same by the time you got on that witness stand, but you always have been a mama's boy." He shrugged. "Do what you got to tomorrow, *boy*. But remember this: I won't be in here forever."

Harm stood up. "That sounds like a threat."

"Does it?" Mr. Macon asked, rising. Harm pushed in front of Dale and me, his hands balled into fists, and the guard bustled over.

"Time to go, folks," the guard said. "Sorry, Macon."

Mr. Macon glared at Dale. "It's okay, Earl. I'm done with him."

Mr. Macon knows how to make words into knives and he knows where to slice. My hate for him blossomed all over again. "Is that why you called Dale over here?" I asked. "To bully him?"

"I didn't call for him," he said, walking to the door. "I want Lavender. Tell him to see me. If he won't come, tell him he'd better watch his back."

"What does *that* mean?" I demanded.

"Shut your motor mouth and do what I say."

My temper went off like the Fourth of July. "You'll get yours tomorrow!" I shouted. "Me and my motor mouth will make sure of it."

His steps echoed down the hall.

My temper's a work-in-progress. So far it's all work and no progress.

Dale slipped his list in his pocket. "I'm sorry, Dale," I said, my anger cooling like a kettle taken off a stove. "He just makes me so mad, and . . ."

"I know," Dale said. "Daddy brings out the worst in people. Also in dogs. It's a reverse talent he's got."

"Forget about him," Harm said, but of course Dale couldn't.

Back in the truck, Dale sat silent as sawdust while Harm and me filled Lavender in.

"Mo's right. He's a bully," Lavender told Dale. "We Johnson men aren't afraid of bullies."

"I am," Dale said. "A little bit."

"I'll be there tomorrow. So will the Colonel." Lavender studied Dale's face. "And as for being a mama's boy . . ." Lavender gave him a gentle shove. "We're nothing like Macon. I'd rather be Rose's son than Macon's boy any day of the week."

That night I plucked the *Piggly Wiggly Chronicles* Volume 7 from my bookshelf, hopped into bed, and picked up my pen. The *Chronicles* go back to my kindergarten days, when I first started writing to the Upstream Mother who lost me in a hurricane flood on the day I was born. I used to think I'd find her. Now I mostly write to keep track of my life, but you never know—she could show up.

> Dear Upstream Mother,
> Dale and me testify against Mr. Macon tomorrow, and I'll be glad to see him go. Mr. Macon's the kind of mean you can taste in the back of your mouth.
> Why Miss Rose ever married him remains a mystery. Miss Lana says time and drink change people, and he used to be a better man.
> Today he threatened Lavender.

I tossed my pen onto my book. I like writing to my Upstream Mother, but sometimes I need immediate answers. I hopped up and padded into the living room.

The Colonel and Miss Lana dozed on Miss Lana's curlicue Victorian settee, her head resting against his shoulder. "Greetings," I said, and they jumped like startled cats.

"Mo," Miss Lana said, blinking. "Can't you sleep?"

I hesitated. "Miss Lana, I know you like me to be sensitive, so you'll be glad to know Harm and me kept Dale company over at Mr. Macon's place today."

"You went to the *jailhouse?*" Miss Lana said, frowning.

"The guard let us in. He likes Mr. Macon." I looked at the Colonel, who had somehow gone to full attention without moving a muscle. "Mr. Macon threatened Lavender. But when we told Lavender, he shrugged it off."

The Colonel sat up. "Threatened him how?"

"He said, 'If Lavender won't come see me, tell him to watch his back.'"

The Colonel frowned. "Stay away from Macon, Soldier. I'll talk to Lavender tomorrow."

"Yes, sir. About tomorrow. Dale's scared . . ."

"I'm taking care of things," he said, and my fear melted like an early snow. He stretched his wiry arms over his head. "Lights out, Soldier. We're fine."

I didn't know it then, but things were already going sideways.

Chapter 2
Trial Day

The next morning—Trial Day—I cranked up the café radiators at six a.m. Our string of Thanksgiving lights glowed a soft swag of halos against the café windows.

Dale's dog, Queen Elizabeth II, sauntered across the room and collapsed near the jukebox. She's been given to sinking spells lately—for reasons Dale and me were keeping Top Secret until school the next day.

"Do I *have* to testify? Are you sure?" Dale asked, trailing the Colonel from the kitchen. "Because I might throw up. Fifteen years in prison seems so long. Daddy's not used to hard time, just lots of little time strung together like a nice necklace. Do you think he can get off?"

Only Dale can accessorize with jail time.

The Colonel answered patient as rain. "Even if Macon gets time, he'll be all right. You and Rose will be too. You have me and Lana, you have Lavender and Mo. As for Macon going free, if the defense can create a *reasonable doubt* of his guilt, he'll walk."

"Can that happen?" Dale asked as I plugged in the jukebox.

"No," I muttered under my breath.

"Anything can happen, Dale," the Colonel replied. "But don't get your hopes up."

Don't get your hopes up? That's the same advice he gave me, only pointed in the opposite direction.

The parking lot stood bumper-to-bumper, cars and trucks bellowing clouds of steam as townsfolk waited for us to open. "Surrounded by wolves," the Colonel muttered, tying his white chef's apron over his court clothes—gray pants, white shirt, and his light-up Charleston tie from a couple Christmases back.

Miss Lana tucked a strand of her glossy Ava Gardner wig behind her ear and wrote the day's specials on the chalkboard. Ava Gardner, an old Hollywood star, grew up just down the road. Miss Lana believes in going local. "Court will be standing room only—which means standing room only here too," she said.

"We should put gossip on the menu," the Colonel muttered. "We'd make a fortune." He had a point.

If Tupelo Landing was a country, gossip would be our national sport.

"Ready, sir?" I asked, heading for the door.

The Colonel studied Dale, his brown eyes serious. "Are you sure, Dale? We don't have to open today."

Not open? My plaid sneakers squeaked to a halt on the clean tile floor.

Dale nodded, stubborn as a brick. "I want everything ordinary even if it ain't."

Miss Lana smoothed her broad-shouldered, tuck-waisted 1940s-style suit. "Places," she called. The Colonel grabbed the coffeepot. Dale snagged an order pad. I positioned myself by the door. "Action!"

I flipped the CLOSED sign.

Truck and car doors swung open, spewing people across the parking lot. A white van yawned and a gaggle of women in bright-colored coats spilled into the crowd. Friends and neighbors surged over the gravel like a hungry, ragged wave and poured into our tiny café, clattering across the tiles, peeling off overcoats and scarves, thumping down around red Formica tables and along the counter.

Out on the highway, a motorcycle slowed to let two cars ease into the lot, and then gunned its engine down the road.

"Welcome," I shouted over the hubbub. "No pushing. Old people and children first. Get back, Jake and Jimmy Exum. You ain't old or young, that's why they call it middle school. Let Hannah Greene's little sister through."

Little Agnes Greene, a kindergarten kid, squirted through the crowd. "Mo, I got a major symptom of dehydration," she said, her small face pinched with worry.

"Water coming up," I said, taking her hand and leading her to a table. "Hey, Hannah," I shouted to her big sister. "I'm hydrating Little Agnes on table number two."

Little Agnes, named for her aunt Big Agnes, went hypochondriac just after Halloween when Hannah read her bedtime stories out of a medical book. Now Agnes believes she catches every disease blowing in the wind. Last Wednesday she thought she had smallpox.

Hannah rushed to her sister as Detective Joe Starr pulled up in his Impala and eased into a skinny parking spot. He and my teacher, Priscilla Retzyl, slipped in to stake out a window table.

I trotted over with waters. "I hope you're coming to court today," I told Miss Retzyl. "Dale and me are testifying. Feel free to give us Extra Credit." She smiled her Not in This Lifetime smile as my archenemy, Anna Celeste Simpson, flounced through the door—a swirl of blond hair, braces, and weasel-esque brown eyes.

"Morning Mo-ron," she said.

"*Attila.*"

She curled her lip and grabbed a window table.

Out of the corner of my eye, I saw a flash of pale blue hair at the door. "Make way for elders!" I called as Grandmother Miss Lacy Thornton strolled through the door in a trim navy blue outfit.

"Thank you, dear," she said, stifling a yawn and taking her regular stool at the counter. She smiled at me over her bifocals. "I barely slept a wink, thanks to the clunking and bumping of my old radiators. But you're looking lovely, Mo."

I smoothed my jeans and red V-neck sweater. "Court clothes," I explained.

"Primary colors," she replied. "Very trustworthy." I poured her water and tried to look like I knew what she meant. "Just toast and coffee, please." The Colonel poured her coffee, grabbed her order, and headed for the kitchen.

"Everybody settle down," I shouted, loading my tray with waters.

Naturally Tupelo Landing's Trial of the Century was the topic du jour.

The Azalea Women, aka the Uptown Garden Club, wedged through the crowd elbow to elbow like a dumpy rugby team and grabbed a table near the jukebox. "I hear Hanging Judge Wilkins has come to Willow Green for the trial," one of them said.

Unlike Tupelo Landing, nearby Willow Green has its own courthouse. Also a traffic light and a hill. Tupelo Landing has a school, a Piggly Wiggly, the historic inn owned by Miss Lana and Grandmother Miss Lacy Thornton, and the café.

A silver bike flashed by the window and Harm Crenshaw hopped off. "Morning everybody," he called, swaggering in and unwinding his scarf.

"Hey," Dale called. Harm's lopsided grin lifted Dale's tension like sunshine lifts fog. Outside, curly-headed Sally Amanda Jones, Dale's girlfriend-in-waiting, walked briskly toward the door, her red Piggly Wiggly sunglasses over her eyes and her breath steaming in the cold.

"Hello, Dale," she said, shrugging out of her plush lavender jacket.

"Hey Salamander," Dale said. "I knew you'd be here for me."

She blushed and took a table. Sal loves Dale like smoke loves fire.

I turned back to the Azalea Women. "Welcome and thank you in advance for your generous tips." Generous tips equals a flat-out lie, but like Miss Lana says, you don't stop pitching just because nobody's swinging. I draped a paper napkin over my arm. "Today, our Get Out of Jail Free Delight features Free-Range Eggs, Potatoes at Large, and Bacon a la Parole. We also got the Colonel's famous Tofu Incognito— a vegan delight featuring tofu scrambled up to look like somebody else. A Special runs six dollars and includes a basket of All Rise Biscuits. May I take your order?"

"Get Out of Jail and coffee," they chorused. "How's Dale holding up?"

Dale and me been practicing that question all week.

"Hang on while I check, *s'il vous plais*," I said. Thanks to Miss Lana, I speak excellent Tupelo French. This can lead to bigger tips or total confusion, depending. "Hey Dale," I shouted. "How *vous* holding up?"

The café swiveled toward Dale.

"Hey," he said, his expression blank as a block of cheese.

I cued him up. "Dale's holding up *trés bon*, right Dale?"

"Right," he said, looking relieved. "I'm holding up real *bon*. So's Mama. In my family we believe everyone's innocent until captured."

Harm winced.

An Azalea Woman sniffed. "Such strong convictions."

"Yes," Dale said, sending a saucer of toast spinning down the counter. "But mostly our convictions are misdemeanors. Daddy's our first Class C felony."

The Azalea Women snickered. I crumpled their order and stuffed it in my pocket.

Mayor Little darted through the door. "Good morning, fellow citizens," he called, shrugging out of his overcoat and smoothing his orange tie over his round belly. "Dale, my heartfelt condolences *or* enthusiastic backslaps, depending on how things go today. No matter which way the legal wind blows, you can count on me."

"Thank you," Dale said, very dignified.

Anna Celeste Simpson sauntered to the jukebox and dropped in a handful of change. Elvis Presley's "Jailhouse Rock" blasted across the café.

I hate Anna Celeste Simpson.

Jimmy and Jake Exum—jeans, plaid shirts, scant eyebrows—jumped to their feet as the Colonel shot through the kitchen door. "No dancing," the Colonel shouted. Jake and Jimmy sat back down. The Colonel stalked across the café and yanked the jukebox's plug out of the wall. Elvis oozed to silence.

Grandmother Miss Lacy's gaze traveled from Attila, to Harm, to Sal. Then to Hannah. "What on earth?" she said, as if she'd just noticed us. "Why aren't you children getting ready for school? You're not all witnesses."

"Mayoral Decree," Dale said, carrying a sandwich to Queen Elizabeth.

Mayor Little patted his lips with a napkin. "You didn't hear, Miss Thornton? I issued my first decree. Mother's tickled pink. Allow me." He headed for his notice on the bulletin board, his buffed burgundy loafers tip-tip-tipping across the tile. "Attention, citizens," he said. "My decree again, by popular demand."

Mayoral Decree

WHEREAS half the town's on the witness list in Macon Johnson's trial, and the other half is dying to see what happens, I—Mayor Clayburn Little—

decree Tupelo Landing closed on Trial Day. The
Colonel can do as he pleases with the café, as there
is no way to stop him.

Vote Mayor Clayburn Little! The mayor who cares!

"I didn't know the mayor could issue a decree," Grandmother Miss Lacy murmured as the Colonel backed in from the kitchen with a load of clean coffee cups.

"He can't," the Colonel said.

The big-haired twins—Crissy and Missy—pushed into the crowded café and zeroed in on the Exum boys' table. At nineteen, the twins have reached and maybe surpassed their full potential. "Excuse us while you move, and thank you," Crissy said. Jimmy and Jake jumped up. Harm gulped, his eyes glued to the twins.

Harm's been thinking of talking to the twins for a couple weeks. For Harm, talking to them is like climbing Mount Everest. He craves the fame and excitement, but mostly he wants to do it because they're there.

"Dare you," Dale said.

Excellent. If anything could take Dale's mind off the trial, this would.

"Double dare you," I added. "But I hope you're wearing Kevlar beneath that sweater, because you're getting shot down."

Harm chugged over to the twins' table. "Morning, ladies," he said, giving them a crooked smile and pushing the hair from his eyes. "Crenshaw. Harm Crenshaw, brother of the noted racecar driver Flick Crenshaw."

"I can't believe he invoked the name of Flick," Dale whispered.

Flick Crenshaw's the dirtiest racer on the circuit. He about killed Lavender last summer by spinning him into a speedway wall. The twins, who keep Lavender company until I'm old enough for dating, saw Flick do it. Now they stared at Harm like he was a cat-gift on their doormat.

"Close your eyes, Dale," I said. "This could be ugly."

"Yeah," Dale said, sounding happy for the first time in days.

Harm took a deep breath. "You're looking doubly fine today," he told the twins, hooking his thumbs in his pants pockets. The twins frowned. "*Doubly* fine. Because you're twins," he explained.

They eyed him up and down. "He's cute even if he is Flick's brother, isn't he, Missy? You're cute," Crissy told him.

"I am?" Harm said, his voice cracking. "I mean, thanks."

Crissy tilted her head. "But you're not mature enough to talk to us," she continued, shifting her gaze to her fingernails. "We're tossing you back like the minnow you are." Dale snickered. "Maybe we'll reel you in when you grow up," she added.

Harm hesitated. Then he gave them a wink. "Catch me later, then," he said, and strolled away.

"Smooth," Dale said as Harm walked by, grinning.

Smooth? In what universe?

"Pathetic," I told him.

"Yeah, but I did it," he said, grabbing an apron. "How can I help?"

My answer was shattered by the squall of tires on the highway, a flash in the parking lot, and a spray of fine gravel on the café windows. Little Agnes shrieked. I reached a window just in time to see a red motorcycle skid through the parked cars, hit a hole, and fly into the air.

The café gasped as the bike landed nose-down, flipping the driver over the handlebars. The driver skidded by, sank a boot heel into the gravel, and popped up to run crazy-legged through the parking lot, arms flailing.

"No! Stop!" Little Agnes shrieked, covering her eyes.

The biker smacked square into the back of the Colonel's Underbird and collapsed facedown across the trunk, legs splayed, still as a bug on a windshield. Papers drifted out of his saddlebag, settling across the parking lot.

"My stars," Grandmother Miss Lacy whispered. "Is he dead?"

"I have a headache," Little Agnes whispered in the silence.

The Colonel and Detective Joe Starr charged the door. "Stay put," Starr said.

We rushed to the window to watch the Colonel and Detective Starr cross the parking lot—trotting at first, then slowing like men who didn't want to see what they were about to see. The driver didn't move. Behind me, Dale whispered a prayer.

Starr bent to peek beneath the heavy helmet and reached for the driver's wrist—and a pulse.

"Oh, no," Sal said, tears pooling in her voice.

The driver jerked away from Starr, and an Azalea Woman cackled like a startled hen. The café answered with a ragged flutter of nervous chuckles. "Not passé at all," the mayor gasped, fanning his face with his hands.

The biker slid onto unsteady legs. The Colonel and Starr grabbed his arms—one on each side—and slowly walked him toward the café door.

The trio stepped inside.

The motorcyclist slipped off the heavy black helmet and shook out a mane of long, curly red hair. "Hello everybody, I'm Capers Dylan," she said with a weak smile. "Is there a mechanic in the house?"

Chapter 3
Capers Dylan

"Mechanic?" the mayor cried. "Do we have one?"

Do we have a mechanic?

Lavender, who's destined for NASCAR glory, keeps every car in town rolling, including the mayor's dented Jeep. "Lavender's world class with the un-running. He can fix anything," I said as my classmate Thessalonians Thompson—orange hair, round face—pushed through the door.

"What's going on?" Thes asked.

"A beautiful motorcyclist just plummeted into our midst miraculously unharmed," Mayor Little said. "I can't wait to tell Mother. Take off your hat, young man."

Thes swiped his gray plaid cap off. Capers Dylan's eyes went red. She sneezed. So did Little Agnes. "You must have a cat," Capers said, and sneezed again.

"That depends," Thes said, his green eyes shifty. "What has he done?" He took a seat at the counter. "Hey, Mo. A fried egg sandwich with a side of okra. We got a twenty percent chance of rain. And I'd love to go to a movie with you."

Thes is a weather freak. "Movies ain't on the menu," I said.

Capers Dylan sank into a chair and unzipped her black leather jacket, which looked like a squirrel had gnawed off most of the left sleeve.

"You're lucky you weren't bad hurt," Sal told her.

Capers Dylan flashed a wide smile. "I'm lucky I didn't get killed. And you are?"

"Sally Amanda Jones. Sal for short."

"Nice to meet you, Sal for short," Capers replied.

I studied her face. Pale skin, soft freckles across broad cheekbones. She had just enough crook in her nose to make her face interesting.

"Actually, Ms. Dylan," Detective Starr said, surveying the parking lot, "you're *very* lucky you didn't get killed. You skidded down the only safe passage through those cars."

"How you popped to your feet, I will never know," an Azalea Woman said.

Miss Lana set a cup of coffee on Capers's table. "I'm Lana," she said. "We spoke on the phone. You're our inn's first guest."

Capers beamed. "Pleased to meet you. I'm here to

cover Macon Johnson's trial for the *Greensboro Gazette*."

The trial! I looked at the 7UP clock. Seven twenty-five a.m.

"A reporter?" the Colonel said, his voice backing up like a cat with wet paws. The Colonel hates reporters. Also law enforcement, health inspectors, and busybodies.

"Why cover Daddy's trial?" Dale asked. "He's mashed potatoes."

"He means small potatoes," I said.

She winked at Dale. "You must be Dale Earnhardt Johnson III."

"Don't say anything else," I warned. "She's researched you."

"And that would make *you* Mo LoBeau," she said, stirring cream into her coffee. "The other half of Desperado Detectives."

As a detective, I ain't used to people knowing more about me than I know about them. So far, I didn't like it. "Capers Dylan. Odd name," I replied.

Her laugh spattered like rain against a pie tin, taking in the entire café. "My mother loved recycling last names and putting them first. It's a Charleston tradition," she said, rubbing her elbow. "Please, everybody: Call me Capers."

Miss Lana's face lit up. "You're from Charleston too?

Let me get you some ice for that elbow." Capers's gaze drifted to the Colonel's sign, above the coffeemaker.

The Colonel—Attorney-of-Sorts

No License, No Guarantees

Questions Taken Thursday Afternoons Only

The way she took it in stride, I knew she'd researched the Colonel too.

"Miss Dylan," Detective Starr said, "what happened out there?" He flipped open the notepad he keeps in his shirt pocket.

Was he giving her a near-death ticket?

"Dale and me wonder too," I said, opening my order pad and picking up my pen.

Capers took in the café faces. "Did anybody see the accident?" We shook our heads. "Well, let's see. A car passed too close. Almost blew me off the road."

Little Agnes frowned. "No. You fell down all by yourself."

"Hush, Agnes," the mayor said. "A near lethal blow-by. Scandalous. Must have been an out-of-towner. We Tupelites pride ourselves on lawliness. Well," he added, "Dale's family is a notable exception, but their farm's outside the town limits."

"Can you describe the car?" I asked.

"A sedan," she said. "Blue, black? I don't know. And I didn't get a license plate number. But I'm sure my insurance will cover any damages to your cars or . . . whatever. If it doesn't, I will." The café relaxed. In Tupelo Landing, we pay our bills unless we're Macon Johnson.

Her pretty smile quivered and her eyes flooded. "Sorry, folks. I'm not normally a crier. . . . I wish I could be more help."

Miss Lana says tears are the universal solvent. It could be true. Harm went into full meltdown. "Crenshaw. Harm Crenshaw," he said. "I'm willing to let you slide."

Let her *slide*?

"Harm, sit down," Miss Retzyl snapped. Harm folded into the closest seat and put his hands on the table. "Miss Dylan, have we met? You seem so familiar . . ."

Capers shook her head. "Like I said, I'm here to cover Macon Johnson's trial, which ties into a larger trial I'm covering later on."

"The trial of the murderer Robert Slate," I guessed. "Captured by Desperado Detectives last summer along with his ugly girlfriend, Deputy Marla Everette."

She laughed. "Well, I've interviewed Marla Everette and I don't find her all *that* ugly. Slate's as ugly as they come." She smiled at Miss Lana. "If you don't mind, I'll just catch my breath—and hope for a ride to the courthouse."

Miss Lana, who doesn't drive as a public courtesy,

elbowed the Colonel. "Colonel, she needs a ride. Where are your manners?"

"Perhaps I left them in the kitchen," he muttered. "I'll check."

The kitchen door swung closed behind him.

Mayor Little smoothed his tie. "Miss Dylan, I'd be glad to squire you about. We'll pick up Mother on our way. She'll enjoy meeting you." A shiver tiptoed up my spine. Myrt Little's the oldest, meanest woman in Tupelo Landing. Her tongue's sharp enough to shred a cabbage at twenty paces.

Capers smiled. "And I'd be grateful for a good mechanic," she said.

"I'll call Lavender and see if he can work you into his schedule," I told her, heading for the phone.

Grandmother Miss Lacy slipped a ten beneath her plate. "Remind him about my boiler, would you, dear?" she asked. "It clunks and bangs every year this time, but it does rattle my nerves."

"I told you to replace that thing last year," the Colonel shouted from the kitchen.

"I'll remind him," I told Grandmother Miss Lacy. Lavender can fix anything, except maybe a broken heart. "Lavender's never too busy for me and mine."

* ⋆ * ⋆ *

Fifteen minutes later, Lavender pulled into the parking lot, the morning sun golden in his hair. He headed for the motorcycle as Capers zipped what was left of her jacket and strolled toward the door.

Dale checked the clock. "Guess I can't put it off any longer," he said. He tiptoed to Queen Elizabeth and tenderly shook her awake.

"We'll be okay, Desperado," I told him. He nodded but didn't meet my eyes.

Testifying will break Dale's heart, I thought. And Dale's heart is my jurisdiction.

I made an executive decision. I sailed to the table Sal shared with Skeeter—tall, glasses, freckles the color of fresh-sliced luncheon meat. "If I testify first, maybe they won't need to call Dale," I whispered. Skeeter stopped peppering her eggs. "I got eight dollars in tips saved up. Get the prosecution to call me first and it's yours."

Sal with her calculator brain and Skeeter with her law books pull strings most people don't even know exist. Miss Lana says they'll run the country one day. The Colonel says he can't wait.

"We'll see what we can do," Skeeter said as an Azalea Woman headed to the window. Outside, Capers scooped up her scattered papers and Lavender examined the motorcycle.

The Azalea Woman narrowed her eyes. "What do you think?"

"I think she's pretty," Harm said.

"Nice dye job," Crissy said. "Missy and me can do that color if anybody's interested."

Dale shrugged into his jacket. "I don't like her."

"Dale!" Miss Lana said. "She's from Charleston. Give her the benefit of the doubt." Miss Lana always says give people the benefit of the doubt. The Colonel says give *yourself* the benefit of your doubts, which you get for a reason.

"I'm going home to change," Dale said, and gave Harm a shy smile. "Thanks for coming today, it means a lot to me. You too, Salamander."

Sal knocked over her milk.

"Come on, Liz," he called, heading for the door. "See you all at the courthouse."

An hour later only Lavender remained, polishing off a sandwich.

The phone rang. "Café," I said. "Hey, Miss Rose."

Dale's mama kept it short and sweet.

"We're on our way," I told her, and hung up. "Your mama's Pinto won't start—again," I told Lavender. "She needs us."

He sighed. He's brought the Pinto back from the dead so many times, we call it Lazarus. "Thanks, Mo."

I grabbed my jacket. "Miss Lana," I shouted, running for the door, "I'm riding with Lavender."

I scooped the last of Capers Dylan's lost papers from the parking lot and hurled myself into the pickup. "What's that?" Lavender asked.

Good question. Tight, blue-inked handwriting crowded the page. A fine tan scribble of mysterious numbers and letters overlaid the words.

"Reporter notes?" I guessed, stuffing it into my bag. "I'll give it to her later."

We took off for Miss Rose's ailing Pinto—and Tupelo Landing's Trial of the Century.

Chapter 4
The Trial of the Century

"All rise," the bailiff called, and Hanging Judge Wilkins swept into the courtroom wearing a scowl and a billowing shade of black. He climbed into his high desk and stood staring down at us, the light playing against the dark planes of his face.

A tornado of butterflies whirled through my belly.

Dale closed his eyes. "Don't throw up, don't throw up," he whispered.

I turned to scan the courtroom. Townsfolk had snagged the good seats. Strangers fringed the room. Capers Dylan sat among the Azalea Women. A knot of thin, chisel-faced men with blond hair—Dale's uncles— lurked near the door.

Johnson men show up for Trial Day. It's a family tradition.

Dale's mama, Miss Rose, smoothed her new dress, and reached for Miss Lana's hand.

"This court's in session. Be seated," the bailiff sang.

Judge Wilkins flounced his robes and we all sat down.

A side door squeaked open.

Detective Joe Starr followed a short, balding man into the courtroom. The man shuffled like an evil penguin, his feet shackled, his hands chained in front.

"Slate," Dale whispered.

Fear rose inside me like a swirl of dirty water.

Dale gulped. "I ain't seen him since we captured him. I guess he's testifying against Daddy too."

"Where *is* Mr. Macon?"

"Probably changing clothes," Dale whispered. "Nobody looks innocent in an orange jumpsuit."

"Good morning," Judge Wilkins said, his voice booming like Judgment Day. "I understand our first defendant will enter a plea."

A plea?

Dale's mouth fell open. Capers peered around the courtroom, her face pale. Skeeter whispered from behind us: "No wonder I couldn't get it set up for you to testify first, Mo. If Mr. Macon pleads guilty, nobody testifies. Including you two."

"Thank you, Jesus," Dale murmured.

My eyes found the Colonel's. He winked.

The judge's gaze raked the empty defendant's chair. "Mr. Bailiff, if you could hurry Mr. Johnson along . . ."

The bailiff bustled out.

In the lull I turned and went into my Upstream

Mother Scan, searching for anybody with my hair, my build, my eyes. Nothing.

A muffled shout broke the silence.

Footsteps pounded up the hall and the bailiff clattered into the room. "Jailbreak!" the bailiff shouted. "Macon Johnson's gone!"

"Everyone stay calm!" Mayor Little screamed.

Dale sprinted for the side door, Harm and me on his heels. We pounded down the hall and skidded to a halt by the jailhouse guard, who lay on the floor. The back door stood ajar, and a cold breeze prowled the room.

Starr shouldered past, pistol drawn. "Call for backup," he shouted at the bailiff. He felt for the guard's pulse as Capers slipped in behind us.

The guard's eyes fluttered open. "What happened?"

"Macon Johnson's escaped," I said.

"Son of a gun," he said, rubbing his head. "I thought we were friends. I sent him in to change clothes. Next thing I knew, *wham!* Hit from behind."

I frowned. "From behind?"

Capers scribbled a note. "He assaulted you and escaped?"

"Laid me out like a side of beef."

I made a note.

Hit from behind. Guard = Side of beef.

"Guess I missed the rest," he added, his hand going

to his holster. He glared at Starr. "Give my pistol back. I had to sign for it."

"Your *pistol?*" Starr said, his gray eyes sweeping the room.

Pistol, I wrote. Gone.

"Anything else missing?" I asked, and the guard patted his pockets.

He closed his eyes and went the color of cement. "My keys."

Dale, Harm, and me rushed the back door. The driveway sat empty as heartbreak.

"Daddy in a black-and-white?" Dale said. He looked at Starr. "I'd like to say on behalf of my entire family that stealing a patrol car is wrong. We know that. It's something we'd show remorse over."

"He took the *patrol* car?" Capers said. "Imbecile!"

"You better set up a search," I told Starr. "Maybe close down the highways out of the county and issue a curfew. He'll probably hide until dark and try to sneak out of the area. He'll go south. His accent would give him away up north."

"Be quiet, Mo," he snapped as the bailiff stepped back in. Starr, who secretly likes me, sighed. "Issue a bulletin: 'Macon Johnson's escaped, armed and dangerous. In a patrol car. Block the highways. Tupelo Landing's on lockdown at sunset.' I'll dust for prints later. Macon may have had an accomplice," he added. "All we have is the guard's word, and he was . . ."

I checked my notes. "Laid out like a side of beef." I went detective-to-detective. "If you ask me—"

"Thanks, but I didn't," he replied. "Get out and let me work. All of you."

We trooped down the hall. "Well," I told Dale. "At least things can't get worse."

Wrong.

Things got worse the instant we stepped into the courtroom. "Dale," Attila shrilled. "Is your stupid daddy on the lam again?"

Dale elbowed Harm. "On a lamb?"

"On the lam. It means on the run," Harm said.

I grabbed center stage. "Quiet down. Desperado Detectives have a statement."

"Allow me, Mo," Capers said, stepping in front of me.

Did she just upstage me? I looked into Miss Lana's horrified eyes. To Miss Lana, upstaging is a capital crime.

Capers continued: "Macon hit the guard, stole his pistol, and escaped, armed and dangerous . . ." She did a dramatic pause good as Miss Lana's. "In a patrol car."

"A *patrol* car?" Attila shrieked like a blond-headed parrot.

"A black-and-white?" Lavender gasped. "You have to be kidding me."

"No," Dale said. "We don't."

My gaze found Dale's mama. Folks say Miss Rose was drop-dead gorgeous before Mr. Macon got hold of her. She still turns heads, but now she's a worn shade of pretty, like an upholstered chair faded by the sun. She stared straight ahead, the crowd's murmurs settling around her like falling leaves.

I stepped in front of Capers, upstaging her right back. Miss Lana applauded.

"Thank you for that introduction, Capers," I said. "It's always good to get a stranger's take on things they know nothing about. As everyone knows, the Desperados helped capture Mr. Macon once. We'll do it again. Anyone with clues may see me or Dale in homeroom or at the café. We have Joe Starr setting up a search and dusting for prints. The lockdown at sunset was his idea, not ours. Just in case you hate it."

"Macon's halfway to Mexico by now," a blond, chisel-faced man shouted.

Dale waved. "Hey, Uncle Austin."

Attila flounced her hair. "On behalf of the *popular* kids in sixth grade, I'd like to say I'm not surprised your father's a felon, Dale, but in a way I hate it because you'll probably follow in his footsteps thanks to the Like-Father-Like-Son Rule."

The courtroom erupted.

Miss Rose stood up. "Stop it right this minute!" she said, her voice ringing across the room. Attila froze like a field mouse in open terrain.

"Not another word about my son," Miss Rose said, her face so strained, her lips had gone white. "This has nothing to do with Dale, and we have nothing more to say. Neither do you, Anna Celeste—not to us. Are we clear?" she demanded, her stare practically melting the turkey earrings dangling from Attila's pink ears.

The courtroom went tight as a full-stretched slingshot.

"Are we clear?" Miss Rose repeated, shifting her gaze to Attila's mother—mean, beige Mrs. Simpson.

Not many people go toe-to-toe with the Simpsons, who are second-generation cul-de-sac. But Miss Rose can stare down a bulldog if she thinks she's right.

Mrs. Simpson licked her lips. "Anna, sit down."

Attila plunked onto the bench as Starr marched into the room. "Curfew sundown to sunup," he said. "If you see Macon, dial 911."

"Sorry Macon gave you the slip," a voice behind me said. "Makes you look bad."

I wheeled. Slate! He's like a snake, I thought. So still, you forget he's there, and poison when you step on him.

Slate scratched his face, his handcuffs flashing. "People always underestimate Macon. He's like little Dale over there—smarter than you think. He's always three steps ahead of you people."

"Except when we throw him in jail," I shot back.

He smiled. "Really? Because I don't see him here. Do you?"

"He has a point," Dale whispered. "Daddy's gone."

Slate's smile broadened. "Let me know if I can help you puzzle things out, Starr. I have nothing but time on my hands. And I admire Macon Johnson so."

"Put a double guard on him," Starr told the bailiff.

Slate's eyes glittered. "Why? What could I have to do with the escape? I was sitting right here. Ask your star witnesses. Hi, Mo. Hi, Dale," he said, smiling like a frog smiles at flies. "I look forward to spending time with you when I get out of here."

The Colonel and Lavender both lunged at him. Starr blocked them like a football lineman, bulldozing them to a halt. "Take Slate to lockup," he barked at the bailiff.

Slate smiled at Miss Rose as the bailiff jerked him to his feet. "Nice seeing you, Rose. Your husband's showing his true genius. Again."

"Get him out of here. Now," Starr shouted. "The rest of you, go home."

Starr stood by the courtroom door, watching the crowd file by. As the Colonel and I drew even, he grabbed the

Colonel's arm. "Colonel," he said, "I'd appreciate it if you'd ride with me today. You know Macon and his habits. I want him in custody before anybody gets hurt."

I waited for the Colonel to say no. He doesn't trust law enforcement and he doesn't much like Joe Starr.

But he looked at Lavender. Then at Dale. Then at me.

"Pick me up at the café," he said. "I want to take my family home."

With Jailbreak on the gossip menu, the café hopped from the minute Miss Lana and me opened the door. The Azalea Women sailed in, pushing Harm aside to grab ringside seats. Then Capers tripped in, rosy with excitement.

"What a day," she said dumping her things out onto a table: notebook, pen, tape recorder, faded *American Heritage Dictionary*, second edition—same as mine, not that I'm lame enough to haul it around. "Great story."

"Like living with a spy, isn't it?" Harm muttered to me as he watched her. "A good-looking spy. But still."

"Everybody pipe down," I shouted, grabbing a tray of waters as Miss Rose's ancient orange Pinto sputtered up. Miss Rose, Dale, and Queen Elizabeth tumbled out, and Lavender pulled away in a cloud of black exhaust.

"The Pinto's developed a death rattle," Miss Rose said, swaying across the room to give Miss Lana a quick hug.

"That's terrible for your deliveries, Rose," an Azalea Woman said, faking a pout.

With her farm tours quiet until spring, Miss Rose makes her money on collards and sweet potatoes. She delivers in the Pinto. "Lavender's taking it to his garage; he'll revive it in no time."

Fear shot darts through my belly. "*He's alone?* With Mr. Macon on the run?"

The Azalea Women perked up.

Miss Rose smoothed my hair. "If you loved Lavender any more, I believe you'd explode," she said. "Lavender's not alone, Mo. Sam's meeting him there." She spoke louder for the Azalea Women: "He's fine."

Sam is Lavender's fellow mechanic. He'd walk through fire for Lavender.

So would Dale and me.

Miss Lana handed Miss Rose our house keys. "Why don't you rest while Lavender works," she whispered. "Unless you want to field every question in town."

"Go on, Mama, I'll help Mo until the Colonel's back," Dale told her.

The two women—one glamorous as Old Hollywood, the other level-headed as twilight—linked arms and strolled to the kitchen door. It's funny how people so different can share the same heartbeat, I thought.

"My homework's on my desk," I called. "Dividing fractions may help distract you from the disaster which is today. Please help yourself."

Miss Rose laughed and the kitchen door swiped closed behind her.

Miss Lana put on her apron. "Being a best friend is a calling and an honor," she told me, watching Dale settle Queen Elizabeth by the jukebox. "Always remember that, sugar," she said, and she grabbed an order pad and went to work.

Dale and me whirled through the crowd like dervishes while Miss Lana and Harm plundered the freezer and cooked. People flowed in and out, rumors trailing along:

Mr. Macon's surrounded.

He's been gunned down.

He's made it to Raleigh.

He called from Charlotte.

He's holed up drunk. "As usual," someone added.

"Don't bother arguing," Dale said, doling out iced teas. "It only makes it worse."

At four o'clock, Lavender cruised up in the Pinto and sauntered in. "Dale? Ready to go?" he asked. "Mama wants to run a few errands before she heads home."

Dale shook his head. "No, I'll help until the Colonel gets back. That's fair."

Our teacher, Miss Retzyl, strolled in as Lavender strolled out.

I darted over to Jake and Jimmy Exum, who were

drinking ice water and sucking our jelly packets dry. The Colonel hates water-only customers. "The Colonel's coming," I said, and they bolted. "A table has just opened up," I called, waving Miss Retzyl over.

Miss Retzyl's smart and pretty. She excels at Average—average clothes, average hair, average car. Average is exotic in my life. I adore her. "Welcome," I said. "Our specials include Miss Lana's world-renowned Leg of Lam, our famous Bustout Broccoli Casserole, and Veggies at Large. Each dish is recycled and fresh-named to reflect current events. What can I start you with?"

"Tea and lamb, please," Miss Retzyl said. "With double veggies."

Capers beamed her a smile. "Low carb. Dieting? Me too."

Did she just call Miss Retzyl fat?

Miss Retzyl studied Capers, serene as a cucumber. I stepped in. "Miss Retzyl, you remember Capers? Capers, Priscilla Retzyl is Joe Starr's fiancée and the teacher of me, Harm, and Dale plus others." Sal smiled from the next table. Jimmy and Jake looked up from a hot dog they'd just conned Thes out of.

Capers did a double take. "You teach these kids? I'm not the only one lucky to be alive."

Miss Retzyl laughed and Capers strolled to her table. "I'd love some background on this town," she said, and Miss Retzyl gave her a smile.

As the day spun by, the gossip wore Dale to a nub.

Miss Lana stopped to tousle his hair as another stranger speculated on Mr. Macon's whereabouts. "Ignore them," she told Dale. "This is a tempest in a teapot. It won't last."

Finally, Joe Starr's Impala cruised into the lot. The Colonel hopped out and a sliver of undercover worry melted from my heart. "Thank heavens," Miss Lana murmured as the Colonel pushed open the door.

"Dale," Crissy shouted from her table, "I hear Macon's wanted dead or alive."

Dale closed his eyes.

"Dead or alive? I knew it," an Azalea Woman cried. "Is there a reward?"

The Colonel's shiny military boots clacked across the tile. "There is no dead or alive, there is no reward," he said. He smiled at Miss Retzyl. "Joe asked me to let you know he'll see you tomorrow."

An all-nighter. So. Once again, Detective Joe Starr is clueless.

The Colonel grabbed his chef's apron and whipped it around his thin body. "Sorry, son," he told Dale. "No sign of Macon—yet. I'll give you a ride home when you're ready." He clapped his shoulder. "Thanks for holding things together here."

Dale stood a little taller.

"Miss Rose is in Mexico with Macon," a voice barked.

"Who said that?" I snapped. "You can't talk about Miss Rose. Stand up! I never went eye to eye with so much stupid before." The Exum boys ducked.

Dale scowled. "This rumor-mumbling has got to stop."

"You mean rumor-mongering," Harm said.

"It's the idea of the word, not the sound of it," Dale said, his voice rising.

The Colonel put a hand on his shoulder. "They'll stop talking about Macon when they find something better to talk about," he said, his voice low. "Hang in there, son. I'll do something stupid before long." He headed for the kitchen as Queen Elizabeth snagged a bit of hot dog beneath Thes's table.

"Liz!" Dale cried. "No junk food! Spit it out!"

I gasped. I'd never heard Dale snap at Queen Elizabeth. She gave Dale a hurt look and spit the treat by Jake's foot.

"Dale needs help," Harm whispered. "He's unraveling."

"True." It could be hours before the Colonel did something gossip-worthy. We needed a diversion *now*. "Dale," I said. "Make your Top Secret Announcement."

"Brilliant," Harm said, and headed for the milkshake machine.

"Now?" Dale said. "But I want extra credit."

For Dale, extra credit is a lifeline on an unfriendly

academic sea. Harm and me float like sea otters.

"Your daddy's an escaped felon with the law on his trail. Miss Retzyl probably feels sorry for you. It doesn't get better than this," I said. "Plus, you'll get people talking about something besides Mr. Macon. And Miss Rose."

"Right," Dale said. "Let's roll."

I stepped onto the Pepsi crate I keep behind the counter for extra height, and raised my hands to silence the crowd. Miss Lana whirled by. "*Own* the stage, sugar. *Project.*"

Miss Lana knows stagecraft like Lavender knows tire rotation.

I willed my personal chi across the room. "Attention everyone and especially Miss Retzyl. Dale has an Extra Credit Announcement."

An Azalea Woman's voice sliced the babble. "Hush! Dale's convinced his daddy to surrender."

"I ain't seen Daddy and I ain't telegraphic," Dale said, taking my place on the Pepsi crate.

"He means telepathic," I said.

Harm drum-rolled his fingers on the counter. A nice touch. He stopped, and a tsunami of silence rocked the café.

"I want you to be the first to know," Dale said. "Queen Elizabeth is great with child."

Capers dropped her pen. *"What?"*

Attila scooted her chair close. "You're thinking of Queen Elizabeth of the United Kingdom. Dale means Queen Elizabeth II, the dog."

"Puppies?" Sal cried, spilling ketchup on her Sudoku book. "Can I have one?"

Dale offered a shy smile. "Lavender says the puppies will arrive around Thanksgiving. And Lavender knows things."

I stepped up beside Dale. "Dale's drawing up the adoption applications. Information will trickle down from Sixth Grade. We'll need references, plus pet photos."

Thes raised his hand. "I never photographed my cat, Spitz. You're good with a camera, Mo. Do you do pet portraits?"

"Pet portraits make me retch, but thank you for asking."

"I have ten dollars," he added.

"I can work you in tomorrow," I replied. Dale was counting on Thes taking a puppy. Thes, who's the preacher's kid, would be good with a dog. Plus, Dale could see the puppy at church every Sunday.

Attila raised her hand. "Who's the daddy?" she asked. "Or is this one of those family mysteries so dear to your heart, Mo?"

Attila's face would be pretty if she didn't live behind it.

"Thanks for asking, metal mouth," I replied. "The

puppies' father prefers to remain anonymous. Dale?"

The Colonel grinned and swiped at the counter. He likes me to think on my feet, and he can't stand Attila Celeste either. I plucked my camera from beneath the counter and lined up a photo for Dale's scrapbook if he ever gets one.

Capers raised her hand. Dale pointed. "Motorcycle woman with crooked nose."

Click.

"Speaking of fathers," Capers said, "any idea where yours is?"

"Don't answer that," the Colonel said, his voice like a hammer.

"Sorry," she muttered, and glanced into Miss Retzyl's eyes, which had gone laser quality. Miss Retzyl's secretly protective of Dale and me when we're in public, though in the classroom it's pretty much open season on both of us. Or else it just feels that way.

The phone rang, breaking the silence. "Café, Lana speaking . . . *What?*"

She turned her back, whispered, and hung up. She snapped into ad-lib mode clear as the Colonel snapping to attention. "Takeout for Rose," she sang. "Colonel, will you deliver?"

My stomach dropped.

We don't deliver. And Miss Rose doesn't order takeout.

"We'll go, Miss Lana," I said. "We'll ride our bikes."

She plunged a special into a takeout bag. "Colonel, do you mind? *Now?*" she asked. She scrawled across her order pad, and handed it to him.

"Ten-four, my dear." He turned it toward me:

Break-in at Rose's. Hurry.

Chapter 6
Break-in at Miss Rose's

The Colonel hunched over the wheel of the Underbird, zipping us past golden soybean fields, dark pine forests, a broke-down car. "That's Uncle Austin's car," Dale said as we screeched around the curve. "I'll tell Lavender."

Lavender's family could keep him in business if any of them ever paid.

We bounced across Miss Rose's dirt drive and into the yard of her old, tin-roofed farmhouse. "Are you all right?" the Colonel demanded, hopping out.

"Just barely," she said, and Dale rushed to hug her.

A gang of dappled, knee-high birds with featherless paste-white faces ran shrieking across the yard. "Guineas," I told Harm, who's from the city. "Dale's new security system."

We hurried to Miss Rose's side. "Macon kicked the back door in," she told the Colonel as we walked up.

"Daddy wouldn't do that," Dale cried. "How can I keep us safe with the door busted in? He knows I'm not good with tools."

Miss Rose watched the Colonel. "I glimpsed the door and the kitchen," she said. "I dialed 911 . . . and you."

911. Starr's on his way.

"We'll check for clues before Starr gets here," I told her as Harm plopped down on the steps and stretched out his long legs.

"Negative," the Colonel snapped. "Up, Harm. Macon could be in the house."

Harm jumped up and wheeled to face the door behind him.

Mr. Macon? *Still here?*

A distant siren pierced the quiet, setting the coyotes in the woods howling and the guineas whirling across the yard. Starr's Impala skidded to a stop by the bird-bath. "Where is he?" he demanded, tumbling out.

"He may be inside," the Colonel said. "Rose keeps her shotgun in the bedroom closet, shells on the top shelf. Be careful."

Several long minutes later Miss Rose's front door swung open. "All clear," Starr said. He marched to the drive and squatted to examine the tracks wheeling in and out. He squinted at Miss Rose's Pinto, under the pecan tree. "Did you drive in this way?"

"Several times," she said. "Lavender too. And the Colonel, just now."

"And a patrol car, if I read these tracks right," Starr said, slapping the dirt off his hands. "Did you notice anything missing inside?"

She frowned. "I'd piled up some of Macon's things to give away. The pile's gone. A hunting jacket, Sunday shoes, an old wallet . . . I don't know what else."

Dale sighed. "Mama and me gave Daddy that hunting jacket one Christmas. Mama tried to give it to Lavender the other day, but he won't wear it."

Of course not, I thought. Lavender's no hand-me-down Macon.

"Why would Mr. Macon take an old wallet?" Harm muttered.

"We don't know it *was* him," Dale said, his voice sharp.

Miss Rose put her hand on Dale's shoulder. "My canned food cabinet's wiped out too—tomatoes, beans, squash. I have no idea what else."

Dale frowned. "Daddy won't eat squash."

She shivered in her gray coat. "The guineas squawked and a car started . . . I saw the kicked-in door and I ran."

She heard Mr. Macon's car start?

"Close call," Starr muttered. He pushed his hat back. "Your shotgun's gone too. I hate to ask, but I need someone to walk through with me room by room. To identify everything that's missing. I'll notify the pawnshops.

There's a chance we can get some of it back."

Dale looked like life had knocked the wind out of him. Miss Rose didn't look much better. "Harm and me know where everything's supposed to be," I said.

Starr surprised me. "Thanks, Mo."

The Colonel nodded. "I'll wait with Rose and Dale."

"Excellent," I said. "As co-investigator, I say we keep this break-in quiet. We got too many rumors already. And someone may mention a detail they shouldn't know, giving us a clue."

Starr ran his finger across his eyebrow. "Good idea," he admitted.

"Right," I said, grabbing my camera. "We're burning daylight."

We stepped inside. Miss Rose's living room told its usual peaceful story: piano, sofa, writing desk, high-back chair by the phone. Not a throw pillow out of place.

Lavender's old room told a different story: Bookcase overturned, closet agape, dresser spitting shirts and socks. "Wrecked," Harm said. "Totally tossed."

I peeped in an open drawer. "Mr. Macon's old shirts and socks—in case Dale ever grows," I told Starr. "This drawer's empty, so Mr. Macon has street clothes."

Harm flipped a chair right side up.

I eased the closet door open with my sneaker. "The

camping gear's gone," I announced. "Sleeping bag, hatchet, lantern. Even the broke cook stove, which Dale and me are more or less innocent."

"Why would he take a busted stove?" Harm asked, folding an old undershirt back into a drawer. Harm's neat, like Miss Rose.

"In a hurry," Starr said, making a note. "Forgot it didn't work."

I spun, canvassing the room. The sagging bed, Lavender's weights and chin-up bar, an old trunk from Miss Rose's little girl days. "Dale's moved the hand weights into his room," I told Starr. "Everything else is good. Let's check out the kitchen next."

Starr scribbled a note. "Okay, but it's pretty bad, from what I saw."

Even with his warning, Miss Rose's normally spic-and-span kitchen punched me like a fist. Back door splintered, cabinets gawking, drawers spewing utensils. "Blood," I said, following the splotches on the linoleum to an open drawer.

"Knives?" Harm guessed, peeping over my shoulder.

"Dishcloths. For a bandage, maybe. Fingerprints should be easy to pull," I said, staring at the blood on the drawer front. "DNA too, if you want it."

Above the drawer, a cabinet door stood ajar. Harm grabbed a spatula and eased it open. Salt, pepper, Dale's goofy ceramic frog jar, its hat crooked. Harm took out his handkerchief, lifted the hat, and went up on his toes. "Empty."

"That explains the wallet," I said. "Mr. Macon took their cash."

As Starr went to the shattered back door, I took out my camera and stepped back for a wide shot. *Click.* I focused on Starr, who stood staring across the backyard and blue-green collard field. Dale's mule Cleo stamped her hooves by the stable. *Click.*

"Macon drove the patrol car back here, to hide while loading up," Starr said, pointing to tracks pressed into the grass. "Then he doubled back, for some reason."

Or we got two cars, I thought, my gaze following the second trail of bent grass to the stable. *Click.*

"Let's check Miss Rose's room, then Dale's," I said. "I hate this for them."

Miss Rose's room looked untouched, all oak and lace. "Just the missing shotgun. I thought he'd tear this room up," I said. "Let's try Dale's room."

I led the way.

Dale's door swung open: Unmade bed, a tangle of jeans, a scatter of dog toys. Hand weights, beanbag chair, pawnshop guitar. A shelf of animal books and Dale's dog-eared favorite—*Manners Girls Like.*

Starr whistled. "Macon turned this place upside down."

"No," Harm said, peeking in the closet. "This is about right."

Starr sidestepped a landslide of music books and made his way to the terrarium. Dale's newt, Sir Isaac Newton, blinked up at him. "Anything disturbed?" he asked.

"Just Newton," I said. "We think he may be clinically depressed."

"I would be too," Starr muttered, sprinkling a few dried bugs at Newton's feet.

The door behind us bumped against the wall and we jumped. "What's taking so long?" Dale demanded. He panned around his room, taking everything in. "Where's my red flashlight? I need it."

His flashlight? How did I miss that?

I turned to Starr, very official. "And the red flashlight is gone."

Dale watched us, his eyes like sky before storm. "Newton's upset," he said, walking to the terrarium and turning his back to us. "You better go."

"Thanks Dale, we're done," Starr said. And we headed for the door.

After Starr roared away, we trooped into the house.

Miss Rose went from shocked to furious in ten seconds flat as she re-examined her kitchen. "Of all the no-good—"

She bit off the end of her sentence, scooped an armload of utensils from the floor, and dumped them into her sink. She leaned against the counter and closed her eyes.

I went woman-to-woman. "It's natural to be angry when a felonious ex kicks in your door," I said, very adult. "If you ask me—"

She held up her hand like a traffic cop. "Excuse me, Mo," she said. "I need to change clothes. Sorry, baby," she added, rumpling Dale's blond hair. "I'm just tired."

Tired of Mr. Macon, I thought. Who wouldn't be?

She bustled back moments later in slacks and a soft work shirt, her dark hair swept up. "It won't take long to set this place right," she said, turning to the sink.

Dale gave her a smile as he scrubbed blood off the drawer front. To me he looked wobbly. I nudged him away. "I seen a million kitchen cuts at the café," I told him. "I got this. Besides, the Colonel needs your help."

He rushed to Harm's side. The boys held the splintered door in place as the Colonel crisscrossed it with duct tape and wedged a chair under the knob.

"That will hold if nobody tries it," the Colonel said as

Miss Rose slammed a pot on the stove. "Why don't you and Dale pack a bag, Rose? We'll clean up tomorrow."

She ran a sink of sudsy water. "Macon will not run me out of my home."

Miss Lana calls Miss Rose independent. The Colonel says she's hard-headed as a railroad spike. He also says to choose your fights. "As you wish," he said. "I'll take the couch. Where would you like Mo to sleep? We won't leave you two out here alone."

Miss Rose glared at him like she could ignite him, which if he stood still long enough maybe she could. The Colonel waited, cool as midnight. Her glare faltered, and she smiled. "What if we call Lavender and see if he can spend the night?"

"I'm on it," I said, and blasted down the narrow hall to the phone.

Lavender snatched up the phone on the first ring. "I said leave me alone," he said, his voice sideways and rough.

My smile died. "Lavender? What's wrong?"

He exhaled like downshifting into a curve. "Sorry, Mo. I thought you . . . It's just that the twins are giving me a fit. What's up?"

The twins make grown men cry, but they never made Lavender *that* mad before.

"Did Mr. Macon call you?" I demanded.

"Let me talk," Dale said, grabbing the phone. "Lavender, we been robbed and the door's only taped on. Mama and me hope you can come over. Now."

I pulled the phone back. "Starr said Mr. Macon might go see you too."

Lavender's voice cracked. "He won't if he knows what's good for him."

"Macon has Miss Rose's shotgun," I added.

Silence zinged through the line. "Tell Mama I'm on my way."

That night I opened the *Piggly Wiggly Chronicles* and picked up my pen.

> Dear Upstream Mother,
>   Mr. Macon busted out of jail. Lavender's in danger and Dale's life is ruined.
>   Lavender charged into Miss Rose's place like the cavalry. He wore his scarred-up jeans and green corduroy shirt, and that denim jacket the exact color of his eyes. Not that it matters.
>   The Colonel and Starr say Mr. Macon will likely sneak out of town tonight if he can. I

think so too. Adios to bad news, I say. Also adios to my hopes for vengeance and a perfect conviction record.

Dale and Miss Rose look stretched as old socks.

Mo

PS: I looked for you in the courtroom, but I didn't see you. Are you in borderline law enforcement like me? Feel free to track me down.

Chapter 7
Puppy Paperwork

The black rotary phone by my bed jangled early the next morning. "Desperado Detective Agency," I mumbled. "Your felonies are our pleasure."

"It's me," Dale said. "I'm glad you're not dead."

"Thank you," I replied. I squinted at my wind-up clock, which had wound down. I gazed out the windows opposite my bed. Dawn o'clock.

"Daddy's probably gone by now," Dale said, "but Mama doesn't want me out on my bike, just in case. Neither does Lavender." I pictured him scrunching into himself, the way he does when he's scared. "You know how Daddy is."

Mr. Macon's cruel as wildfire. I squinted at my windows—all three unlocked.

The Colonel says most things worth having come double-edged like a sword. With an A+ imagination, the good side is, you can solve mysteries. The bad side is, you can scare yourself senseless. "I ain't worried," I lied.

"Lavender's driving me to school," he continued.

"We'll pick you up. Be careful. Miss Lana and the Colonel too. Good-bye." The line went dead.

I bounded to my windows and locked them—one, two, three—not looking out in case Mr. Macon was looking in. I opened the living room door and listened for signs of life. No voice, no snore, no clatter of stiletto heels. I turned my Detective Senses toward the café. Not even the rattle of a pot.

Can a person be more or less orphaned twice in the same lifetime?

I lunged for my phone and dialed the café.

"This is the Colonel. Speak to me."

My fear melted like ice cream on a July sidewalk. "Good morning, sir," I said, very casual. "I assume Miss Lana's alive too?"

"She's alive and a vision of caffeinated loveliness," he said, and I heard her laugh. "Would you like to speak to her?"

"Not necessary, sir. See you in three shakes."

A few minutes later I blasted onto the porch, running a comb through my hair. The Colonel sat smiling in our porch rocker, his short, bottle-brush hair still flat on one side from dreaming. "Morning, Soldier," he said. "I suddenly longed to see you. No word yet about Macon," he added, rising and scooping me into a hug.

The Azalea Women say the Colonel doesn't give a flip about people. They're wrong. He just doesn't give a flip about Azalea Women.

We fell into step, heading down the walk and around the side of our building. "Heads up, Soldier. The crowd's ugly today," he whispered, opening the café door.

The early morning crowd stared at me like sag-faced snapdragons caught by frost. Capers Dylan, on the other hand, smiled fresh-faced as a pansy. "Hello, Detective," she said, looking up from her oatmeal. "Care to join me?"

The kitchen door swung open. "Morning, sugar," Miss Lana called as she twirled in, her skirt flaring and her Marilyn Monroe wig glistening. "Grab some silverware and join Capers. Space is tight this morning. Everyone's starving for Starr's report."

"Yes, ma'am," I said. Miss Lana lowered her tray to show three breakfast plates. I chose the grits and eggs.

"Hey," a stranger called from the counter. "Where's my grits and eggs? Did Macon Johnson steal those too?"

Strangers can be rude.

"Keep your shirt on," I shouted, unrolling my silverware.

Miss Lana gave me a quick kiss. "Lavender will be here in ten, sugar."

Capers tried to smooth her crumpled blouse. "You and Dale got the same wrinkled sense of style," I said.

"Guess I need an iron," she said, smiling. She leaned forward and whispered, "Sorry to hear about the break-in at Rose's. What happened?"

The back of my neck tingled. How did she know about that?

"Lana told me," she added, like she could read me. "I helped her with the café after you all took off like bats. I know Starr let you in on the investigation. He'd be crazy not to ask Tupelo Landing's most successful detective for input."

Blatant flattery. My favorite kind. Not that I like being questioned.

"You been researching us," I replied, grabbing my milk. "Why?"

She laughed. "You're like me. You'd rather ask than answer. Fair enough, Detective. You interview me first."

More flattery. Excellent. "How come you're a reporter?"

"I get paid for being nosy."

"Speaking of noses, yours is crooked. Why?"

"Bicycle crash when I was a kid. I was trying to stand on the seat and fly like a bird." I felt a sudden surge of respect. "Most spectacular wipeout in the history of Rainbow Road," she said.

"You mean Rainbow Row," I told her, and Miss Lana winked at me from a couple tables over. I shot Capers a new question: "Who's your best friend?"

"Well . . . my sister, I guess. My turn," she said, unleashing dimples.

"One more thing," I added, lowering my voice. "The break-in at Miss Rose's: We're keeping it quiet for now. Totally off the record. I hope I can count on you."

She tilted her head, considering. "It's obvious Macon did it. Give me the details later and it's a deal."

"You're on," I said as the café door swung open. Lavender!

"Morning, Doc," Capers called. "How's your two-wheeled patient today?"

Lavender sauntered over like a big golden cat. "In critical condition," he said, reaching into his pocket. "Here's the estimate. Sorry it's so expensive, but . . ."

She barely glanced at it. "Let's do it." She plucked an envelope from her saddlebag. "Will this get you started?" she asked, flashing a fat wad of green.

The café gasped. In Tupelo Landing we don't pay for car work until we whine the price down. "Great," Lavender said, swallowing his surprise. "I'll order the parts."

"And where can I rent a motorcycle 'til you're done?"

"You can rent a *car* in Greenville. That's about it." He smiled at me. "Dale and I are ready when you are, Miss LoBeau."

Capers watched him stroll out—and she wasn't watching in a fix-my-bike way.

Out-of-state competition? Is that fair?

"Cash was nice of you," I whispered, grabbing my messenger bag. "Lavender's recent full-blown seed tick infestation has set him back. Don't mention I told you."

Her expression went sunshine to rain. "Seed ticks?"

"You hardly see them until you go chronic. What's that?" I asked, squinting at her collar. Her laugh sounded tinny as she brushed her hand across her neck. "It's just as well," I said. "Lavender don't like older women." A total lie. Lavender likes every woman he ever met and most of the ones he only heard about.

I swung my messenger bag onto my shoulder. "Bye, Miss Lana," I shouted.

The Colonel stuck his head out of the kitchen as I snagged my lunch from the counter. "Stay alert, Soldier. I'm on standby if you need me."

Dale just finished doing his homework wrong when we coasted to a stop in front of our brick, two-story school. Attila Celeste minced across the schoolyard with her posse of fifth-grade Attila-wannabes—same clothes, same walk, same maniacal hair toss.

"Maybe I should go back home," Dale said. "We could hunt for Daddy."

Lavender stuffed Dale's homework in his backpack and

hooked it shut. "Walk in like you mean it, little brother. Did you bring the puppy forms?"

Dale nodded as he watched Attila.

"Then stop worrying. If I know Macon, he's running by now."

"Then why are you driving us around like babies?" Dale asked.

Lavender grinned. "Same reason you're going to school. Because I'm Rose's son and she said so. Go on, and let me fix Mama's door. This will blow over, same as always."

We found Harm standing by the steps, shivering in his sweater and moth-bitten scarf. "You look like you're freezing," I told him.

"Coolest guy in middle school," he said, his breath steaming in the cold. "Who am I kidding? I'm freezing my begonias off. Let's go inside." Lately Harm's using flower names as off-color words—a trick Miss Lana taught him. He says it keeps his grandfather, Mr. Red, off his back.

"I wish I didn't need adoption applications," Dale said as we headed up the steps. "If the puppies had homes with my best friends . . ."

"I can't," I told him for maybe the hundredth time. I held the door open for Attila and let it go in her face just as she got there. "There's too much traffic around the café."

"And Gramps said no because he's Gramps," Harm said. "Plus, I can't afford one. Pups need medicine, food . . ."

We stepped into the school's steamy heat. The hall smelled like waxed floors and gossip. "I want Skeeter to check my adoption form," Dale said, leading us to the office.

Skeeter has a cushy teacher-appointed office job.

"I've been expecting you," she said as we dropped into teacher-quality chairs. "We'll need to be discreet. I don't normally conduct business at school. It makes it hard to discuss my fee."

As if on cue, Sal popped in from the hall. "You'll want to trade for our services?"

Dale slipped close. "I got two boxes of windshield scrapers, excellent for use on bugs year-round and snow if we ever get some."

Windshield scrapers? Has he lost his mind?

"Excellent choice," I said.

Skeeter swiveled her deluxe leather chair, leaving her back toward us. Sal shook her head. "That's what you gave us for Christmas."

"Ouch," Harm said.

"Actually," Sal said. "I was hoping . . ." She gazed at Dale, her eyes glistening. "I always wanted a puppy, Dale."

Skeeter swiveled back around. "Me too. Queen Elizabeth is top-of-the-line. Smart, good family, nice sense of humor. You'd have visitation rights, of course."

Perfect! Skeeter and Sal are prime puppy candidates. Still, in Dale's universe, asking for a puppy equaled asking for family. Harm and me waited.

Dale gave them a quick nod. "Deal."

Sal clapped and bounced up on her toes.

Skeeter smiled. "I'll have this back to you right after lunch."

Skeeter ran true to her word. She grabbed me as we filed from a lunchroom awash in gossip. Dale let it roll off him like water off wax. I'm more of a sponge person, and I'd just about had my fill.

"Mo, I want you to see something," Skeeter said, handing me a neat stack of applications as the crowd surged on. "Check out Dale's rough draft, on top of the stack."

I stared at the mutant baby scrawl. Dale's never liked writing, but *this?*

"Maybe it's the stress of the trial or having an armed-and-dangerous father on the run," she said. "I typed it as a professional courtesy, but if his homework went in like this . . ." She shrugged.

"I owe you," I said. "Heard any news on Mr. Macon?"

Skeeter's Cousin Information Network blankets the state. If a sparrow burps, she hears about it. "Not a word—which is odd," she said as the tardy bell rang.

I skidded into Miss Retzyl's room. "I'm glad you could join us," she said.

Teacher Sarcasm. Danger.

"Thank you," I replied. "I love your outfit. Is it new?"

"Have a seat, Mo. Everyone, take out your science books."

Science books? Mine was under my bed. "I think we're on the biology chapter," I said, opening my history book for cover. "Which reminds me, Dale has an extra credit science announcement. Go," I whispered, sliding the applications to his desk.

"There is no biology chapter, Mo," she replied. "We're discussing isotopes. Who can define an isotope?"

"Unless I'm turned around, Isotope's a barbecue joint off I-95," I said. "Dale has an item of scientific interest."

Dale beamed at the class. "Who wants a puppy?"

The class exploded. "I do!" Jake shouted above the hubbub.

I smiled at Miss Retzyl, who I adore. Or whom I adore, whichever is correct.

She sighed. "Hurry," she said. "We have a lot to cover."

Dale nudged the applications toward me.

I blasted down the row, handing out papers. "To be considered for a puppy, please fill out this form. Dale will select a few lucky applicants. He's waiving the application fee for sixth graders, but don't let it get around."

I tried to look innocent as I smiled at Dale. "Does this waiving apply to Miss Retzyl too?" I asked—a softball lob with Home Run Suck-Up Potential.

Dale pursed his lips and studied Miss Retzyl. My stomach went into a tuck-dive.

"Say yes," Harm hissed.

"Yes," Dale said.

"Congratulations," I told Miss Retzyl, handing her an application. "We're talking puppies of outstanding beauty and poise."

Susana Lowery from the third row held out her hand.

"Thank you for considering adoption," I told her.

"Look who's thanking," Attila muttered. I strolled to the bulletin board and pinned up an application:

Puppy Adoption Form by Dale

• Name of Human

• List all biters in your home

• Will you allow visits from Dale?

• Names of pets?

• Why do you want a puppy?

• Pet History with Photos

• Extra Credit: Do puppies have spirit lives?

"This is the stupidest thing ever," Attila muttered, crumpling her application and tossing it to the waste-basket.

"Thank you for pre-crumpling," I said. "It saves Dale and Queen Elizabeth the trouble of destroying your application themselves. And thank *you*, Miss Retzyl. I yield the floor to you at this time."

Miss Retzyl exhaled the way a karate instructor does before he breaks a board. "Science," she said. "Isotopes and radiation. Who knows how they're connected?"

Jake raised his hand. *"Jake?"* she said, smoothing the surprise from her face.

"Isotope would be a good name for a puppy. I could call her Iso."

Dale pulled a tiny notebook from his shirt pocket and made a small black X by Jake's name.

"Queen Elizabeth's offspring need royal names, which could mean research," I said. Research is to Miss Retzyl as bird seed is to squirrel.

"Mo," she snapped. "We're talking about—"

"Isotopes," Harm said, very smooth. "Unstable atoms release particles called isotopes. Radiation's pretty much made out of them, which is hard to imagine because you can't see it. But like bad breath, it's still there," he added, smiling at Attila.

Attila snarled, but when he turned away she breathed into her cupped hand.

Dale gave me a thumbs-up.

I relaxed. My keen Detective Senses told me Mr. Macon was gone from our lives, maybe forever. Life would settle back to dull normal. The Desperado Detective Agency would find a new case, one that would bring us wealth and glory.

Naturally, then, the next break-in hit me broadside.

Chapter 8
The Next Break-in

"Glad *that's* over," Harm said as the school door closed behind us and Dale tripped down the steps. "Dale, how do you stay cool, with people talking like that?"

Dale flipped his collar up. "I'm Tupperware," he said, very suave.

Harm's smile froze.

"He means Teflon," I said. "Nothing sticks."

"Hey Harm, where's your bike?" Dale asked as we headed across the schoolyard, Attila on our heels. "Is Mr. Red scared of Daddy too?"

"He's a little jumpy, yeah," Harm said. "He dropped me off this morning. Most folks did," he said, hooking a thumb at the empty bicycle rack.

A nearby Buick tootled its horn. "Yoo-hoo, Desperados! Over here," Grandmother Miss Lacy called, just as Attila's mother's stealth beige Cadillac oozed to the curb.

Mrs. Simpson purred her window down. "Good news, Anna," she called, sneering at Dale. "They found Macon Johnson's camp stove on the side of I-95. He's gone, and good riddance to white trash. Hop in, honey. I'm late."

White trash? Who does she think she is?

"Hey you!" I shouted before I could think of anything to say. "Most witches ride broomsticks. How'd you rate a Cadillac?"

Attila puffed like a blowfish and dropped her books. I started for her, my hands balled into fists. Harm grabbed the back of my jacket and spun me toward the Buick as Dale opened the front door. Harm slung me in and slammed the door. The boys dove in the back, and Grandmother Miss Lacy put the pedal to the metal.

"Anna will get you for that," Harm warned, sounding happy.

"Yeah," Dale said. "Thanks."

I been fighting for Dale since our Diaper Days. He hates fighting. I, on the other hand, enjoy it—especially if Attila's my target. Dale leaned across the seat to study Grandmother Miss Lacy's face. "Is it true Starr found our camp stove?"

Grandmother Miss Lacy, who ain't much taller than me, sits on a pillow to see over the dash. "It's true. And I should warn you. Capers's jailbreak story is front-page news all over the state. The café phone's ringing off the hook. Reporters, gossips . . ."

"Is that all she wrote?" I asked, thinking of Miss Rose's break-in.

"Should she have written more?"

So, Capers Dylan kept her word.

Grandmother Miss Lacy went for a change of topic. "How was school, Dale?"

"School lasts twelve years and people are trashing us worse than ever and I hate it, but except for that it was fine," he replied. "We gave out adoption forms. I'm hoping Mo will take glamour photos of Liz so we can post them too," he added.

Being a best friend carries a heavy price. "Sure," I mumbled.

"Miss Thornton, may I offer you a puppy?" Dale asked, in a move straight out of *Manners Girls Like*. "It could grow into a watchdog and keep you from being an old maid."

An old maid? Definitely not in *Manners Girls Like*.

Harm gasped. "Dale," he said. "I don't think that came out right."

"Dale means . . ." I said. I stopped, trying to think of an end to the sentence.

"Alone," she said. "He means I wouldn't be alone. Thank you, dear, but some things are worse than being alone. Being chewed up, spit on, and covered in dog hair come to mind. Harm, I'll drop you off first if no one objects."

"I'm sure Grandpa Red won't mind," Harm teased. "He misses you."

"I've been busy at the inn, dear," she said, pointing the Buick toward the edge of town. "Lavender's finishing up another room for us. So much dust!"

Lavender can fix anything. It's only a matter of time before he gets his new second-hand racecar fixed up, and wins at Daytona. I will cheer from the stands.

Grandmother Miss Lacy puttered past the old store and turned onto a rutted path leading through the woods, to Mr. Red's dirt yard. "My word, Harm Crenshaw," she said, gazing at the small homestead. "You two have been busy."

Harm grinned. "Check out the new steps. Gramps built them himself."

"Very handsome," she murmured as Mr. Red spotted us. He straightened his barn jacket and wiggled his cap tighter on his head.

"Those plaid ear flaps are a good look for him," Dale said.

Mr. Red opened her door. "Lacy," he said, like a prince opening a carriage door.

"Red," she replied, smiling up at him. "The place looks nice."

"Come in and see what I've been doing," he invited.

She shook her head. "Not today. I want Mo and Dale home before people start worrying. And talking." She put the Buick in reverse and we bounced down the path.

"Are you going to marry him?" Dale asked as we hit a rut that bounced him almost to the roof.

"Marry Red?" she said. "What on earth are you talking about?"

"I hope not," he said. "You're Mo's honorary grand-mother. If you marry Mr. Red and adopt Harm, that would make Harm Mo's uncle. I don't think you can go to sixth grade in the same class with an uncle. It sounds illegal to me."

Dale's mind works in mysterious ways.

"I hadn't thought of it quite like that," she said.

Nobody thinks quite like Dale.

Five minutes later Dale and me blasted through the café door. "Miss Lana," I called, "guess what! We passed out puppy applications and—" I skidded to a halt.

"Hello Detectives," Capers Dylan said, stuffing her papers into her saddlebag. The café had gone World War II Paris—khaki napkins, Sherman Tank salt and pepper shakers, Maurice Chevalier on the jukebox. "What's cooking?"

Dale sniffed. "Mama's collards?"

"Where's Miss Lana?" I asked.

"Piggly Wiggly," she said. "It's amazing how much food a café runs through. The Colonel had already taken the phone off the hook and stomped out. Lana asked me to watch the place. I hope you're not hungry, because I don't cook."

Miss Lana left the café with a rookie?

"You're relieved of duty," I said. "Café Command requires expertise. When you deal with the public, an infinite number of things can go wrong."

As if to prove my point, a red sports car wheeled into the parking lot—flashy hubcaps, spoiler, air freshener dangling from the mirror. Flick Crenshaw rolled out, an ugly stick of dynamite begging for a light.

"Speak of the Devil," Dale said, heading for the ice cream.

Flick shoved through the door. "Hey, Dale," he said. "Who's your friend?"

"You know Mo."

"I mean the good-looking one," he said, winking at Capers. "Coffee, Mo."

"We're out."

His gaze lingered on the full coffeepot. "Not my day," he said. "Came over to join Starr's search. I'm civic-minded that way. Only he can't use me."

Flick's civic-minded like the Colonel's take-out-the-trash-minded—meaning he ain't. He smirked at us. "You don't know, do you?" he asked. "Some detectives you are. Macon Johnson robbed Creekside Baptist Church."

The ice cream scoop clattered from Dale's hand. "What?"

"Check your police scanner," he said—like we had one. "Creekside Baptist is your church, isn't it, Dale? Doesn't your mama sing in the choir or something? Bet she won't after this."

"Get out of here," I said, my temper popping.

Flick's face went switchblade serious. "Don't tell me what to do, you little—"

"Leave her alone," Capers snapped. She tucked her saddlebag against her body, shoved her right hand inside, and pointed the bag at him. "I mean it."

"Gun," I whispered, "get down." I turned to Dale.

"Down here," he whispered from behind the counter.

Flick glared at Capers, spun, and slammed the door behind him.

"What's in there?" I demanded as Flick fishtailed across the parking lot, headed for town. "We don't allow firearms unless you're Joe Starr."

She plopped into a chair. "Just my writing gear. Total bluff." She flipped open the saddlebag. "See for yourself. What's wrong with that guy?"

"Mama says he's unsavory," Dale said, grabbing the

phone and dialing. "Harm? Meet us at Creekside Baptist," he said, and hung up.

I looked at Capers. Smart, good bluffing skills, bold. And she kept her word to me. Maybe she's café material after all. "You're in charge," I said, snagging my camera. "We'll fill you in when we get back."

"Deal," she said, and we flew out the door.

Dale hopped on my handlebars light as a bug and I pedaled toward town. Flick's car roared by, headed back toward the café.

"Where's *he* going?" I looked back a moment later to see Capers and Flick in the parking lot, her finger in his bantam chest. "Look," I said, skidding to a halt and pitching Dale to his feet.

Capers hauled back and slapped Flick hard enough to stagger him sideways.

"Wow," Dale said. "She's got a temper bad as yours. And a way better right hook."

Suddenly I liked Capers Dylan. A lot.

Chapter 9
He Could Have Just Asked

At the church steps Dale vaulted off my handlebars. "Hey, Thes," he said as Harm blasted up on his silver bike. "What happened?"

"We've been robbed," Thes said, his voice swollen with tears. "All of us. Daddy, me, you, Jesus, everybody." He sat bundled on the top step, his orange cat, Spitz, winding around his feet. Starr's Impala lurked in the parking lot.

"Don't worry, Thes, the Desperados are on it," I said. "What walked off?"

"Sunday's collection—maybe a hundred dollars," he said, scooping Spitz into his lap. "Detective Starr's checking for fingerprints." He scowled at Dale. "If your daddy needed something, all he had to do was ask."

Dale's face went the color of river sand. Dale loves that church good as he loves his own house. So does Miss Rose.

Thes knows that.

"I hate it same as you," Dale said. "And it's going to break Mama's heart."

Thes and Spitz stared at us, the silence stretching tight. "I'll do Spitz's photos first thing tomorrow," I said, to break the tension. "I hope you land a puppy."

"No," Thes said, turning away. "I don't want a puppy anymore."

Dale looked like he'd kicked him.

"Thes, you don't mean that," Harm said. "Let's talk tomorrow."

"I said I don't want your puppy," Thes said, glaring at Dale. "Not after this."

"You'd never get one anyway," Dale shot back. A total lie. "Queen Elizabeth and me didn't rob this church. If you're punishing us for something we didn't do, you ain't puppy material."

"Fine," Thes said, his voice harsh. "Go on, then," he added, giving Harm and me an eat-dirt look. "All of you. Get away from me." He pulled his cat close.

Spitz hissed.

We balanced on a silence rocky as a rowboat on a choppy creek and I searched for just the right words. Nothing came. I went with what I had. "Your cat is ugly," I said, very cool. "Excuse us. We got a case to solve."

We stepped into the church and gasped. The pulpit

lay on its side, its purple skirt crumpled. The candlesticks had rolled across the floor—one under the piano, the other beneath a pew. Reverend Thompson kneeled in front of it all, wiping the floor.

"Desperado Detectives at your service," I said. "We came soon as we heard."

He lumbered to his feet and tossed the rag into a bucket. "Thes is around here somewhere. He likes you kids. Especially you, Mo," he said, giving us a sad smile.

"Yes, sir," I said. "When did this happen? Does the church have enemies?"

"Besides Satan?" Dale added.

Reverend Thompson smiled. "I suspect Satan has bigger fish to fry. This strikes me as man-made mischief. I'll let Starr figure out *which* man. As for time, I locked up late last night, and opened two hours ago. Someone took the collection—and the plate."

The collection plate?

"That giant gold plate?" I said. "It must be worth a fortune."

He shook his head. "Not in dollars. It had a different kind of value. Someone donated it to honor a loved one."

"But why take *that*? You can't fence a collection plate," Dale said. "Anybody that's been to our family reunion knows that. Daddy ain't a rookie."

The *Daddy's a Professional Thief Defense*. Harm winced.

"Good point," Reverend Thompson said, very easy. "The bandit may have been a rookie, which would certainly eliminate Macon. Or he could have another motive."

Like getting even with Miss Rose and Dale for going against him, I thought.

"I'll give you a hand with the pulpit," Harm said. Dale and me darted to help. "Now," Harm said, and we muscled the pulpit into place.

I cased the sanctuary one last time. Starr's already de-clueing the office, I thought. I made a note: Add police scanner to Christmas list. "If you find clues, give us a call," I said, heading for the door. "Come on, Desperados. We'll search outside."

I led the way out the side door and along the building. "Hey Mo, did you just call me a Desperado in there?" Harm asked. "You said 'Come on, Desperados.'" He tried to act like he didn't care, same as when Attila calls him an outsider.

I crooked an eyebrow at Dale, who bobbed his head.

"You're on probation until we solve The Case of the Missing Daddy," Dale said. "I'd say you have a good chance unless the stress crumples you." Harm revved up his swagger as we rounded the side of the cinderblock building.

"Over there," I said, pointing to Thes's rabbit box.

Someone had shoved it beneath the bathroom window—which gaped open.

"Whoever went through there is thin," Harm said. He plucked a snarl of brown thread from the windowsill. "Off a hunting jacket?" he guessed. "Mr. Macon's hunting jacket's missing. And he's thin."

"So are you," Dale said, frowning. "And I see a hundred of those jackets every hunting season." Dale touched Harm's sleeve. "You got to keep an open mind to be a detective. Settle down. If you weren't a natural we wouldn't have drafted you."

Being in charge suits Dale when he knows the rules.

Dale walked down the back of the building, studying the ground. "Weird footprint," he announced.

"Footprints?" Starr said, rounding the corner. I shoved the thread in my pocket. "What are you kids doing? Because if you destroyed my evidence . . ."

"We didn't," I said. *Destroyed* and *in my pocket* are two different things.

Starr knelt and measured the footprint Dale had found. "Size nine dress shoe."

My heart dove to my sneakers.

Mr. Macon wears a size nine—I knew it from our first case. Starr pulled a frame from his bag and placed it around the print. "Perfect," he said, tipping a bottle of green goo over the print. I stepped back, pulled out my camera, and lined up a long shot. *Click*. Then the foot-print. *Click*.

Dale frowned. "But that's just *one* print. And it's in the only clear space back here, and it's totally flat—no shoe-bend to it. Who would leave a print like that?"

"Somebody standing still, like you are. What size shoe does Macon wear?" Starr asked.

Dale studied the graveyard, the river. The quiver of his chin put him a heartbeat from crying. *He knows his daddy's shoe size good as I do.*

It's hard being a good son to a bad man.

I stepped up beside him. "Dale and me don't track shoe sizes. We enjoy a reverse-flair for trivia. We're below average at best."

"Way below average," Harm said. "It's sad, really."

"Well, Rose will remember," Starr said.

A slime-ball move.

"Daddy wears a nine," Dale blurted. "But that's circumstantial."

Starr made a note in his clue pad.

"Come on, Desperados," I said. "Let's ride."

Dale went quiet as the bottom of a well as we pedaled back to the café. Queen Elizabeth, who waited by the café jukebox, brought him back to life.

"She showed up at the door," Capers said, rearranging

her papers. "I assumed she was looking for you," she said as Dale gave Liz a hug.

"Liz is psychic," I explained. "She always knows where Dale is."

Dale rubbed Liz's head. "She's been craving odd foods lately," he said. "Mama says it's normal when you're expecting. She may need ice cream."

Capers laughed. "A psychic pregnant hound. Great detail for my article."

As Dale trotted behind the counter and opened the ice cream case, I snuck a peek at Capers's notebook. She closed it. "Congratulations on your great right hook," I said.

A blush crept up her neck. "You saw that? Flick's a foul-mouthed worm. He had it coming." She gave Harm a smile. "I'm surprised he's your brother."

"Me too," Harm said. "I'm also surprised you're still in town with no trial to cover. I know Lavender's still got your motorcycle, but . . ."

Smooth. Good way to *not* ask a question when you *do* want an answer. Harm will be a great detective one day.

"I'll file updates until we see what Macon does," she said. "Speaking of updates, you promised me a report."

I hesitated. Mr. Macon robbed the church, but how could I say it and still be a good friend to Dale?

"I got a quote," Dale said, setting a bowl of vanilla ice cream by Queen Elizabeth.

Dale, who hates to speak up in class, will talk to a reporter?

The hair on the back of my neck stood up.

"A *rookie thief* robbed Creekside Baptist last night," Dale said. "The Desperados take this personal. We will track this no-talent to the ends of the earth if we can get a ride that far, but hopefully the thief will stay local so we can ride our bikes. Thank you."

I relaxed. That could have gone worse. Way worse.

"Hey," Dale said, his face lighting up. "I just thought of something else."

"No you didn't," I said, very fast. "This concludes our press conference," I added as the Colonel came in from the kitchen and heaved a bin of silverware onto the counter.

He dealt Capers a look that could freeze lava. "Leave these kids alone. Fork Duty," he said to us, whipping a stack of napkins out of the cabinet.

Harm followed us to the sink to wash up. "Good job," he told Dale.

I grabbed a knife-spoon-fork trio and quick-rolled it café-style. "Wow," Harm said, nudging in beside me. "You're blazing fast."

"It's in my blood," I told him.

Beside me, Dale folded his napkin into his customary Diamond Fold Pouch and tucked the silverware inside.

Dale watches PBS, the only station Miss Rose allows. He can also turn hand towels into animal shapes. "Nice," Harm said, watching him. "But your way's easier, Mo. Teach me?"

I snagged another handful of silver as Miss Lana flew in with vinegar cruets. "Dale? Invite Rose for supper, honey," she said. She opened a jar of red pepper flakes and added a pinch to each cruet. I read the specials board:

AMERICANS-IN-PARIS SPECIAL:
Baked ham avec cloves, macaroni au fromage, collards a la zing. $7.95

"'A la zing,'" I told Harm. "Tupelo French for red pepper."

Dale hung up. "Mama can't come, but I can," he told Miss Lana. "Her new boyfriend's keeping her company. I'd feel like a spare tire around them anyway."

"You mean a fifth wheel, honey," she said. "And it's not so. What do you think of him? I haven't met him yet—which is starting to hurt my feelings."

"He's nice on the phone," Dale said. "But he makes her different."

Miss Lana swept him into a hug. "We'll like him. If we don't, we'll drive him mad and he'll go away." She rumpled his hair as Starr stalked in, his collar turned up against the cold. "What'll it be, Joe?" Miss Lana asked, smiling.

"Two burgers and coffee. To go," he said, sliding his thermos across the counter to Harm. Normally Starr doesn't drink coffee after three p.m. due to chronic jitters. His ordering coffee now can mean only two things: love or law.

"You got a date with Miss Retzyl?" I asked. "May I recommend the house fries with extra ketchup? You don't want to look cheap around a schoolteacher."

He smiled. He's not bad when he smiles. "No date, but the fries sound good. Pickles on the burgers." Queen Elizabeth's ears perked up.

"No date? You're on stakeout, then," I said, very smooth.

"Stakeout?" Capers echoed from across the room. "Where?"

"Sorry—classified information," he said as Miss Lana speed-wrapped his burgers and popped them in a bag.

"Seven dollars even."

Starr put a ten down and turned for the door. Queen Elizabeth shot from the shadows like a heat-seeking missile and grabbed his cuff.

"Liz!" Dale cried as she tugged his pants leg. "No!"

Dale grabbed the pickle jar, fished out a pickle, and waved it near her nose. She rolled her eyes sideways to stare at it. "Let Starr go," he coaxed. "Good girl." She released Starr's cuff and delicately plucked the pickle from Dale's fingers.

"Cravings," Dale explained, smiling up at Starr. "She'll be embarrassed when she has time to think this through."

Harm opened the door for Starr. "Our associate Anna Celeste Simpson will handle your dry cleaning bill."

Harm's going to fit in good.

We watched Starr's Impala ease into the night as a pack of strangers filed in, discussing Capers's story and the jailbreak.

"Starr's not headed for the church," Dale said as his taillights disappeared. "He's staking out Daddy."

"I doubt it, Dale," the Colonel said. "If Starr knew where Macon was, he'd arrest him. Finish that silverware. The supper crowd's on its way."

As we worked, Dale whispered: "Mo, something's wrong at church."

True, I thought. Your daddy robbed it and you can't say it.

He wrapped a set of silverware wrong, unwrapped it, wrapped it again. It scared me. Dale and me been wrapping silverware since second grade. Stress, Skeeter had said. First the jailbreak. Now Mr. Macon robbing his church, Thes turning on him, people white-trash-talking his family.

He looks like a candle burning out, I thought.

"Things are . . . wrong," he said. "I can't *think* it yet

but I can feel it. Right here," he said, laying his hand just below his ribs. "In that place that folds up like a lawn chair when you're scared."

"I know that place," Harm said, his voice soft.

I didn't say it, but I knew it too. The place that folds in on itself when I think Upstream Mother's never coming, or that the Colonel and Miss Lana will get so wrapped up in each other, they won't need me anymore.

"Don't tell Mama about the footprint," Dale said. "She's upset enough."

"Deal," I said, watching the Azalea Women's van wheel across the parking lot. She knows by now anyway, I thought, as they surged for the door.

> Dear Upstream Mother,
> Dale's daddy robbed Creekside Baptist. The talk's all over town.
> School takes in late tomorrow thanks to a so-called Teacher's Work Day. Word on the street is Line Dancing is involved.
> I'm getting scared for Dale. Me and him been outsiders all our lives but I never seen it as bad as this.

I grabbed my phone. Harm picked up. "Hello?" he said, his voice sleepy.

"I'm worried about Dale."

He yawned. "Me too. Come over tomorrow. Breakfast is at eight. How's Lavender? I didn't get to ask you at the café."

"Lavender?" I said, sitting up. "Has something happened to Lavender?"

"No. But Macon's his daddy too."

What kind of future wife am I? I hadn't even thought about Lavender! "I was just going to check," I said. "Fortunately I have his number seared into my brain."

I prepared a few sensitive off-the-cuff remarks as I dialed. Sadly, he didn't answer. "Lavender's home, Crissy speaking. With whom are you?"

Crud. A twin.

"It's Mo," I said. "I hope Lavender's hair loss problem isn't as contagious as people say. You're brave. Do you have a diagnosis yet?"

The phone clattered to Lavender's end table and his front door slammed.

"Crissy?" Lavender called. He picked up. "Who the heck is this?"

"It's Mo. I just called to check on you. Crissy sounded like she had a little hairball in her throat, which can happen in her line of work."

I could hear his smile. "I'm sure she didn't, but thanks for checking on me, Mo. I'm okay. Once the chin-wagging stops, life will go back to normal. It always does."

I hesitated. "Dale actually thinks Mr. Macon didn't rob the church."

"I know," he sighed. "Truth is, Macon probably hit it for cash on his way out of town. Listen: Dale and I are helping Mama break collards first thing in the morning, and then we're trucking them to Ayden. Want to ride?"

Me? Spend the morning with Lavender, who I will one day walk with in the evenings, discussing our adopted children and our foster parrot, Cliff, whose behavior problems keep us awake at night?

I sighed. Miss Lana says canceling one date for another is tawdry, which if I ever look that up, I'm pretty sure it will be bad.

"I hate to break your heart, but I got a breakfast date."

I heard his grin. "Say hey to Harm for me. 'Night Mo."

Harm? How did he know it was Harm? I returned to my letter:

> Just talking to Lavender settles my soul.
> Scaring off a twin scores double. Faking hard-
> to-get scores triple. When you meet Lavender,
> you'll see why.
>
> Breakfast with Harm tomorrow.
> Mo

Chapter 10
Breakfast at Harm's

I still had Dale on my mind as I knocked on Harm's kitchen door.

"Just in time, LoBeau," Harm said, swinging the door open. His dark hair still glistened from his shower. He wore a white T-shirt neatly tucked into dark jeans. "Help yourself to juice. We eat in five."

Harm looks at home in a kitchen, spinning from sink to stove. Before Harm moved in, Mr. Red's kitchen held towers of dirty dishes and watched the world through grimy panes. Now a potted begonia sat in the center of the polished oak table and curtains hung neat at the sparkling windows.

I grabbed an orange juice. "Where'd you learn to cook?"

"My mom." He flipped a pancake and slid the black iron griddle to catch it. "She'll be a big singer soon as she gets a break."

"That's where you get your good voice," I said.

He grinned. "The point is *somebody* had to cook."

His string-bean arms are filling out, I thought, watching him tip a pancake onto the spatula and flip it. "You been lifting Dale's weights."

"A little," he said, grabbing his wrist and flexing his muscles.

"Show-off," Mr. Red said, shuffling in to wash his paint-covered hands at the sink. Miss Lana says always compliment your host's home. "Nice shade of . . . pink," I said, watching the pink paint swirl down the drain.

He gave me a look from beneath white eyebrows. "Just sprucing up the place," he said. "Pink is Lacy's favorite color."

Pink? Is he mad?

"Used to be, anyway," Harm said. "Seventy or eighty years ago."

Mr. Red smiled. "I'm making things nice for Harm and me. If Lacy likes it too, so much the better." He dried his hands, leaving a faint pink smudge on the towel.

"Breakfast is served," Harm said, placing his pancakes on the table. I sat and whisked my paper towel into my lap.

"Bless the food, bless the cook. Amen," Mr. Red muttered, and shoved the pancakes my way. "Where's Dale? He usually trails you like a shadow."

I loaded up on pancakes. "Helping Miss Rose and Lavender."

Harm stacked his flapjacks neat as Tuesday. Mr. Red forked up a landslide.

"Miss Lana said invite you for Thanksgiving dinner at our house," I said, and they smiled identical smiles.

"What else do you do around here to celebrate?" Harm asked.

"A school play, most years," I told him.

"Hope not," he muttered. "I get stage fright."

We continued on, hitting the highlights: Macon's escape, the scarcity of clues, Dale's guineas. Mr. Red shocked me on the guineas. "Smart idea. Dale has brains, he just has a gear most of us can't find."

Harm looked at his grandfather. "Gramps, Dale doesn't think Mr. Macon robbed the church."

Mr. Red frowned. "It's tough, hearing your father did something you can't imagine," he said. "Are people treating Dale right?"

Harm shook his head. "School's a freaking nightmare. I don't know how he walks in there. Mrs. Simpson called Dale's family white trash and Mo tried to fight. Thes has turned against Dale—and against us too, if I read him right yesterday."

Mr. Red's fork froze in midair. "Thes? The preacher's boy?"

"He's even turned on Mo. And he *really* likes her," Harm said, his voice teasing.

I flipped a speck of pancake at him.

"Eat it or leave it, but don't throw it," Mr. Red muttered, and drowned his pancakes in syrup. "Don't let that church turn on Dale. He's not tough enough."

"Dale's plenty tough," I said. It's a reflex, standing up for Dale.

Mr. Red grinned at me. "You remind me of somebody I used to know."

"Miss Lacy Thornton," Harm guessed. "You caught a bad break when you were a boy, Gramps. Just like Dale's catching one now."

Mr. Red has a moonshine past with some ugly stories hooked in. He shrugged his thin shoulders. "I've known Dale all his life. Macon used to bring Dale by when he was no bigger than a minute. Macon was a better man then," he said. "But he can't let things go. He's never satisfied. Everything feels like a slight to him. It doesn't matter how much he drinks or steals or makes Rose cry, nothing will ever fill Macon up."

Dale never mentioned moonshine shopping with his daddy. But Dale never mentioned a lot of things.

"Keep standing up for Dale like Lacy did for me," he said. "And square things with Thes if you can. Gossip's like a ship—hard to turn and harder to stop. Dale needs that church sailing with him."

Harm buttered his pancakes. "Make nice with Thes.

We can do that," he said, and then gave me his faux angel look. "Good thing we didn't insult his cat."

Crud. Spitz.

Mr. Red hopped up and ferried his plate to the sink. "Put in a word for me with Lacy, will you, Mo?" he asked, his old eyes twinkling.

Miss Lana says love's like time travel. Could be. Just saying Grandmother Miss Lacy's name put a spring in Mr. Red's step as he headed for the door.

"There's Thes," Harm said a few hours later as we headed across the school grounds. "Let's make nice, like Gramps said."

"Thes," I said as Dale slammed his bike into the rack. "How's the weather?"

Normally Thes babbles weather. Today he studied the sky and wandered away. "Anna," he shouted. "Wait up. I got a forecast for you."

My blood ran ice. "He's crossed over to the dark side," I told Harm.

Dale sprinted up. "Hey," he said. "Do you think anybody filled out a puppy application? Liz is a nervous wreck."

Queen Elizabeth? Nervous?

Hannah opened her satchel. "Question answered, Dale. This is from Little Agnes," she said, handing him a form. "If you give her a pup, I'll help her."

Dale smiled, very shy. "Thank you. I'll keep her in mind," he said, and slipped the application into his backpack.

Little Agnes was the first of many.

Dale glowed as the applications rained across his desk. "Thank you," he said. "We'll be in touch. Thank you. Thank you . . ." The kids filed by: Sal with two apps—one for her and one for Skeeter—Susana, Jimmy and Jake . . .

Jake placed a Snickers bar on his. Dale turned his head. Jake slipped the candy back in his pocket and Dale slid the application into the pile.

I gave Thes my best insincere smile. He took his blank application from his notebook, crumpled it, and tossed it at the wastepaper basket.

Thes and Attila kept the church rumors buzzing like chain saws the rest of the day. Dale ignored them. He skimmed applications behind a wall of open schoolbooks until the bell rang and we sprinted for freedom.

"You sorting those today?" I asked as we hit the playground. "We could post the Puppy List tomorrow. Miss Lana says strike while the iron's hot."

He jerked his bike out of the rack. "Maybe tonight," he said. "Today I got a surprise for Miss Thornton. Plus Lavender invited us over to see his new car." He frowned. "Did I forget to tell you?"

Dale makes me crazy.

If I'd known Lavender had invited us to Grandmother Miss Lacy's old garage, where he fixes cars, I'd have worn my other sweatshirt—the one without the gravy monogram. Miss Lana says Fate keeps us humble. The Colonel says he'd hate to meet her in a dark alley.

We dropped our bikes by Grandmother Miss Lacy's dogwood. I grabbed my camera from my basket as Dale tore to the garage. The front door squeaked open and she stepped out, smiling.

"Hey. Lavender invited us over," Harm said, "and Dale brought you a surprise."

I avoided her eyes. Dale's surprises can stun.

Dale struggled toward us with a pet carrier, his slight body leaning against its weight. He set the cage by the steps and opened the door. Two guineas popped their heads out—paste-white, wrinkled skin, cherry-red dots on each cheek, a sparse tuft of feathers on their tiny heads. They darted out, and screamed across the yard.

"Those are the ugliest birds I've ever seen," Grandmother Miss Lacy said, blinking.

"Yes, but they make up for it by being loud," Dale said. "Guineas are the best watch animals next to a dog. You alone in this big house isn't safe. I'm the man of *our* house and I thought I'd help you too, until you and Mr. Red . . . You know. Go steady."

The guineas shrieked. An Azalea Woman opened her front door and peered out.

"How . . . generous," Grandmother Miss Lacy said. "How do you get them back in the cage?"

"You can't," Dale said. "It's not mine. They'll sleep in your trees. I'm glad you have two, because one would be lonely."

A guinea flapped across the ground, catapulted into the air, and slammed into the side of the garage. It picked itself up and ran off again.

Grandmother Miss Lacy took a deep breath. She's going to kill Dale, I thought, and stepped back. Harm stepped back too—good instinct.

Instead of killing Dale, she wrapped him in a fierce hug. "Thank you for caring about me. Do come in while I find my coat."

We stood in the hall as she ravaged her closet. "Somebody robbed Creekside Baptist yesterday," Dale said. "People say it was Daddy, but it wasn't."

Her radiator clunked. I held my breath, hoping Dale wouldn't ask me to back him up on the Macon's Innocent claim.

"Yes, dear, I heard." The pipes clanked. "That heater has me at my wits' end. I may *have* to buy a new one. That one's old as I am."

"It's probably still under warranty, then," Harm said, and she laughed.

Where did Harm learn how to flirt?

Moments later Lavender beamed at us. "Allow me to introduce you to the latest number 32 car," he said, jacking the car up a notch and kicking the jack stands out of the way. "Don't ever go under a car without jack stands, little brother," he said, letting the jack down. "Because if the jack slips, you can be crushed or trapped, and . . ."

"I know," Dale said. "You told me a thousand times. How's she looking?"

Lavender grinned. "I think you'll appreciate her lines *and* her pipes."

I aimed my camera and he pulled back the tarp like a magician.

We gasped.

Miss Lana says reality is like cheap shampoo. Sometimes it takes a while to sink in. This was one of those times.

Click.

The car slumped like a refugee from a junkyard—dingy, tired, lonely for paint.

"Dang, son, that's old," Harm said.

"Classic Monte Carlo," Lavender replied, glowing. "Well, she'll be classic when I'm through. Bought her off a driver in Tar Heel, North Carolina. I love Tupelo Landing," he said, "but this car is my ticket to bigger things."

He leaned against the car. Lavender, who's dazzling in coveralls, leans better than anybody I know.

Click.

Dale kicked a tire. "Does she roll?"

"The body needs work, but she sings like an angel." Lavender reached through the window and turned the key. The engine roared to life.

"Yeah, boy," Harm said, leaning into the sound.

"She's lovely," Grandmother Miss Lacy said. "What color will you choose?"

"Black," Harm and Dale said together.

I shook my head. "Purple, like your last car."

The door flew open behind us and a cold swirl of dead leaves swept into the garage. "I vote green," Flick Crenshaw said. "The color of a dead man's car."

"A dead man's car!" Grandmother Miss Lacy cried.

Harm glared at his big brother. "That's an old racing superstition, Miss Thornton," he said. "And it's bull. What do you want, Flick?"

"That's a lame ride," Flick said, scouting the car.

"Good enough to beat you," I said.

"Really? Name the time and place. I bet a hundred bucks on me."

Normally Lavender doesn't have two words for Flick Crenshaw—not two Miss Rose allows, anyway. To my surprise, he nudged Dale. "What do you think?"

Smart. A race would give Dale one more thing to think about until the Mr. Macon hoopla dies down. Sometimes I think Dale and Miss Rose shape every decision Lavender makes. Then I see him with a big-haired twin and I think twice.

"Me?" Dale said. "Yes, I think so. Beating Flick is always good."

"Miss Thornton?" Lavender asked.

She shrugged. "A hundred-dollar wager hardly seems worth getting out of bed for. But what do I know? I'm only the sponsor."

The sponsor?

"Well, the inn is, technically," she said. "Lana and I feel it's only a matter of time before Lavender wins at Hallelujah."

"Talladega," Dale said.

"A thousand bucks then," Flick said, and Harm did a double take.

"You're on, Flick," Lavender said, smooth as if he had a thousand dollars. "Now get out of my garage—and stay out."

٭ ٭ ٭ ٭ ٭

That night I grabbed Volume 7 and a green ink pen formerly known as Attila's.

> Dear Upstream Mother,
>
> Good news: I'm on Team Lavender and the race is on!
>
> Bad news: Thes ain't making up. Now I wish I hadn't called Spitz ugly, but like Miss Lana says, you can't unsay words once they're launched any more than you can un-shoot an arrow.
>
> Did I get my mouth from you? If so, feel free to take it back.
>
> Mo

Chapter 11
No. Yes. Maybe.

The next morning, Thes strolled into school with a newspaper under his arm. "Did everybody see this?" he asked. He snapped the paper open and showed the headline to Capers's article: *Tupelo Landing Stunned by Church Heist. Escaped Con Top Suspect.*

Dale didn't look up from his applications. In fact, he didn't look up all day.

"Help," he said as we stumbled out of school, brain-fried from reading bar graphs. As if bar graphs could survive in the real world. Dale opened his backpack and tipped it toward us. "More applications. Skeeter had them in the office."

Harm's mouth dropped open. "How many have you got?"

"A brazillion," Dale said.

"Dale," I said, "Brazil is a country. Not a number."

"If you want to go nit-picky on your best friend," he said, his voice rising. "I thought applications would be easy, but when I read these, I get brain glob." He whirled to face us. "Why did I put essays on the application? Do I think I'm a teacher?"

"Calm down, Dale," Harm said. "Maybe we can help."

"Good," Dale said. "I deputize you both onto the Puppy Committee. First meeting starts now." He hopped on his bike and zipped toward home.

Harm looked at me, his dark eyes full of surprise. "The Puppy Committee? Congratulations," he said, and we sailed off behind Dale.

As Dale dealt out the applications in his room, the living room phone rang. Miss Rose answered, her voice drifting to us.

"She's talking to Bill," Dale said, listening. "Her new boyfriend."

She laughed easy as water over stones. I'd forgotten how much I missed the sound. "She sounds happy," I said. "Harm and me will screen the applications, but the final decision's up to you. We'll divide them into No, Yes, Maybe."

Outside, the guineas squawked. "Hold on, Bill," Miss Rose said as someone tapped on the front door. "Dale," she called. "More flowers, baby."

More flowers?

Dale trotted out as Susana Lowery zipped past the window and jumped into a getaway Chevy at the road.

"Flowers?" Harm said. "Does Susana like Dale too? I thought Sal liked him. And since when do girls give guys flowers? Never mind," he said before I could answer. "I like tulips in case you ever want to know."

"Mums," Dale announced, setting a flowerpot by the terrarium. "I got more on the back porch if you want some. Also candy and the book *What Sign Is Your Pet?* From kids wanting puppies."

Dale's getting puppy kickbacks?

"Mums?" Harm said. "They're cheery. Gramps might like them."

Dale nudged the bright yellow flowers to him, unwrapped three candies, and pushed them into his mouth. "Tuh committee is nah in session," he said. And we went to work.

An hour later we had one sprawling, ragged pile of applications and a tiny pile. Harm slumped in his chair, flipping through *Life Cycle of the Newt*.

I lined up another glamour shot. "This way, Liz," I said. She looked over her shoulder. *Click.*

Dale tossed his last application into the No pile. "Jerome named his hamster Assassin. What kind of message does that send?"

I lowered my camera. "That's all of them, then," I said, staring at the applications slip-sliding across the bed. "Who made the Yes pile?"

"Sal. And Skeeter."

I looked at Queen Elizabeth, whose sides bulged like she'd swallowed a bucket of bolts. "We need more than two homes." I rustled through Dale's rejects. "You're not giving Miss Retzyl a puppy? Have you lost your mind? She's a *teacher*."

"She's too strict," Dale said, flopping back on the bed.

I pawed through the papers. "And Little Agnes? What's wrong with Little Agnes? Hannah will help her with a puppy, you know she will."

"She failed her essay," Dale said, and clamped his mouth closed like a turtle.

I flipped to the essay page. "She wrote on that stupid baby paper with the dotted lines," I said. "She used a fat pencil." I read her essay:

I will lov a puppy every day. Agnes

"You took off for *spelling?*" I demanded. "Little Agnes is only five."

"Exactly," he said, his voice filling with tears. "There's something wrong with every single one of these. Except maybe Sal. Liz is family and you can't just let family go. You have to know they'll be okay."

"But Dale—"

"Dale's right," Harm interrupted.

Dale's right? Is he kidding?

Harm stood and stretched his long arms above his

head, grabbed the pot of chrysanthemums, and headed for the door. "They're your puppies, Dale. You let us know. Come on, LoBeau. I'll race you home."

I followed him to our bikes. "Harm, we need to post that Puppy List while everybody's excited. There's no telling how many puppy homes we'll need."

"I know."

I followed his gaze to the window. Dale stood by his terrarium, strumming his guitar. "He's singing Newton to sleep," I said.

Harm swung his leg over his bike. "Dale's having a rough time. He isn't like us. We lost our first worlds all at once, in an instant. You in the flood on the day you were born, me when Flick dumped me here to make a life if I could. But Dale's losing his an inch at a time. He'll let go of the puppies when he's ready."

I hadn't thought of it that way.

"Race you, LoBeau," he said, and blazed down the drive.

It was near dark by the time Harm and me pedaled into town. Harm rode with no hands, lean and comfortable as a knife cutting through the wind. "I got to swing by Grandmother Miss Lacy's and pick up some photos," I called. "You want to come?"

"Better not," he shouted, leaning into a turn, the mums cradled in his arm. "See you tomorrow. Remember: Tulips."

Like I'd ever care.

A half beat later I bounded up Grandmother Miss Lacy's steps. "Come in, dear," she said, smiling me into the hall. I gave her a quick hug. Grandmother Miss Lacy feels fragile as a hummingbird in my arms.

"I came to pick up the photos we worked on last night. If they're dry, I mean."

We headed for the darkroom. "Excellent candid shots," she said, peering at the photos clothes-pinned to the line. "And are these evidence?"

"Photos from the church." I sighed. "Dale thinks his daddy didn't rob it."

She stacked the photos. "What do you think?"

"I think Mr. Macon's guilty as sin. And I also think Dale's my best friend." She slipped the photos into an envelope. "You stood by Mr. Red back when his daddy was accused of a crime," I said, watching her. "Did you know he was guilty?"

"We all had suspicions," she said. "But Red was a friend. I like always to be both, but sometimes you have to choose. Would you rather be right—or kind?"

"I'm a detective," I said. "It's my job to be right. But as a friend . . ."

She smiled an inscrutable Old Person Smile. "Your choice, dear."

I headed for the door. "You coming to supper? It's

Miss Lana's Morocco Night—a collard stir-fry."

She laughed. "How many ways can Lana cook Rose's collards? I'll meet you there."

I scampered down the steps and grabbed my bike. As I turned, my glance raked the garage. Lavender, standing in the shadows by the door!

He turned his collar up to his hat, and the skin across my shoulders pulled tight. Lavender is hair vain. He doesn't wear a hat.

The wind blew and the shadows shifted across the man's face.

Mr. Macon? Flick? A stranger?

I dropped my bike. "Stop! You're under arrest," I bellowed in case it was Mr. Macon. I charged across the yard, the guineas shouting from the treetops. The man faded into the shadows.

"Stop!" I shouted again, rounding the garage.

A hand snaked from the dark and clamped my arm. A leg swept my feet from beneath me and the world spun upside down. I landed in the leafy arms of a camellia bush as the prowler ran away.

"Macon Johnson? Are you sure?" Starr asked ten minutes later, letting the curtain fall at the parlor window.

"Yes. No. Maybe," I said. "By the garage."

He headed for the door. "Stay inside, both of you. I mean it."

Grandmother Miss Lacy and I watched his light play along the edges of the garage. "He's found a clue," I said as Starr knelt. "Cover me."

"With what?" she asked as the door clattered shut behind me and I stealthed to Starr's side.

He jumped to his feet. "I told you to stay inside," he snapped.

"What did you find?" Grandmother Miss Lacy asked, strolling up behind me.

Starr whipped his hat off. "Don't you people ever follow directions?"

Interesting. Miss Retzyl asks the same thing.

Starr clicked his pen against his pad. "Running toward danger is a boneheaded move, Mo," he said. "Don't do it again. Miss Thornton? Keep your doors locked."

He tipped his hat and walked away.

Chapter 12
Wrong Twice, Just Like That

"I'm not sure who it was," I told Dale and Harm first thing the next morning, at school. "Mr. Macon's my best guess. And if it was him, it's a definite clue."

"Did you see his face?" Dale asked, frowning.

"Sort of."

"Sort of?" he said. "You're naming Daddy on a sort of?"

I felt heat walk up my neck. "He was Mr. Macon's height and he wore a hat. It could have been Flick or a stranger, but Mr. Macon's . . . you know. Mr. Macon."

Dale narrowed his eyes. "You saw a man in a hat, and guessed Daddy. Detectives don't guess, Mo, we prove."

From there, things careened downhill.

Miss Retzyl smiled at us as we settled in our desks. "Thanksgiving's just around the corner," she said. "Normally that means a play . . ."

Someone moaned. Maybe me.

Jake's hand shot into the air. "We found the first Thanksgiving menu. Extra credit!"

Last time the Exums went for extra credit, they blew up the classroom. The front row rustled like sitting ducks as Jimmy tucked his shirttail in and carried their paper up to Miss Retzyl.

"It *does* look old," Miss Retzyl said. No surprise. The Exum boys do top-notch forgeries. "This brown ink is wonderful." She held it to the light. "Is it coffee, or tea, or lemon juice?" Jimmy blinked innocent as a fawn. "It's lovely. And the way the paper's singed on the edges. . . ." She gave him a hundred-watt smile. "How did you do it?"

Jimmy opened his mouth.

"Don't answer," Jake whispered.

Jimmy closed his mouth.

Miss Retzyl read the menu. "Sorry, boys," she said. "I don't believe the Pilgrims served green Jell-O."

"They didn't?" Jimmy said, his eyes going round. "Mama does."

Jake raised what would have been his eyebrows if he hadn't already blown them off. "It's not real? We're shocked!" He went for a diversion—a good move. "Can we do a Thanksgiving play, then? Jimmy does a good turkey. Show them."

Jimmy hunched his shoulders and gobbled. Harm and Dale clapped.

Attila flounced her hair. "For heaven's sake, sit down,"

she snapped. "You're as lame as Miss Lana in her Pilgrim outfit. Where does she get those things anyway?"

"The *Mayflower*," Dale said. "I think she looks nice."

Dale standing up for Miss Lana after I'd practically turned Mr. Macon in on a whim made me feel worse.

I passed Dale a note: I'm sorry.

He read it and nodded without looking at me. Crud.

"We *could* have a talent contest this year," I suggested.

Attila stuck out her lip. "You're just saying that because Dale and Harm have talent and I don't."

True.

"That's not true," I replied. "We all got talent. You, for instance, got that incredible goldfish imitation." She whipped around to stare at me, her mouth half open and her eyes slightly bugging. "See?"

"Actually," Miss Retzyl said, "we'll skip the play this year. We're behind in our studies thanks to the Exums' . . . explosive history presentation last month." Jake and Jimmy smiled like stuffed animals. "I just wanted to mention the short week ahead, and your math test on Wednesday. Please take out your science books."

No play?

I raised my hand. "Excuse me. Nobody hates school plays more than me, but now that we can't have one, I feel like I lost something I might enjoy in a parallel universe. For me, public humiliation is part of the holidays."

Harm twisted in his seat to stare. Sal glanced up from her book, *Deciphering Codes*. "I think we should vote."

"Sixth grade is not a democracy," Miss Retzyl said. "Science books. Now."

That afternoon we found Queen Elizabeth curled by our bikes. "How many little royals you think she's carrying?" Harm asked, running a hand across her tummy.

"Somewhere between two and twelve," Dale said. "I've been thinking about names. So far I got George, Victoria, Mary Queen of Scots. Not Henry VIII," he continued. "He failed with family issues."

Understatement. Henry VIII ran through wives like a coyote runs through chickens. Dale and me saw the PBS special.

Hannah strolled by. "How about African royalty? King Tut? Or royalty from another planet? Leto II?"

"Ming is good," Sal said, sailing up. "From China's famous Ming Dynasty. Here, Ming," she called, clapping her hands. "Good Ming."

Queen Elizabeth thumped her tail.

"Liz likes it." Dale smiled at me. "You want to work on the Name List today?"

"I'd love to," Sal said, her voice soft.

"I meant Mo and Harm," Dale said, grabbing his bike. "The Names Committee."

Another committee?

"Dale," Harm said, "Sal could be on it. Or—"

"No. It wouldn't look right," Dale said, his voice stubborn.

Sal stomped her boot. "We have a deal," she said. "I'm a puppy shoo-in."

"Shhh," Dale said, casing the schoolyard. "Nobody knows that. Sal, I like you, but you hanging with the committee doesn't look right for the puppies."

"Doesn't *look* right? You never used to care how things look," Sal said. "It was one of your best traits."

"I never had puppies to watch over before."

Sal put her hands on her hips. Or where her hips will be when puberty hits. "You've changed, Dale. And not for the good." She slid her Piggly Wiggly glasses over her eyes and stalked away.

Dale stared after her. "What just happened?"

"We'd be old men before I could explain it," Harm told him as Sal turned to glare at Dale from the edge of the playground.

I hopped on my bike. "I got to help at the inn. We can think up names over there."

"Race you, Casanova," Harm said.

Dale frowned as Harm sped away. "Casanova? What kind of name is that?"

* * * *

We pedaled out of town and down the curved, cedar-lined drive to the ancient, two-story inn just outside town. It looks nice, I thought as I hopped off my bike. White clapboards, tall windows, a wide porch lined with rocking chairs. We pushed inside to red-gold pine floors, high ceilings, and ancient leather sofas and chairs facing a fireplace and piano.

"Make yourselves at home," I invited, and grabbed a dust cloth.

A half hour later Harm collapsed in the inn's parlor, a history book on his lap. "Maybe you could add Queen of Sheba to the list," he said, flipping a page as Dale and I dusted. "Margaret, Beatrix, Francis, Louis . . ."

The front door swung open. A thin bald man and a plump rosy-faced woman stepped into the vestibule, smoothing the ride from their clothes. "Welcome," I said as the Colonel struggled in behind them with an ironing board under his arm.

"Blast it," the Colonel shouted as the door slammed on the end of the board. "Capers asked for this. Don't ask me why. She looks like she slept in her clothes."

"Maybe that's why," Harm said.

The Colonel stomped upstairs and I smiled at the strangers. "Welcome to the inn. We prefer cash but will accept US dollars. Sign here," I said, offering the guest book. "Your room includes supper. Tonight we feature Miss Lana's famous collard bisque."

Upstairs something crashed.

"There's a Holiday Inn in Greenville," the woman said, edging toward the door. "The newspaper says there's rumor of a reward for Macon Johnson and I'd love to spot him, but I'm not this curious."

"A reward?" Dale said, going pale.

I was losing them. Crud.

"In addition, our senior guide Dale is conducting a walking tour of Tupelo Landing at seven tomorrow morning, weather permitting."

Dale shook his head. Dale carries his stress in his shoulders, which now nearly touched his ears. "Tips are encouraged," I said, and he relaxed. He nodded. "Sign here," I said, pushing the guest book toward them. "The bellhop will carry your bags for five dollars."

Harm hopped to his feet.

"Five dollars is outrageous," the woman said, and Harm sat back down.

"Blast it!" the Colonel bellowed upstairs. Another crash. The Colonel dragged the ironing board across the floor and bumped down all thirteen steps.

Harm closed his book. "You know, Colonel, we could

put that at the end of the parlor. I saw a screen that would look nice."

Harm carried the board over, reached underneath, and gave a smooth dip. The legs clicked down. "There you go, sir," he said. "Where's the iron?"

The vein in the Colonel's forehead rose like a newborn mountain range. "I'll get one," he said, barely moving his lips. "As soon as I take out the trash."

Some folks are cut out to be innkeepers. Other folks are the Colonel.

"A reward?" Miss Lana said an hour later. "There was a rumor earlier in the day, but it's died down," she said, giving Dale a quick hug. "Strangers brought it to town."

She beamed at me. "And you signed in new guests? Wonderful!" she cried, hurrying a bowl of collard bisque to Lavender's mechanic, Sam. "I'll make sure they have fresh towels."

Attila perched by the window sipping something a putrid shade of green.

I glanced at the Specials Board:

COLLARD SMOOTHIES! $2

"I'll handle the towels, Lana," Capers said, jamming her papers in her notebook. "I'm going to the inn anyway. We Charleston women have to stick together."

"We also offered them a town tour tomorrow, *weather permitting*," I said, glancing at Thes, who sat hunkered at the counter.

A stranger rattled his newspaper, flashing a headline: *Racecar Driver's Father Is Escaped Con*. "A tour?" the stranger said. "Does it include Macon Johnson's farm?"

"Daddy doesn't have a farm," Dale said. "It's Mama's."

"*A tour?*" Miss Lana shrieked. "When will I have time to give a tour?"

Attila smiled, her mustache a shimmering green.

"Don't worry, Miss Lana, the Desperados will give the tour," I said. "Thes, you're famous for your weather skills and television-worthy suit," I said, trying to make nice. "What's the forecast?"

He ignored me.

"Thes," Miss Lana snapped. "Weather report! Now!"

"Ninety percent chance of rain," he said. "Egg sandwich and okra to go."

Outside, Attila's mother tooted her horn. Attila plunked two dollars on the table and smirked at Capers. "I wish you'd stop writing about us. You bring too much riffraff to town. And I, for one, think a reward is a lovely idea. I heard somebody spotted your daddy today, Dale. It turned out to be your uncle Austin. Pity." She swayed out, her hair swishing like a blond curtain of evil.

"That girl's a piece of work," Capers said, watching the

Cadillac prowl away. She stuffed her dictionary in her saddlebag. "Oh well, what goes around comes around."

A paper slipped from her bag and I scooped it up. Another odd collection of numbers and letters. "What is this?" I asked.

Dale peeked over my arm. "Numbers," he said. "Sometimes I feel like they're stalking me."

She snatched the paper from my hand. "Just a game. Like Sudoku," she said, and hurried into the night.

"Must be a city game," Dale said, heading for the door.

"Dale, wait," I said, grabbing his arm. "I'm sorry I named Mr. Macon last night. You're right: I couldn't see who was standing outside Lavender's garage."

He looked out over the parking lot. "I forgive you," he said, "but we got to start thinking different, Mo. If we don't, this case will pull my family under."

Chapter 13
Footprints Never Lie

I awakened the next morning to thunder galloping across heaven and curtains of rain pounding across my roof. I dreamed up a To-Do List: Make nice with Thes, Avoid giving a tour, Find a new lead.

Thes had nailed the forecast—a chance to make nice. I grabbed my phone. He picked up on the second ring. "Good job," I said, and hung up.

I dressed, grabbed my Graceland umbrella, and sloshed to the café. Capers's little rental car already sat outside. "Happy Saturday! Great day if you're a duck," I called, splashing through the door.

Was Capers wearing Miss Lana's sweater? Does Miss Lana think every woman from Charleston is her sister?

I looked into Miss Lana's stricken eyes and my To-Do List fell to dust. "What's wrong?" I asked. "Where's the Colonel? Is he okay?"

"He's fine," she said. "Mo, Priscilla just called."

That's all. A teacher alert. My heart slowed to normal.

"I can explain once I hear the baseless accusations

against me," I replied, brain-scanning the past few days for academic crimes.

Miss Lana took a deep breath. "Another break-in—"

Capers cut in, smiling like she was announcing a birthday party. "You'll never guess who got hit. You'll love this. That snooty girl who was in here yesterday."

"Anna Celeste?"

"Mo, she's fine," Miss Lana said, shooting Capers a Be Quiet Look and putting an arm across my shoulder. "Someone broke in while they were sleeping. And there's nothing to love about it, *Capers,*" she said. "It's dreadful."

Capers scowled. *"Someone* broke in?" she shot back. "Macon Johnson broke in."

While they were sleeping?

"I got to get to Attila's," I told Miss Lana. I stared out at the pouring rain. One good thing about being a kid: You get to ride your bike everywhere. One bad thing about being a kid: You got to ride your bike everywhere.

"You're in luck," Capers said, like she could read my mind. "I can drop you off on my way to town."

The door slammed against the wall and Dale and Harm blasted through, both of them dripping. "Good news," I said. "No tour. We're rained out."

Dale bobbed beneath his yellow slicker like a happy duck.

"Bad news," I added, grabbing my camera. "Break-in at Attila's."

Dale gasped.

"Capers is giving us a ride to the crime scene," I said, and scoped the takeout bags lined up by the cash register. "Miss Lana, I'm starving."

"Here you go, sugar," she said, handing me the mayor's bag. "I'll make Mayor Little a new one."

Excellent. Mayor Little and his mother eat huge.

"Forgive my mess," Capers said moments later, scooping an armful of papers off the front seat for Harm. We piled into her tiny car. "Bird-watching's a junky hobby. Just push everything on the floor."

She's a definite pack rat, I thought, shoving the backseat jumble aside—binoculars, fedora, gray leather gloves. I checked out the dashboard: road map, half a fast-food burger. I tilted my takeout toward Dale, who grabbed a cheese biscuit.

Capers chugged to the road.

"Take a right," Dale said as I bit into a bacon and egg sandwich.

Harm pushed his hood back, the rain curling his hair. "Who do *you* think's doing these robberies?" he asked Capers.

"Macon Johnson. Sorry, Dale. Most people agree."

Dale polished off his biscuit and fished in the bag.

"Your articles make it seem that way. But a lot of people thinking *flat* don't change *round*," he said. "Christopher Columbus proved that."

It's surprising what Dale picks up at school. Sometimes I wonder if we're in the same classroom.

"Besides, why would Macon risk a break-in?" Harm asked. "If he's smart, he's long gone from here."

She shrugged. "Adrenaline's addictive. That's why criminals get more daring—they crave the rush."

Dale went the color of stale oatmeal. Mr. Macon's good at addiction.

She turned on Cul-de-Sac Drive. "So, an adrenaline junkie might go from robbing an empty house, to robbing a church, to robbing an occupied house, to . . . who knows?"

"Interesting," Harm said. "But that doesn't mean it's Mr. Macon." He pointed to Attila's house. "We'll hop out here."

Capers squeaked the little car to a halt. "Listen, I'd love to tag along, maybe pick up a quote or two. What do you say?"

So that's why she offered us a ride! "No paparazzi," I said. "Sorry."

We scrambled out and I popped my umbrella open. Harm and Dale crowded close. "Nice digs," Harm said as she pulled away.

"Very nice," Dale said from somewhere inside his yellow hood.

True. The two-story brick house sat back from the street, overlooking a manicured lawn. Starr's Impala loafed on the long brick drive. We sloshed to the door and rang the bell. The door swung open. Mrs. Simpson stared down at us—perfect makeup, excellent hair, shiny beige robe.

"Greetings," I said. "Desperado Detectives extends our deepest sympathies on your losses, which we assume as rich people you have insurance. We are here out of respect to a classmate. An enemy is almost as dear as a friend."

"And we're sorry," Dale added.

She narrowed her eyes. "You should be sorry," she said, her voice like a knife.

Harm interrupted. "Mrs. Simpson, may we come in?"

"Anna," she shouted over her shoulder. "It's Mo and Dale and that tall boy."

That tall boy? Give me a break. She knows Harm.

Anna Celeste came to the door, her eyes puffy and red-rimmed. "You," she said, glaring at Dale. "What do you want?"

"We want to see if you're okay," Dale said.

"Oh." Niceness confuses Attila like bright light confuses raccoons. "Somebody broke into our house last night," she said, her voice going off-key. "While we were *sleeping*. He took my jewelry and Daddy's cash off the laundry room counter. Why would he want my jewelry?" she demanded. "What's wrong with you people?"

"Anna," Harm said, "we want to help. If you tell us exactly what's missing . . ."

"You know what's worse than what he took? Knowing he picked up things and left them behind." She took a step toward Dale. "Your daddy came in my house," she said, her voice rising. "He touched my life with his filthy white-trash hands. You don't know how that feels," she shouted, her pretty face twisted.

"I do know," Dale shouted. "He came in my house too."

His words slapped me across the face. I hadn't thought of it like that.

Attila slammed the door.

We stood on the porch, listening to the patter of rain. "That could have gone worse, but I don't see how," I said as Joe Starr barreled around the corner.

"What's all the noise?" He stared at us bleary-eyed. "What are you doing here?"

Joe Starr ain't hitting on much without morning coffee. "We're detectives. This is our life's work," I replied. "And we're checking on an alleged friend."

"Two dogs with one bone," Dale explained.

"Or two birds with one stone," I continued. "Your choice."

Joe Starr blinked.

"We have clues, if you want to swap," I said. Not exactly a lie. More like a bargaining position. "First, we know the crime occurred after nine—Attila's bedtime." A guess. "Let's see," I said, flipping open my blank clue pad. "We got missing jewelry—mostly ugly costume stuff. Hideous turkey earrings, suggesting a thief with bad taste. A little pocket change from the laundry room and . . ."

"And a laptop," Harm said, smooth as cream. An excellent ad-lib.

"Really?" Dale said. "Because I didn't know—" Harm elbowed him.

Starr flipped open his own pad. "Laptop?" he said. "I don't think so. Jewelry, most of it NOT costume jewelry. Cash. A couple of clean shirts and a pair of pants. No laptop. In fact, no electronics, which seems odd. Just Anna's bicycle."

Anna's pink show bike? The one with showroom treads? The one she never rides because her mother hauls her all over town like a princess?

"Right," I said. "You probably dusted for prints."

Starr yawned. "No fingerprints. Just a footprint."

"In *this* rain?" Dale asked, frowning.

"See for yourself," Starr said, leading the way. "Same as at the church."

Dale stared at the lone footprint under the eave. I grabbed my camera and backed up for a wide shot. *Click.*

Dale shook his head. "Who wears the same shoes to two robberies in a row?"

Thieves have fashion etiquette? I made a note to tell Miss Lana.

"Who walks flat like that and makes just one print?" Dale demanded. "He stole a collection plate he can't fence. He's wore the same shoes to two robberies, hooking the break-ins together. He left a footprint at both crime scenes, where you'd see it for sure. This is rookie. Not Macon Johnson. Tell him, Mo."

My heart hammered. Of course it was Macon Johnson.

I remembered Grandmother Miss Lacy's words: Would you rather be right or kind? I went for both. "Macon Johnson's a top-notch professional in his field," I said. "And he has the record to prove it."

Dale nodded, very regal.

"We're keeping an open mind," I added as Harm crooked a brow.

Starr shrugged. "Really? Here's how I see it. Macon connects to every crime scene. He lived at one, he married in one, and he knows this house holds money."

He pointed to the ground. "Then there's this. Sorry, kids, but footprints never lie."

Dear Upstream Mother,

    Capers's story hit the newspapers late this afternoon: <u>Prominent Family Robbed While Sleeping. Macon Johnson Still at Large.</u>

    Dale can't sag much lower.

    Harm and Mr. Red stopped by the café this afternoon.

    Mr. Red says not to let Dale's church turn on him. Harm and me are going tomorrow, but I don't see what we can do.

    Can you sing? Neither can I.

    Mo

Chapter 14
Am I Dying?

I woke up Sunday morning with Starr's words caroming around my mind: Footprints never lie. Poor Dale.

Tap-tap-tap. "Soldier?"

"Colonel?" I sat up, wide awake.

He opened the door and peeped in. "Breakfast in twenty minutes. Look sharp. Church at 1100 hours. I want us there at 1030 hours, at the latest."

Did he say *us*? The Colonel's going to church?

The hair on my arms stood up. The Colonel never goes to church, preferring the natural cathedral of ocean and mountain and sky. I shot into the living room. "You're going to church, sir? Are we at war? Is Miss Lana sick? *Am I dying?*"

"At ease, Soldier." He sat on the settee, buffing his black shoes to a high sheen. He held them to the light, lowered them, and gave them another swipe. "Today's the first Sunday after the church break-in. Lana and I thought we'd support the community."

My panic fell away. "Support Miss Rose and Dale, you mean."

"As you wish," he said. He put a square of newspaper on the floor and placed his shoes on Capers's last article. He headed for Miss Lana's door, the threadbare plaid bathrobe I gave him years ago swinging on his spare frame. He tapped. "Lana," he called, "Georgian toast or omelet?"

"Georgian toast, honey. And thank you," she called.

Honey?

She stumbled into the living room and collapsed on the settee, her curlers hidden beneath her scarf. "Everybody in town will come to church today for one reason or another." She sighed. "Poor Rose. I do wish Macon had robbed the Episcopalians instead." She shook her head. "That didn't come out right, sugar. I need coffee."

"On it," I said. I sniffed the air. Coffee. I followed the scent into our own personal kitchen and snagged a mug the Colonel liberated from the Guatemala City Ritz. Or the Fayetteville flea market—I'm never sure which.

I filled it, loving the smell of our own personal coffee and our own private bacon in our own actual home. "What's that?" I asked, glancing at an odd-shaped package on the counter—an awkward pileup of brown wrapping paper and masking tape.

"Strictly need-to-know," the Colonel said, whisking it

under the counter. A quick smile softened his whiskery face as he turned the bacon. "Always remember, Soldier. There's more than one way to settle a score."

We rolled into the church parking lot right on schedule. "There's Dale!" I said as the Colonel rocked the Underbird into park. I scooted for the door. "Don't forget this," I said, grabbing the odd package off the floorboard.

"Put that down, sugar," Miss Lana said. "Dale's coming."

Dale's coming? So what?

Dale ran toward us, Queen Elizabeth waddling furiously behind. "When's Queen Elizabeth going to have those puppies?" Miss Lana asked. "She looks ready to pop."

"Hey," Dale said, opening my door. He saw the Colonel and froze. "What's the Colonel doing here? Did somebody die?"

"Can't he come to church?" Miss Lana teased, rising from the car like royalty. She cupped Dale's face in her hand. "You're so handsome. Are you singing a solo?"

Dale shook his head. "Me and Liz are congregation today. But Mama's playing."

"Wonderful," she said, and she and the Colonel sailed toward Miss Rose like boats across smiling waters.

They look good, I thought. The Colonel in his dress

blues, Miss Lana in her 1940s suit and seamed stockings. Miss Rose opened her arms to them like she hadn't seen them in forever.

Attila brushed by. "Dale, Mother says tell Miss Rose to cancel our Thanksgiving order. She's buying our greens in Kinston. It's not because your daddy robbed us. Miss Rose's produce simply isn't up to our standards.

"By the way," she continued, "I hear Reverend Thompson's preaching on the Eighth Commandment today in honor of your family."

When it comes to church, Dale's an A+ student. I ain't.

"The Eighth Commandment?" I whispered.

Attila shot me a look that would incinerate a sparrow in full flight. "Thou shalt not steal, Mo-ron."

Dale stuck his hands in his pockets. "I like the next one too, where you don't lie about your neighbors."

She sashayed away as a camo pickup rattled into the lot.

"No way," Dale breathed as Mr. Red hopped out, smoothing his gray suit. "The Colonel *and* Mr. Red? In the same church? With neither one of them in the take-out box?"

"Yep, not a coffin in sight," Harm said, swaggering over. "Eerie, isn't it?"

Mr. Red reached out to shake Dale's hand. "Morning, Dale."

"Hey, Mr. Red," Dale said. "Thank you for coming. It means a lot to me."

"Proud to be here," he said, watching the Azalea Women clot by the front door. "People talk, Dale. But that doesn't mean your friends are listening. Stand tall. Your true friends will stand with you." He winked at Dale. "Excuse me, son, Lacy Thornton's looking my way," he said, and hurried away.

We strolled across the parking lot, neighbors and strangers milling around us.

"There's Lavender," I said, and darted to his side.

"My favorite pit crew," Lavender said, adjusting his tie. "I hoped you three could help us test 32 at the Carolina Raceway today," he said, and we bobbed our heads like a trio of yo-yos. "You'll ride in the lowboy with Sam," he told Harm as Capers strolled by. "Mo, you're with Dale and me. We leave at two."

"Outstanding," Harm said as Lavender veered toward a twin. "Come on. I want a good seat. I've never heard Miss Rose play and I want her to see us listening."

Dale frowned. "See us listening? Why?"

"Because," Harm said. "Mothers like that."

As the church filled, Miss Rose played proud as an angel—straight-backed and sure, her fingers coaxing hymn after hymn from the old piano. Hannah and Little Agnes went up to light the candles.

Thes scooted in behind us and leaned forward to whisper: "With no collection plate, Daddy's passing his *fishing hat* today, the one with the hooks dangling off of it."

Dale and Harm didn't turn around. I did.

It's hard to make nice and defend your people at the same time. I looked into Thes's eyes, willing every ounce of me into a Don't Mess With Us Stare. "There ain't no weather in heaven," I whispered. "Good luck."

Thes gasped.

"Very mature, LoBeau," Harm whispered, but I could hear his grin.

"Where's the Colonel?" Dale asked, reaching down to rub Queen Elizabeth's ears. She sat with her legs jutting at an odd angle to accommodate her round belly.

The Colonel brought us here and then went AWOL?

I peered down the row. Miss Lana sat with her hands folded in her lap, her hat's half-veil draping her eyes. I cranked around to run a quick Upstream Mother Scan as I searched for the Colonel.

"Eyes forward," the Colonel whispered, sliding in from the other end of the pew.

"Busted," Dale snickered as Miss Rose pounded an intro on the piano.

We rose and hurled ourselves into "I'll Fly Away." I almost felt like I could fly too, that many voices bouncing off the walls and coming back to lift me up. I sang between Dale and Harm, riding their magic carpet of song. Underneath pulsed the Colonel's bullfrog tune and Miss Lana's steady melody.

Two hymns later, Reverend Thompson launched into his scripture readings—not on Thou Shalt Not Steal, as Attila predicted, but on forgiveness.

"Here we go," Harm whispered. "It's pass the fishing hat time."

Miss Rose tilted her head a smidge higher. Dale did too.

Reverend Thompson looked at us. "You never know what's good and what's bad as it happens," he said. "A break-in at our church can turn into something wonderful—like a packed house on Sunday. Thank you for your love and support."

The congregation rustled.

"And you'll never guess what I found in my office today—an anonymous gift." He reached beneath the pulpit and lifted up a shiny new collection plate. Dale gasped. A crumple of brown wrapping paper and masking tape fell to the floor.

Reverend Thompson started the plate around, and said what he always says: "Put something in if you have it. If you need it, please take something out."

I looked at the Colonel. He stared straight ahead. So did Miss Lana.

This is what we do in our family, I thought.

I squared my shoulders and stared straight ahead, my heart soaring.

Sunday morning brought a truce, but it was short-lived. In fact, the afternoon hit the Desperados like a one-two punch, leaving us reeling.

Lavender cruised into the café parking lot at two and tooted the truck's horn. "Gotta go," I bellowed, grabbing my camera.

"Back before dark," the Colonel said as I pounded out the door.

I dove in, crawling over Dale and Queen Elizabeth to sit by Lavender.

He wore his ripped jeans and scuffed cowboy boots.

If there's a sweeter hour than the one it takes to rumble to the Carolina Raceway with Lavender, I ain't found it. I also ain't looking for it.

"We have the track to ourselves today," Lavender said as we chugged through the chain-link gate. "I want to wind her out for a few laps, see what we've got." We headed for the infield, where Sam was already backing the 32 car off the lowboy.

She wore new tires all around, and a pox of pale body putty. "I wish you'd paint that car," Dale said. "She's embarrassing."

"Will do," Lavender said as Sam tossed his race suit to him.

"Wear this, just in case of fire," Sam said. "You never know."

Lavender stepped into the suit, wiggling it up over his hips and shrugging it across his shoulders. I lined up my shot as Harm slung the battered toolbox onto the pickup's tailgate.

"Hold it!" I said. Lavender smiled. "Perfect." *Click, click, click.*

"I'll go easy the first couple laps and then wind her out," Lavender said, and swung in through the driver's window. "Can't wait to see how she runs."

The new 32 roared to life. He clamped on his helmet and fishtailed to the track.

"She sounds great!" Dale said, springing onto the tailgate between Harm and me. Lavender put his foot into the second lap, the engine roaring on the straightaway and whining in the turns.

Sam closed his eyes and listened like a musician tuning a fiddle. "She already sounds better than any car we've ever had. We'll be ready for Flick in two weeks if the talk about Macon keeps driving our business away."

I frowned. "What do you mean?"

"People are bailing on Lavender like he's the *Titanic*. A thousand-dollar prize money will definitely help out until our business comes back." He gave me a smile. "Mo, see if you can find a stopwatch. Let's time these laps."

I popped the battered toolbox open. A folded square of pale blue paper stared up from the jumble of wrenches and screwdrivers. I unfolded it.

RITE FRONT TIRE SLIT?

"What's this?" I looked into Sam's shocked face.

"Don't know and not taking chances," he said. He spun to the track. "Stop!" he shouted, waving his arms. He charged toward the edge of the track, the three of us on his heels. "Lavender, stop!"

Too late.

The right front tire exploded in a cloud of smoke, spinning the car up the track toward the wall. "Turn," I screamed like Lavender could hear me. "Turn!"

The car veered like it had been hooked, and wobbled into the infield.

Lavender's hands shook as he read the note. "Who wrote this?"

Harm quickly slid beneath the car. "It's slit, all right," he said. Lavender crouched by the tire and ran his hands along the inside wall. "Here," Harm said.

"Son of a gun," Lavender muttered as Harm hopped up.

Sam glared at Harm. "Who would be mean enough to do that?"

"Don't you look at Harm in that tone of voice," I said.

Sam slapped his cap against his leg. "Why not? What did you tell me Flick said when he busted in the garage? *Paint it the color of a dead man's car?*"

"Flick wouldn't do this," Harm said. "He wants to beat Lavender. He wants Lavender's thousand dollars."

"Maybe he's more worried about losing his own money," Sam said, his face going red. He stepped toward Harm.

"Calm down, Sam," Lavender said, looking up from the note. "Anybody recognize this handwriting?"

Dale shook his head. "It's not Daddy's. Mo saw somebody outside the garage. There's strangers in town and you've been in the papers. It could be anybody."

Lavender slipped the note into his pocket. "That tire feels sliced, but we won't know for sure until we pull it and take a look."

"I'll get the jack," Harm said, heading for the lowboy.

"Stay away from that car," Sam snapped.

"I trust Harm," Lavender said, his voice easy. He popped the car's hood and leaned in. He exhaled long and even, the way old men exhale cigar smoke. Not that Lavender will ever smoke.

He slammed the hood. "Let's get out of here until we know what's going on. Whoever slit that tire could have done way worse too."

I turned to case the stands one last time. The afternoon shadows slashed deep and sharp across the empty stadium. My pulse jumped. *What was that?* The pines swayed behind the chain-link fence. A swirl of red leaves tumbled behind the stands.

Just my nerves, I thought.

"Lavender," Harm said, "if that tire's been slit . . ."

"We need to bag it for evidence," I said. "Because somebody's trying to kill you."

The slit tire knocked the wind out of us. The second half of the one-two punch landed on our way back home. And it landed hard.

The sunset flowed orange in the rearview mirror as the raceway faded behind us. "Don't worry, Lavender," I said. "Desperado Detectives will sort this out."

He tapped his fingers on the steering wheel. "Thanks, Mo, but I don't want my favorite sixth graders mixed up in this."

"We can handle ourselves," I told him.

"Mo and Harm can," Dale added, smoothing Liz's ears. "I still need help."

"You do fine, Dale," Lavender said, turning on the radio. The announcer's voice blasted into the cab: "Now for

Stupid Crimes," the announcer said. "A man robbed the First Carolina Bank at the Tarboro mall yesterday, shot at the security guard—and dropped his wallet. The wallet's ID says—Macon Johnson."

"Daddy?" Dale cried as Lavender swerved off the road and bounced back on. We stared at the radio like it might change its mind. "Daddy would *never* take a wallet to a crime," Dale said. "This isn't fair."

Dale kills me. Mr. Macon ain't been fair to anybody long as I've known him.

Lavender clamped his jaw so tight, the muscles stood out like rope.

I sat still and quiet as the glass in the windshield, all the way home.

Chapter 15
Things Get Worse

Joe Starr didn't return my calls about Lavender's tire all evening.

"I've told you, Mo," Miss Retzyl finally said as she answered my third call. "Joe's investigating a bank robbery. He'll see Lavender at the café in the morning. Think about something else. Why don't you do your homework?"

We had homework?

"I already did it," I said, and hung up.

By the breakfast rush, news of the robbery had topped the gossip list. Lavender flowed in NASCAR handsome, and the Azalea Women circled like buzzards.

"Lavender," one said, laying a flashy hand on his arm, "I'm glad you're here. I'd love to use Rose's produce, but plans change. Tell her to cancel my order. She'll understand." She caught wind of the Simpsons canceling, I thought.

Her friend's gaze flicked over Lavender. "Cancel mine too."

"And mine."

Miss Lana closed her eyes. "I do not curse," she said. "But those women make me want to learn how."

Lavender swung onto a stool. "Don't change for *them*, Miss Lana," he said, giving her a break-my-heart smile. "I couldn't stand it if you did."

She poured his coffee. "On the house," she said. "And the Underbird needs a tune-up."

"Thanks, but I tuned it up last week," he said.

"It needs another one," she insisted as Starr sauntered in and read the Specials Board: Collard Quiche.

"Just coffee, Lana. Sorry I couldn't come sooner, Lavender," he said. He took the pale blue note Lavender offered him, carefully holding it at the corner—like I'd forgot to do. "Recognize the handwriting?"

Lavender shook his head. "But that tire's slit. I pulled it and checked. You can pick it up for evidence if you want it."

Capers looked up from her omelet.

"That ain't for the papers," I said, and she winked.

Starr slipped the note into a clear bag.

"My fingerprints are on that note," I told Starr as Miss Lana splashed his cup and headed down the counter. "Also Lavender's, Dale's, Harm's, and Sam's."

"And the twins'," Lavender added, looking sheepish.

"Great," Starr muttered. "Any idea who wants to hurt you?"

Lavender shook his head. "Flick wants to race me, so not him, unless he's realized he's going to lose. And no matter what he said there's no reason for Macon to hurt me, if he's even here."

I pointed to a table of strangers. "And thanks to Capers's news stories we got a bumper crop of suspects in town."

Starr stood. "Listen up," he said, his voice stifling the café chatter. "I'm passing around an evidence bag with a note in it. Don't open the bag. Just see if you recognize the handwriting."

He sent it down the counter. Thes shook his head no and passed it on. No, no, no down the counter and then to the tables.

"How long until you get the ballistics report on the gun used in the bank robbery?" I asked.

"Not long. I'll let you know if it matches the pistol from the jailbreak."

"That would tie Macon Johnson in for sure," Capers murmured, sipping her coffee.

Miss Lana glanced at the clock. "Time for school," she called. Every kid in the café stood up and scratched for money.

Thes dropped his cash by his plate and shot out the door as Miss Lana handed me a tiny package from the freezer. "Here you go, sugar," she said. "Good luck making nice with Thes. Tell him to keep it cold."

"Thanks," I said, dropping it into my messenger bag.

Lavender smiled at an Azalea Woman. "I can get to your car today," he said.

"That won't be necessary," she said, cutting her bacon careful as if she was doing brain surgery.

"You?" he asked the woman beside her, and she shook her head.

Capers gave him a smile. "My motorcycle?"

He headed for the door. "Your parts got caught in a Chicago snowstorm, but they'll be in tomorrow. Looks like your bike will get my *undivided* attention."

He smiled, but the smile didn't find his eyes.

Starr tossed a five on the counter. "Get a lock for your garage," he told Lavender. "And use it. I'll stop by for the tire. Everybody seen the note?" he asked, looking around the café.

"Over here," Tinks Williams said, passing it on.

Mayor Little read it, gasped, and knocked his chamomile tea to the floor. He looked around the café, his face white as the napkin tucked into his collar. "This is Mother's notepaper," he said. "She's a murderer and I never suspected a thing."

"Idiots," Mrs. Little said a few minutes later as Starr and me settled on her sofa.

She could be right. I glanced at her clock. Twenty minutes until school starts and Miss Retzyl hates tardy like St. Pete hates gatecrashers. But Dale would never forgive me if I passed up this chance at a break in our so-far pitiful case.

I smiled. Mrs. Little is the oldest, meanest person in Tupelo Landing. She almost liked me a couple months back, but fondness, like peanut butter, has a shelf life.

She sat in her rocker like a queen vulture, the sunlight glinting off her lemony bun as she examined the note.

I tried to picture her slithering beneath a Monte Carlo and slitting a tire.

Nothing happened.

"*Rite* front tire slit?" she said, glaring at Starr. "Do you think I can't spell?"

"You spell excellent," I said. "But is it your notepaper?"

"Excellent*ly*. I have notepapers like this. So do a million other people," she said, hooking a small drawer of her writing desk and pulling it open. An army of bloodred pens lay beside her papers. "What are you accusing me of?"

"Nothing," Starr said. "But I'd like to search your home if you don't mind."

Search Mrs. Little's house? The hair on my arms stood up.

"I have to go," I said, jumping to my feet. "I can't stand being late for school."

"Liar!" she cried, jabbing a finger at me.

I shot through the thorny plants that make up her yard, grabbed my bike, and pedaled like I was racing for heaven.

Dale loitered by the bike rack. "Did you bring the Puppy List?" I asked.

He patted his backpack. "I'm ready." He sniffed. "What stinks? Is that you?"

"It's a peace offering for Thes," I said as Harm rocketed up. "Listen: Starr's checking the ballistics on the gun used in the robbery, and Mrs. Little owns blue notepaper like in the toolbox. But she doesn't have the same pens—not with her paper, anyway. Starr's searching her house now."

"Brave man," Harm said, grinning.

"Understatement," I said. "We'll pump him for information if he survives."

Thes wandered by. His father had turned the church in Dale's favor with his Forgiveness Sermon. I didn't want Thes turning it back.

Here goes nothing, I thought, and tried to look sorry.

"Thes," I said. "Please accept my apology for my oral misfire. I hope you will forgive me, which your father says is good. Here," I said, lifting Miss Lana's freezer packet from my messenger bag. "For Spitz. Nothing says 'I'm sorry I called you ugly' like liver."

He wrinkled his nose. "Thanks," he said, looking like I'd handed him a bag of liver, which I had. "I've been thinking about that sermon too. And . . ." He looked at me. "I forgive you, Mo. Spitz does too. We'd love to go to a movie with you."

He looked at Dale, and he walked away. It was a start anyway.

As we slung ourselves into our seats Thes twisted in his desk. "Dale," he whispered. "Are you posting the Puppy List soon? I'd like to talk to you first."

Dale put a pack of rubber bands on his desk. Stress relievers. Miss Lana says worriers mostly wear rubber bands like bracelets and pop them against their wrists when frazzled. Dale does it different. He zinged a rubber band, barely missing Attila's replacement turkey earrings.

"Announcements?" Miss Retzyl called.

Attila raised her hand. "I wish it was Career Day," she said. She turned to Dale. "Your father could talk about robbing my house. That would be fascinating."

Zing.

A tap at the door. Capers stepped in, clasping her notebook—and a takeout bag. "Sorry to interrupt. Mo forgot her lunch. . . ."

Collard quiche. Like the Colonel says, not everything left behind is forgotten.

"Capers," Miss Retzyl said, placing my lunch on her desk, "we'd love to know more about your work. We don't meet many reporters in Tupelo Landing."

"Uh, yeah," she said. "We could talk Fourth Amendment issues or . . ."

Attila sniffed. "You mean *First* Amendment issues—freedom of the press. What do you know about Macon Johnson?"

Miss Retzyl opened her gradebook and picked up her red pen. Attila shrank away. Red ink is to Attila as water is to the Wicked Witch.

"We'll find a time for a school visit then, Capers," Miss Retzyl said, smiling. Capers bolted, dropping her notebook. It exploded in a flurry of pages. She scooped them up and ran. But not before one lonely page swirled beneath Miss Retzyl's desk.

Suck-up points. I smiled and waited for the bell.

"Remember," Miss Retzyl said as I practiced to see how long I could go without blinking. "Whenever you solve a problem, check to make sure you know the givens. What's true. If you have the wrong givens, you'll end up with the wrong answer. Mo," she said. "Blink."

The lunch bell sounded. I zipped over and slid my toe beneath her desk. "Capers dropped this," I said. "I'd be glad to return it with your regards."

"Thanks," she said, handing me my so-called lunch.

"I live to serve," I replied, and trailed Harm and Dale into the lunchroom. Attila and her posse sat at the Popular Table. We headed for the Detectives' Table.

Dale looked over as I opened the note. "What you got?"

"Hopefully it's that numbers game we wanted to show Harm." I looked at the paper. "Crud. It's a messy letter dated 2-6—February sixth."

"February?" Harm said. "This is November."

Sal scooted in beside Dale. "Hello Dale, what's that?" She leaned closer. "Why are you walking around with a 2-6 word code, Mo?"

My world screamed into a backspin. "A what?"

"A 2-6 word code," she said, stabbing her milk with a straw. "See?" she said, pointing to the numbers at the top of the page. "It says so right here. This is a very old cypher. The two means start with the second word. The six means use every sixth word. Where'd you get this?"

"Capers dropped it."

She ran her finger along the page. "Maybe she codes notes to her editor to keep nosy people from reading them. She's trying to work out the code here . . . This must be her rough draft."

Her finger trailed down.

"And down here she gets it. I'll read you the entire

message, and then the hidden one." She smoothed the page and read: "Darling, I am alone here but I am not too slow to settle in. I do hope you can send me some letters, just little messages about your own sweet life as I am bored with mine. Arranged with Lana to pay cash. Babe."

"Capers doesn't talk like that," Harm said. "Who's Babe?"

Dale leaned close. "So when you put it all together . . ."

Sal plucked a pencil from behind her ear, skipped a word, and underlined every sixth word: "I am in. Send messages as arranged. Babe."

"Wow," Harm said. "What are you, a genius or something?"

"I guess this could be to her editor," Sal said, blushing. "But why sign it Babe?"

Skeeter beelined for the Popular Table. "What's Skeeter doing at Attila's table?" I muttered. "Office assistants don't eat with sixth graders."

"Hold on, I'll read Skeeter's lips for you," Dale said, squinting. "Looks like . . . 'Anna's hit a foul ball.'"

"More like 'Anna has a phone call,'" Harm said as Attila followed Skeeter out.

Dale unwrapped his brownie, broke it, and gave half to Sal. "I'm sorry about the Puppy Committee disaster. I was wrong."

Sal blotted the crumbs from his waxed paper. "You're under stress, Dale. It's okay, but don't do it again." She looked at me. "Are you giving that letter back to Capers?"

"Never betray a teacher's trust when you can get caught," I said, opening my collard quiche. "I'll give it to her soon as Skeeter makes us a copy."

Attila strolled in after lunch, smirking. Not a good sign. "I have an announcement from Mother, but I'll wait for the end of class."

"She's angling for Maximum Impact," I whispered.

Dale frowned. "Angling for who?"

The afternoon crept by. "Language arts homework," Miss Retzyl finally said. I tried to will the clock to move faster. Fifteen minutes to freedom. "Who can define a metaphor?"

Dale, who sat studying his Puppy List, slid low in his seat. "Harm?"

Harm shifted his long legs. "Thanks for thinking I might be able to do that," he said. "A metaphor is something poets use to walk ideas across paper."

Sal raised her hand so hard she practically levitated. "Miss Retzyl? I wrote one: 'Dale's smile strolls barefoot across my lonesome porch.'" She blushed.

"Wonderful!" Miss Retzyl cried. "You turned a smile into a barefoot visitor."

"Hopeless," Attila muttered. "Here's mine: 'Mr. Macon's guilt rises like putrid fog over a cesspool.'"

"Simile!" I shouted, pointing at her. "She said *like* putrid fog!"

"*I don't care!*" Attila bellowed. "Mother called. She's offering a reward for Mr. Macon's capture and the return of our things. Two thousand dollars." She looked around the classroom. "Think what you could do with that much money."

The classroom erupted.

"Daddy didn't do it!" Dale yelled over the din. "Leave us alone!"

Something had to change. Fast. I leaned over, grabbed his Puppy List and headed for the bulletin board. "Thank you, Anna. The Desperados look forward to collecting the reward and throwing a class party." The Exums applauded. "Now for today's *really* important news: The Puppy List is posted," I said, pinning it to the board.

The room's attention swarmed to it like fruit flies to an old banana.

"We got six names, but we may add more. Our sympathy to the unlisted."

"Who's on it?" Hannah asked. "Did Little Agnes make the cut?"

Miss Retzyl sighed. "You might as well read it, Mo."

I skimmed the notice.

PUPPY LIST
• Sal
• Skeeter
• Little Agnes and Hannah
• Miss Retzyl
• Susana
• Jimmy and Jake maybe but
  don't get your hopes up

"I *would*," I said, "but I like to foster reading skills in my classmates."

"She's afraid unlisted kids will kill her before she makes the door," Attila said.

True.

"That's a lie," I replied as Harm and Dale stuffed their books in their backpacks and perched on the edge of their seats, ready to run.

The bell rang. The class stampeded the board.

Dale, Harm, and me shot to the door. I gazed at the cloud-heavy sky and shivered. "The café's the closest safe haven," I shouted. "Ride like the wind!"

Chapter 16
Be Careful What
You Wish For

I was still panting as I stared into Miss Lana's gray eyes. "Go into the deep woods?" I said. "But it's freezing out there. And it looks like rain."

"And we want to hide," Dale added.

"You don't need to hide," Miss Lana said. "The mayor *assures* me Macon is in South Carolina."

The mayor? What does he know?

She smiled at me. "Chop-chop, sugar. I need autumn materials for Thanksgiving centerpieces. Colorful leaves, pine needles, pinecones. Not the petite pinecones, the large ones. The small cones are so tense."

Her glasses slipped down her nose. "And Mo, I'll want the long-leaf pines from the bluff overlooking the river. The ones that whisper susurrus in the wind." She winked. "Onomatopoeia, my little Kiplings."

"Bless you," Dale replied.

"Normally we'd love to go, Miss Lana," I said—not so much a lie as a possible truth in a parallel universe.

"But we got metaphors to write and—" The phone rang, cutting me off. Miss Lana scooped it up.

"Café . . . Oh." She held the phone toward Dale. "It's for you."

Dale trotted to the phone. "Hello? Oh, hey, Thes. . . . *How many kids are after us?*" He frowned. "No. I appreciate the warning, but I don't feel like I owe you a puppy." He turned to us, his eyes quick with fear. "Three kids and a lunchroom worker are hunting us. And we got a fifty percent chance of rain."

Harm scouted the empty highway outside. "This is the first place they'll look."

I snatched up the collection bags. "Come on, Desperados. Let's roll."

The Colonel says the worst possible thing usually happens at the worst possible moment. As we blasted across Fool's Bridge, I stood up to hyper-pedal.

Bam. My bicycle chain slipped off.

I landed hard on the seat. No brakes! I veered into the drive of the old general store and rocketed toward an ancient gas pump.

"Jump!" Dale screamed.

I jumped, dug in, and slung my bike in a half circle at the store's front step. The dust settled around me like a skirt.

"Mo!" Harm said, skidding up beside me. "Have you lost your mind?"

"No," I replied, very smooth. "My chain." I looked at the empty highway. "Let's fix it now in case we need a fast getaway."

We flipped the bike over and fed the chain back into place. "That will hold until Lavender can take a look," I said, and tossed Harm a collection bag.

"Great tin art," he said, checking out the metal ads nailed to the store's walls. "The Lone Ranger. That's probably worth real money."

Ever since I met Harm, he's been trying to make money. He's even tried to get a job from the Colonel. "Why do you always want money?" I asked.

"Don't you?" he asked, and gave me that lopsided grin.

"Catch, Dale," I said. He whirled to grab his collection bag, brushing the cobwebs veiling the old door. "Ick," he muttered, swiping them away.

Dale can't stand cobwebs.

"The path's over here." We rolled our bikes behind the store and scuffed along the leaf-covered trail into the forest.

Dale made his voice high and swiveled his hips like Miss Lana as he walked up the trail. "Bring nice pine-cones," he said. "Not the petite ones. They're so tense."

He shoved his hands in his pockets as we headed down the trail. "Organic leaves for a woman who wears fake hair," he muttered.

Harm shot Dale a puzzled glance. "That's not like you, Dale."

Dale sighed. "It's the reward. People are mean enough without adding greed. I just wish we had some clues."

My back prickled, the way it does when Attila sneaks up behind me. "Shhhh." We froze, listening to wind and creaking branches. "Sorry," I said, feeling foolish. "Just the wind, I guess. Let's go."

A few minutes later we paused at a fork. The left trail meandered along the river. The right trail rose to a sandy bluff—home of the long-leaf pines. "This way."

"The river's high," Dale said, studying the muddy swirl from the top of the rise. The trees on the bank stood waist-deep in water, trailing their fingertips in the current.

He sniffed the air, which had gone sharp with the scent of rain. "It's going to pour. We better hurry," he said.

Behind us, the leaves crackled.

"Who's there?" I cried, wheeling. Brown eyes stared back through the brush. Brown eyes, broad body, antlers. A buck pawed and snorted.

"A wild deer," Harm whispered, grabbing my elbow.

A wild deer? Versus what? A pet deer? Harm's so city.

Dale raised his arms and whistled as he slapped them to his sides. The buck shot into the forest, zigzagging through briars and gracefully leaping a tall hurdle. He landed in a ragged tattoo of sound and galloped away.

I levered my arm out of Harm's grip. "You're cutting off my blood flow."

"Sorry," he muttered. "What's that he jumped over?"

"Fallen tree, maybe," Dale said. We pushed through the woods to a head-high mound of brush. Something silver glinted beneath the branches.

"One of Mr. Red's old stills?" I guessed.

"Maybe," Dale said, looking around. "There's a boat ramp a little ways down the river. That would mean easy transport. If Mr. Red wasn't retired, I mean."

"He'd better be retired," Harm muttered, "or Miss Thornton will kill him."

I studied the brush pile as thunder rumbled overhead. Slowly the glints and shadows took shape. "That's not a still," I said. "It's a car. With lights on top."

"The patrol car," Dale said, his voice faint.

"Well, you said you wanted clues," Harm told him, crashing toward the car.

Dale bit his lip. "Yeah. Mama says to be careful what you wish for."

We dragged the branches away and I knocked the sheet of mud off the driver's window. I peered inside.

"Empty," I said. I slid my new Graceland handkerchief from my pocket. "Elvis on polyester," I told Harm. "Polyester is eternal." I draped it over the door handle. "I'll check the interior. You two check the trunk."

"No," Dale said. "There could be a body in there."

Dale already feared clowns. Now it looked like he was adding random bodies in car trunks to the list. As best friend, I try to be sensitive. "Okay. I'll take the trunk and you search the car," I said. "I just hope there's not a clown in the backseat."

Dale sprinted to the rear of the car. "Okay," he called. "Pop it."

I tugged open the mud-smeared door. I slid behind the wheel, draped Elvis over the trunk latch, and popped it.

"Got it," Harm called, sliding his jacket sleeve over his hand and lifting the lid.

The car's interior looked spit-and-shine, ready for patrol. Not a scrap of paper, not a scuff. Just a skull-and-crossbones air freshener—minus half a crossbone—dangling from the rearview mirror. I crawled into the backseat. "Nothing here," I called, "except for the air freshener, which ain't county-issue."

Harm strolled over. "Those things? Two-fers at any auto store in the world."

I wrapped it in my handkerchief, eased out of the car,

and bumped the door closed with my hip. "Anything in the trunk?"

Harm sighed. "You better take a look."

Dale looked up as I rounded the car. "Our old camping gear," he said. He moved a blanket with a stick. "Daddy's clothes. A can of squash. I told you he wouldn't eat it."

Harm turned in a circle, surveying the woods. "But how did he drive in?"

"Over there," Dale said, pointing to a leafy thicket behind the car. He squinted, studying the thicket. "Those limbs got cut with an ax and stacked up there."

An ax?

Harm gulped so hard, I heard it. "There wasn't an ax in the car. We need to get Starr. Now."

"No," Dale said. "Let's stake out the car. If it's Daddy, we can get him to turn himself in."

Harm looked at me. "An ax guy versus three kids with pillowcases. You're the tie-breaker."

I made an executive decision. "Run!"

Ten minutes later we blasted through the café door. "Miss Lana! Colonel!"

Capers dropped the phone on the hook. "I was just calling in my story and *you* just missed your folks. The Colonel's gone to Kinston, and Lana and Miss Thornton ran over to the inn to welcome some guests," she said, taking my leaf collection from my freezing hands. "Lana's working too hard. She needs some help over there." She looked from me to Harm to Dale. "What's wrong?"

What's wrong? Just an ax murderer and the biggest clue of our lives—not that I wanted any of that in the paper.

"Nothing," I said. "When's the Colonel coming home?"

"Soon, I hope. I'm on cake duty and I don't bake."

Excellent. A diversion opportunity.

I sniffed. "Cake? Is that what's burning?"

"Oh my gosh, it better not be," she said, scrambling for the kitchen.

I looked at Dale. "Follow her," I whispered. "Keep her busy. Don't give our clues away. And don't mention the car. Harm will help."

I grabbed the phone and dialed as the door swung shut behind them.

Miss Retzyl answered. "Hello?"

"It's Mo. I'd love to talk metaphors, but I need Joe Starr pronto."

She sighed. Sometimes her sighs last exactly as long as it takes to count to ten. Interesting. "Joe," she called. "It's Mo. For you."

From the café's kitchen, I heard a crash. "I'm sorry," Dale cried.

"We'll help clean that up," Harm said.

"Detective Starr," Starr growled into the phone.

"Hey," I said. "We need backup. Pick us up at the café. And keep this confidential."

"I'm not your backup," he snapped. "I'm a law enforcement professional. I don't taxi kids around."

My temper growled like a wolverine. I counted to ten.

"I understand," I said. "We found the missing patrol car and we'll bring it in once we're old enough to drive. It won't be long. Harm's already twelve."

I hung up and glanced at the 7UP clock on the wall. Starr should be here in two minutes flat. I loaded fresh film into my camera. Another crash from the kitchen. With that much noise, Miss Lana's cake will fall flat as Louisiana.

Exactly two minutes later Starr skidded into the parking lot, siren wailing. "Where's the patrol car?" he demanded, blasting in.

"Patrol car?" Capers said as Grandmother Miss Lacy's Buick fishtailed up.

Miss Lana bounded through the door. "Mo? What's wrong?"

"Your red velvet cake fell," Dale reported. "It must have been the noise from the siren."

Capers frowned. "What's going on? Joe? Desperados?"

Please. Does she think we cough up leads easy as Spitz coughs up a hair ball?

Dale smiled. "We found the patrol car with our camping gear and Daddy's clothes in the trunk," he said. He looked at me. "That was a secret, wasn't it?"

Capers grabbed her notebook. "Let's go," she coaxed, giving Starr a smile. "I won't write a word until you say I can."

My temper popped. "Until *he* says you can?"

Capers snagged her jacket. "Sorry. Until *the Desperados* say I can. Grab your camera, Mo. A photo will look great with my article. Your byline will too."

"Mo," Miss Lana whispered, "she'll find out anyway."

Good point. And like Miss Lana says, if you can't get out of it, get over it. "I'm over it," I said, grabbing my camera. "Let's roll."

"Hang a right," Dale told Starr. "We'll come in the back way, on Fish Camp Road, so we don't have to walk so far."

An uneasy silence crept over us. "Did the bank's ballistics report come back yet?" I asked to break the tension. Outside, a giant combine purred across a soybean field.

Starr slowed. "I meant to tell you. The bullets match the jailbreak gun."

"That means Macon," Capers murmured. "Sorry, Dale."

"Fingerprints?" Dale asked.

Starr shook his head. "Whoever robbed the bank wore gloves."

"Then you can't say it was Daddy," Dale said. "It could have been anybody. There's the path," he added, pointing toward a gap in the pines.

Dale hunched forward in his seat, studying the dirt path, and I caught a silver glimmer in his hair. I plucked it out. "Cobwebs," I whispered. "From the old store."

He sniffed them. "They smell bad."

I smiled like he was normal.

Starr eased onto the rutted path, the briars scraping the sides of the car. "What's down there?" Harm asked, peering down a narrow wooded lane.

"An old fish camp," Dale said. "There's an old marl pit back there too, where farmers dug up ancient shells to sweeten the soil. You can't get to it anymore."

Starr spun his wheels in a soft spot. "We checked the fish camp the day Macon escaped. This path too. Did you kids touch anything at the crime scene?"

Just the entire car.

"Please," I said before Dale could confess us. "We're borderline professionals."

Dale pointed ahead. "It's past that boggy spot. We better walk."

We piled out. Harm, Dale, and I darted past a clay-stained cement boat ramp angling from the path, into the river's swirl. We scrambled up the rise, rounded a bend, and slammed to a halt.

The branches that once hid the car lay scattered and crushed, their white bones and dull leaves littering the path. "It's gone," I said, my heart dropping.

"Somebody stole our stolen patrol car."

Starr slapped his hat against his leg and stared into the forest. "*This* is why I don't want you messing with my cases," he snapped.

"Because we find things you can't?" I demanded.

"Because you could have gotten killed. *Obviously* Macon was watching you."

Dale glared at him. "Even if it was him, he wouldn't hurt us."

"Really?" Starr said. "Because that's not the way I remember him."

In truth, that's not the way anybody remembers Mr. Macon. Starr clapped his hat back on and stared at the tire tracks leading from the hiding place, toward the highway. "Did you see anybody back here?"

"A buck," Dale said. "A nice eight-pointer."

I remembered the prickle of a stare against my neck. Somebody *was* watching us. When will I learn to listen to my detective instincts? "Dale's right," I added. "Anybody walking through here could have took that car."

"Really?" Starr said. "Did you look inside? Was the key in the ignition?"

Mentally I surveyed the car's dash. The ignition sat empty. How did I miss that?

"No?" Starr guessed. "Then it must have been in the pocket of whoever was watching you. Any idea why *someone* might move the car *now*?"

Harm went the color of raw pastry. "He may have heard me say we needed you."

"That could have spooked him," Dale said. "A little."

"Do you think so?" Starr asked, his voice like a whip.

"Come on, Joe," Capers said. "The kids found the car. They didn't drive it away. At least you know where it *was*, which is more than you knew before."

Starr took a couple of deep breaths. The red seeped from his face.

My detective instinct quivered. This time I went with it: "I'd put a bulletin out if I was you." Starr turned tomato red and stomped back to the Impala.

"At least things can't get worse," I said.

"I wish you wouldn't say that," Dale muttered. "You're always wrong."

We drove toward the highway. My gift of gab had deserted me. Dale and Harm stared out opposite windows. Only Capers seemed at ease. "Stop," she said.

Starr slammed on brakes. "What?"

She pointed down the curving offshoot path, to the

old fish camp. "Where's the best place to hide something? Somewhere already searched. Just like Macon hid that car on a path you'd searched. You searched the fish camp too. I say we try it. That car has to be somewhere, Joe. It didn't fly away."

A shot at redemption. "The Desperados concur," I said.

"Be quiet, Mo," Starr growled.

We hiked to the old fish camp, our feet squishing in the mud. Its shack slumped by the river, half covered in vines. Two broke-through chairs sat on the porch, admiring a snaggletooth dock zigzagging into the river.

The air smelled heavy and sharp. "Coyotes," Dale said. "Smells like they sleep here. They used to stay at the marl pit."

Harm gulped. "I guess they wanted nicer digs."

Starr shoved the shack door open and shined his light inside. "Nothing," he said. "It was worth a shot," he told Capers. "Let's get back to the Impala before somebody steals that too." He hesitated. "I'd just as soon not read about this in the newspaper."

"No problem," she said. "I wouldn't have written about it anyway," she whispered to me, and shoulder-bumped me.

Comforted by a stranger. My life has come to this.

⋆ ⋆ ⋆ ⋆ ⋆

Dear Upstream Mother,

Today I found the biggest clue of my life. Then I lost it. I hope you aren't ashamed.

I am. I think Dale and Harm are too.

Miss Lana says to live in the moment, but this one's a nightmare and tomorrow looks even worse.

I am available to spend the rest of my life with you.

Mo

Chapter 17
Attila Goes Nice

The Colonel says there's two ways to meet Disaster: backing away or head-on.

"There's no backing out of sixth grade, so we might as well meet this head-on," I told Dale and Harm the next morning as we huddled by the bicycle rack.

Hannah and Attila walked by, whispering and holding their books in a sophisticated high school way.

"Morning, ladies," Harm said, giving them his best smile.

Hannah, who likes us, shot Dale a look and sped up.

Harm's smile crumpled. "It's hard to look good after you lose a patrol car."

Dale yawned. "This is easy compared to having Macon for a daddy. Gossips are like snipers," he said. "They run out of bullets after a while. Plus we got other things to think about. Queen Elizabeth is getting . . . rounder," he said, very delicate. "We may need more kids on the Puppy List."

We walked up the steps and opened the door.

The crowded hallway went dead quiet. Then whispers shot down the hallway like lightning down a raw wire. I would have marked it up to Standard Middle School Sniping, except for one blood-chilling thing: Attila went nice.

"Shhhh, there's Dale," she hissed, grabbing Hannah's arm. Attila's gaze found Dale's, and quickly skated away. "It's probably nothing," she said, too loud. Her posse nodded like robots plugged into the same brain.

"What's nothing?" I demanded.

"Nothing's nothing, Mo-ron," she said as Jimmy and Jake jogged by.

"Mama told me," Jimmy told Jake. "There's a body in the car. Oh," he said, freezing. "Hey, Dale."

"Don't be dumber than you have to be, Jimmy," Attila said. "Nobody actually *said* there's a body in the car."

"It's on Mama's police scanner. Possible body."

Harm did a double take. "Your *mother* has a police scanner?"

"Mama says she'll need one when we're older and she might as well start learning it now," Jimmy said. "A fisherman ran his boat up on a car, in the river. Near the boat ramp on Fish Camp Road. Starr called for a wrecker, and divers from Goldsboro. And EMTs."

Divers? EMTs? Starr *does* think there's a body, I thought.

"We better get over there," Dale said, the blood dropping from his face.

"You can't. It's time for homeroom," Attila told him. She looked at him. "Good grief," she muttered. "How can I get even with someone who won't even fight with me? Go, Dale," she said, shoving him. "I'll cover for you. But don't ever mention it again."

Attila knows how to cover?

"Thanks," Harm said. "You're . . ." She put her hand on her hip and glared at him. "Thanks Anna," he said again, and we ran for the door.

If there's a speed record for getting from the school to the boat ramp, we broke it.

We ditched the bikes beneath a bay tree and ran to the small knot of men pacing at the river's edge. "What's going on?" I gasped. "What's happened?"

"Not much," Sam said, tugging his knit cap down over his ears. "The divers went in. They took the hooks from the tow truck. Ain't nothing to do but wait." He shoved his hands in his jacket pockets. "I know your daddy, Dale," he said. "Macon didn't go down with a car. But you kids maybe shouldn't be here."

Dale shouldered past him, headed for the water's edge.

Lavender's truck skidded into the clearing and he scrambled out. "Where's Dale?"

I pointed to the water, and Lavender said a word I'd never heard him say before—one Miss Rose would never allow even in her barn. He ran to Dale and put his arm around Dale's shoulders. He bent low to talk in his ear, and herded him back up the hill.

"I want all three of you over here, out of the way," Lavender said, like a mother hen herding baby chicks. "I'll call you when I know something."

"But," I said.

"No buts." He put his hands on Dale's shoulders and bent to look into Dale's eyes. "Nobody knows whose car that is. It's just like Daddy to ditch a car, but it is *not* like him to be in it when he ditches it," he said, his voice even.

Hearing Lavender call Mr. Macon "Daddy" scared me clear past my backbone. Lavender ain't called Mr. Macon "Daddy" since he moved out of that house two years ago.

A woman stepped from the group and crossed her arms. *Capers Dylan.*

"How did Capers get here so fast? She ain't rescue," I muttered.

"Somebody must have told her at the café," Dale said, his eyes following Lavender. The wind swirled across the river, rattling sycamore branches like bones. We stepped closer to Dale. I could feel him shivering, and I knew it wasn't from cold.

Even from our distance, we could see.

They jacked the car onto the ramp inch by inch, the rusty cables creaking and straining, spooling tight as my nerves. The back of the car broke the muddy surface first, the bumper crisscrossed by branches, the back windshield covered in mud. The current grabbed the front of the car and jerked it at an angle.

The cable screamed and the driver gunned the tow truck's engine.

Capers looked at her watch, opened her notepad, and started scribbling. I grabbed my camera. *Click.*

The truck chugged into a deeper gear for a harder pull, and the car sloshed forward. "It's a black-and-white," somebody called. "And somebody's . . ." The voice trailed away.

"Don't be in there," Dale whispered, his eyes glued to the swirling water. Dale sat flat down and pulled his knees to his chin. He leaned forward and pressed his face against his knees. Harm and me folded down beside him. "Please," Dale said.

I bit my lip and watched the car slide up the ramp, its front wheels torqued near sideways by the current. A large, dark form bobbed against the driver's window.

"Jeez," Harm whispered.

"Don't look, Dale," I said.

The men on the bank stood like scared boys, staring.

Lavender squared his shoulders and headed for the car. "Lavender," Sam shouted. "Stop."

Sam pushed past Lavender and splashed into the shin-deep water. He grabbed the driver's door, closed his eyes, and yanked it open. The river rushed him like a rapid. Lavender grabbed Sam's arm to keep him from toppling over, and then stooped to look in the car, his face a throw-up shade of gray.

"Please," Dale whispered.

Lavender turned to look at Dale. For a half beat I thought Lavender would cry. Then his face stretched back to its regular shape. "Just his hunting jacket," he shouted. "He ain't in here."

Dale burst into tears.

"Not now," I told Capers as she buzzed toward us. "Dale needs a minute."

"Sure," she said. "I just have a theory I want to run by you."

Lavender bounded up. "Capers, Starr's looking for you. He wants you double quick." As she walked away, he dropped to his knees. "Dale?" he said, putting his hand on Dale's shoulder. Dale sobbed, and he wrapped him in a hug. "It's just a jacket that got caught in the door."

Dale looked up, his eyes wet. "I'm sorry," he said, wiping his face on his sleeve.

Lavender gave him a gentle rock. "Don't be sorry." He looked over at Capers, who stood at Starr's elbow. "Harm, throw the bikes in the truck. I can use a hand at the garage and you all could use a day off."

Harm grabbed his bike.

"Mo, I'd appreciate it if you and Harm rode in the back to keep the bikes steady. Dale, you're up front with me," he said.

Harm and me loaded up.

"Lavender," I said, looking back at the people milling around the car. "What did Starr want to talk to Capers about?"

He grinned. "He didn't. I took a page from the Mo LoBeau Handbook of Diversions. Let's get out of here before she figures it out."

Nobody knows me like Lavender.

We spent the rest of the morning sorting tools and straightening up Lavender's garage, the guineas chirping and chattering outside.

Dale didn't say a word as he worked beside Lavender, lining up wrenches and ratchets. I stacked cans of paint, primer, body putty. Harm sanded the car's body, his brown eyes smiling over the top of his mask.

By the time we taped plastic over the windshield and fenders, the blush had found Dale's cheeks again.

Just standing beside Lavender reminds Dale who he is.

Lavender slipped over to me as I tackled the boxes by Capers's wounded motorcycle. "Dale seems better," he said, his voice low.

"True." I picked up a box of clutter. "What's this? Candy wrappers, papers, a scratched beach music CD . . ."

"Trash from the mayor's Jeep," he said. "I meant to throw it away."

I snared a piece of pale blue paper. "Glad you didn't," I said. "This is a perfect match for the toolbox note. Now we know how it got in your shop. I guess Mrs. Little didn't slide under the car and slit that tire after all," I said, pocketing the paper.

He gave me his old grin. "Not this time anyway." He looked around the garage. "That's as clean as I can stand," he said. "Anybody hungry? Barbecue cures every ill known to mankind."

"Sal says it makes a good lip gloss too," Dale said, and we headed for the truck.

An hour later Harm and me found Grandmother Miss Lacy unloading groceries from the Buick as Dale and Lavender headed to the garage, to paint the 32 car. I grabbed a Piggly Wiggly bag.

"Thank you. Come in and get warm," she said. "Then we'll prepare your alibis."

"Alibis?" Harm said, hooking a gallon of milk. "Why do we need alibis?"

"You're truant," she said, heading for the door. "The news is all over town."

Truant? Doesn't that mean jail time?

"What in heaven's name?" she murmured, screeching to a halt. A familiar-looking pot of mums sat by her door. "Such nonsense," she muttered, her eyes sparkling. "Read the card," she invited, and I opened it.

> *Roses are red,*
> *And I'm Red too,*
> *I can't write a poem,*
> *But these are for you.*

She laughed. "Oh, for heaven's sake," she said, whisking them into the house.

She put the mums on her kitchen table, filled her blue kettle, and lined up three cups. "Mo, I developed your film," she said as her boiler clunked. "In fact, I've made your contact prints. I don't know if you have time today, but . . ."

"I've never seen a darkroom," Harm said, his voice quick with excitement.

"That settles it," I said, and swiped one of Grandmother Miss Lacy's old jokes. "We'll pop in and see what's *developed*."

As it turned out, what developed came as a total shock.

While Grandmother Miss Lacy bustled about setting up the darkroom, Harm and I used magnifiers to examine the tiny images on my contact sheets, to pick the ones we'd develop into photos. "Queen Elizabeth takes a good glamour shot," he said. He grinned and scooted his magnifier along the images. "Capers does too. Nice smile."

"She shows up a lot," I admitted, looking through the evidence photos. "In the café, at the inn, at the river . . ." I checked out my wide shot at Attila's. "What's that?" I asked, squinting at a blip at the edge of the photo.

"We have an enlarger, dear," Grandmother Miss Lacy said. "Let's find out."

She slipped the photo's negative into the old enlarger— a giant insect-looking machine hulking on the counter— and gave it a crank. The image widened and, with another crank, zoomed into focus.

At the edge of the field across from Attila's stood a woman. "What's that she's holding?" Grandmother Miss Lacy asked, squinting at the grainy image.

"Binoculars," Harm said, his voice shocked.

"She's spying on us," I said. "Capers was spying."

A couple hours later, with my newly developed photos hanging like flags on the darkroom drying line, Lavender pulled into the café parking lot and I hopped out.

"See you tomorrow," I shouted as Harm helped me drag my bike from the back of the truck.

They pulled away as I pushed through the café door. "I'm home," I called. A group of strangers looked up from their burgers. One read a newspaper article: *Old Inn Profits from Crime Spree.*

Miss Lana says the articles are good for business. The Colonel says they're a plague. I tend to side with the Colonel.

Miss Lana tapped her chalk against the Specials Board and smiled her hello. The overhead light glinted off her short platinum blond Jean Harlow wig and flapper dress—1920s Hollywood, all the way.

"Where's Capers?" I asked. "I got some questions for her and her binoculars."

"At the inn," she said. "We'll see her at supper."

A stranger headed for the cash register.

"I got this one," I told Miss Lana, and smiled at the pasty young man, who wore a pink Mohawk. "I am Mo LoBeau—a possible orphan saving for college—and I'll be ringing you up today," I said. He plunked down a five as I grabbed his bill and read Miss Lana's neat handwriting. "A Tupelo Burger with a side of collards. That's four dollars and one cent. Avoid the horror of Unexpected Change," I added, nudging my tip jar forward and counting ninety-nine cents into his hand.

He leaned toward me, his breath reeking of collards, his Mohawk glinting. "Who's the weirdo with the bizarro hair?" he asked, cutting his eyes toward Miss Lana.

"That would be you," I replied.

He shoved the change in his pocket and slammed out. Sadly for me, the door swung open again almost at once.

"*Mo LoBeau,*" Miss Retzyl said, her voice like ice.

My life screamed into slow motion. *Why did I spend all afternoon in the darkroom? Why didn't I have an alibi for missing class?*

I zipped back into Real Time. "Welcome," I said. "I was just thinking what an excellent role model you are. May I treat you to supper with double desserts?"

She slammed a stack of papers on the counter. "You, Dale, and Harm. Truant."

The strangers looked up. So did Miss Lana and the Colonel.

This is the last time I'm trusting Attila Celeste to cover for me, I thought.

"Anna did her best to cover for you, Mo," she said with a terrifying display of All-Knowing Teacher Wiles. "But it's hard to cover for three people at once, even with Anna's skill set. Joe told me where you were and I understand why you went there," she said. "But if you cut school again, you'll suffer consequences. *Real* consequences."

I looked at the folders. "I hope that's my punishment homework," I lied.

"It is." Her eyes went softer. Or else I imagined it. "I know Dale's your best friend," she said. "But dropping this case might be the kindest thing you can do for him. Let Joe do his job, and let Dale focus on his puppies and homework."

Drop the case? Is she mad? That's the *last* thing Dale wants.

"You're very wise," I said.

She snorted. The door slapped shut behind her.

I looked at Miss Lana. "I can explain this."

"No need, sugar," she said. "Capers stopped by to tell us you went home with Lavender." She looked at the Colonel. "As father figure, perhaps you'll say something of a disciplinary nature?"

He looked like she'd slapped him with a cat. "Don't break any more laws, Soldier," he said, his voice stern. Then he smiled. "And thanks for standing by Dale. You're a good friend and I'm proud of you."

"Well, I'm glad that's settled," Miss Lana said, tapping her green chalk against the Specials Board. "Let's do something creative with Rose's collards tonight," she said as the Colonel loaded the coffee machine. "How do you spell *salade de chou*?"

"S-L-A-W," he said.

"Collards again," I said, watching her. "I'm not the only best friend in this café."

Another stranger handed me his check.

"I'm merely a cog in the cosmic wheel, sugar," Miss Lana said. "Rose's business is off because of Macon. Because of Macon, strangers eat here and boost her business. The wheels on the bus go round and round. Wouldn't you say so, Colonel?"

"No," he said, and headed for the kitchen.

She smiled at me. "Why don't you invite Dale and Harm for supper? You can do your catch-up homework together."

"Excellent," I said, ringing up the stranger: "Double collard casserole with sweet potato pie. Six dollars and one cent."

"Aren't you the stupid kid that lost the patrol car?" he asked.

I counted to ten while I pretended to study his check. "Maybe I am stupid," I sighed. "I added wrong. That's *seven* dollars and one cent," I said, and nudged my tip jar forward.

Dale and Queen Elizabeth sauntered in with the supper crowd. "You said we got punishment homework," he said as Queen Elizabeth settled by the jukebox.

"Metaphors," I said. "Harm's staying home. Mr. Red needs him."

Miss Lana rumpled Dale's hair. "Poetry. Perfect for you, Dale. Your lyrical nature, your timeless perspective, your spiritual *je ne sais quoi*." Sometimes Miss Lana talks like a blizzard. You have to shovel your way through and even then, when you look back it's hard to see your own tracks.

"Just remember Cinderella, and you'll be fine."

Cinderella?

"Cinderella. Because . . ." My voice trailed away.

She smiled. "The Fairy Godmother turned the pumpkin into—*poof!*—a carriage. Mice into—*poof!*—horses. Poof one thing into another and you have a metaphor. As Shakespeare used to say, 'All the world's—*poof*—a stage . . .'"

"Poof," Dale said. "Why didn't somebody say so?"

Mayor Little shot through the door, smoothing his

plaid tie. "Mother's down," he said. "The stress of Starr searching our home, strangers prowling about town trying to cash in on that reward. Mother's immune system's flat as that cake," he said, eyeing Miss Lana's fallen red velvet. "All thanks to Macon Johnson's shenanigans."

"That's not a cake," I lied. "That's a Discus Delight. The Colonel mashed the calories out of it."

"Not fattening?" an Azalea Woman asked, her sketched-in eyebrows arching.

"Where did the calories go?" Dale asked, looking around. Dale is to ad-lib as Queen Elizabeth is to ballroom dancing.

"The Colonel blowtorched them," I replied as Sal strolled in.

Hannah and Little Agnes zipped in behind her. I handed Dale three waters. "Please take these to table three." Dale swaggered over and took a seat.

"I'll have a fat-free dollop of discus," the mayor said.

"Whipped cream and chocolate sauce?"

"Mercy, yes," he said, putting his napkin in his collar.

An Azalea Woman watched Dale shrug out of his jacket. "I just hate it that little Dale has to wear Lavender's hand-me-downs," she said. "If only Macon—"

"Dale's a musician. He enjoys vintage outfits," I said. "Besides, Miss Lana says most everything in life worth having is handed down."

Miss Lana nudged me aside. "I've got this table, sugar. You get Thes."

Thes sat at the counter, his chin in his hands. "Burger and fries. Sorry you lost the car, Mo. Tough break. I wanted to ask you something," he said, green eyes serious.

"Car loss happens. And I will not go to a movie with you."

"It's not that. I'm over you."

Over me? Has he lost his mind?

"Do you think Dale might add me to the puppy list? He could see the puppy every Sunday at church and more if he wanted. I'd do a good job. And I'm sorry for what I said at the church the day it got robbed. I was wrong."

"You broke Dale's heart, not mine. Apologizing to me won't help."

He slumped. "But I'm like you," he said. "I hate to admit it when I'm wrong."

By mid-rush, I'd bribed Sal and Hannah into doing our homework, and the mayor's flu talk had gone full-blown. Two Azalea Women felt feverish.

"This could be a pandemic," the mayor fretted. "Don't tell that horrifying reporter. Tupelo Landing has never had so much bad publicity."

Miss Lana dabbed oil of cloves behind her ears and

then mine, to ward off germs in case the talk proved true. "No, thank you," Dale said, ducking away. "Real boys don't smell like cooked ham."

The first odd call-in came around six p.m.

"Attention everyone," Miss Lana sang. "Starr says they've found Macon Johnson's orange prison jumpsuit in South Carolina. He's gone south," she said, looking at Dale. Dale took it like an eleven-year-old trying to be a man.

"Our crime wave's passé," the mayor cried, and the café applauded.

The second weird call-in came moments later. Miss Lana snagged me. "I need you and Dale to handle room service, sugar."

"*Room service?* Since when do we offer room service?"

She snapped a takeout bag like cracking a whip. "Capers has fallen ill too. She just called and she sounds terrible. Let's surprise her with comfort food." She plunked a container of practically organic soup in the bag and cut a wedge of macaroni and cheese.

"Normally we'd love to risk our lives for Capers, but I'm feeling puny. Dale too."

Dale sniffled.

Little Agnes looked up from her kindergarten homework. "Do I have a fever?"

Hannah touched her little sister's ear. "You're fine. Drink up," she said, sliding her shake closer and handing her a straw.

"Stop worrying, Agnes," Miss Lana said. "Here, Mo. Just in case." She reached under the counter and handed me a box of germ masks. I peeled a mask from the box.

Little Agnes jutted her small face forward.

"Me too," she said.

I slipped the mask over her pug nose and gently popped the rubber bands behind her ears. They bent forward, giving her the look of a spindly, masked bat. Hannah slipped the tip of her straw under the mask.

They say it takes a village to raise a child. In Little Agnes's case, it may take a metropolitan area. Charlotte, maybe. Or Washington, DC.

Miss Lana handed me the takeout. "Don't dawdle, sugar. Leave the food by Capers's door. And don't forget the masks."

Fifteen minutes later, Dale and me oozed down the inn's curved cedar drive. "Slow down," he said, looking back. "We about lost Liz."

"Slow down? Any slower and we'd be backing up." I dragged my sneaker's toe-cap across the gravel. Queen Elizabeth panted her way to Dale's side.

"The books say exercising her will help the birthing go

good," Dale said. "We mostly walk. We tried yoga, but she ain't as flexible as she looks."

"Unless I'm mistaken, NPR is saying yoga is for cats," I said, grabbing the takeout.

"Stay Liz," Dale said, and Queen Elizabeth curled up by his bike.

We scampered across the porch and pushed open the heavy door. The inn's radiators hissed as we trotted up the stairs.

"Masks," I whispered, and Dale wiggled his into place. I put the bag in front of Capers's door and raised my fist.

"Wait," he said. He fluffed his hair around the mask's rubber bands. Like Lavender, Dale is hair vain. "Okay."

"Mo and Dale to Go," I called, knocking. "Tips welcome."

"Tips. Good," Dale whispered.

Inside the room, a door slammed. A thud. Muffled curses. The doorknob rattled. Capers opened the door far enough to peer out with one eye. I could just make out Miss Lana's frilly *Gone With the Wind* bed jacket. She opened the door wider, revealing a red flannel nightgown beneath the bed jacket—definitely not Miss Lana's.

"Room service," I said. "Throw your tip on the floor. We'll disinfect it later."

She tugged a tissue from her pocket and took in a

couple quick breaths. Dale scuttled back like a frightened crab, tripped, and crashed to the floor.

"AhhhhHHHHCHOO!"

I ducked like I was dodging bullets. Which maybe I was.

"Nice boots," Dale said, staring at Capers's feet.

I looked down. Motorcycle boots peeped from beneath her gown. "What the . . . ?"

She kicked the bag inside and slammed the door.

"Boots with a nightgown?" I said as we tromped down the stairs.

"Probably near-death-experience boots so if she goes out of body, her feet won't get cold," he said as we headed for the front door. I nodded like Dale was a regular kid.

Dale closed the inn's heavy door behind us. "Where's Queen Elizabeth?" he asked. "Liz! Here, girl!" A cold moon watched us from beyond the pines. From near the river a pack of coyotes howled out their raw, twining song.

I cupped my hands around my mouth. "Liz!"

A faint echo bounced from the forest. The coyotes yodeled back.

They're death on lone creatures, I thought.

"They're hunting. We have to find her," Dale said, panic edging his voice. "Queen Elizabeth counts on me."

"Those coyotes are miles away," I said, hoping I was right. "Don't worry, Desperado. We'll find her."

We didn't.

An hour later, we climbed up from the river, our voices hoarse from calling. We'd looked everywhere: springhouse, dance pavilion, even the edge of the old cemetery. My heart and my feet felt like ice.

"I've been hovering," Dale fretted as we headed for the inn. "She's run away."

I looked at the inn and my heart exploded like fireworks. "Dale. Look."

A lumpy, triangular silhouette darkened the edge of the inn's porch. The lump tilted its nose to sniff the wind.

"Liz," Dale said, relief sweeping his voice. He broke into a run. As he hugged Queen Elizabeth, a voice sliced the night.

"Deal with it," a woman said.

Capers?

"I thought she was sick," Dale whispered. "What's she doing out here?"

"Shhhh." I peeped around the side of the inn. "Let's find out."

"Stay, Liz," he murmured. "I mean it this time."

We slipped behind the boxwoods and crept down the side of the inn. Capers stood in the moonlight, her gown flapping in the breeze. A man walked to her, his body a shifty gray shadow in the moonlight. "Moves like a wolf," Dale whispered.

The man slipped close to Capers . . . Did he hand her something? Take something? I squinted as he stepped away. "It's too dangerous," he told her. He turned and disappeared into the woods.

Dale frowned. "Too dangerous? What's too dangerous?"

Capers strolled toward us. We flattened against the clapboards.

She sniffed the night like a wild animal. Then she froze, her attention focused dead ahead, the wind trifling with her hair. Slowly I turned my head to look.

Queen Elizabeth strutted across the yard like a hired gun. She snuffled the crisp night air, wagged her tail— and waddled for Dale.

The Colonel says sometimes you got to turn the tables while you got a table to turn. I stepped into the moonlight: "You don't look sick," I said. "Explain yourself."

She jumped. "Jeez Louise," she gasped. "What are you doing here?" She wrapped Miss Lana's bed jacket tight around her. Was she hiding something against her rib cage? "Okay, you got me. I *am* sick, but I came out to meet a source."

Does she think we're blind *and* stupid?

I smiled, pretending to be both. "What source? We didn't see anybody. Did we, Dale?"

"No?" he guessed. "What did he say?"

"Sorry," she said, trying to brush past. "A journalist always protects her sources."

"Off the record, then," I said, stepping in front of her.

Dale stepped up beside me. "We took you to the patrol car that wasn't there—off the record," he added.

Good move.

She tilted her head and the breeze caught her curls. That ain't Sick Bed Hair, I thought. She's lying from here to Christmas. But why?

"I've said too much, Desperados," she said. "I'm sick and I need to go back to bed. But I'll tell you this: His lead will help your father, Dale—if it plays out."

Smart. That's exactly the bait to reel Dale in, I thought.

Dale stepped aside and she swept past us, the inn's door locking behind her.

Five minutes later we stood in Harm's kitchen, warming our hands at the stove.

"A shadowy wolf-looking guy with Capers?" Harm said. He shoved his hands in his pockets and leaned against the counter—a good look. "And you told her you *didn't* see him?"

"Yeah," Dale said, looking at me. "Why did we do that?"

"Because detective work is half what you know—and half what other people don't *know* you know." I held my palms to the stove, loving the heat's sharp bite. I shook my head. "I can't quite explain it, but there's something about Capers."

"She's smart, hot-headed, and nosy. Reminds me of you," Harm said, setting a cookie jar on the table and opening it.

"I don't like her either," Dale said, taking a cookie.

What?

"She's like you on the outside, Mo, but not on the inside," he said. He gulped his cookies, filled a bowl with water, and headed for Queen Elizabeth.

"What did she say about spying on us?" Harm asked.

"At Attila's, with binoculars," I said, to fill Dale in. "I forgot to ask her," I admitted. I frowned. "What *do* we know about Capers, really?"

Dale shrugged. "People like her. Guys like her because . . . you know," he said, and Harm nodded. "And the town likes her. Normally the town hates strangers, but she wrecked and nearly got killed—but didn't. She's a miracle and everybody loves a miracle except the Devil. And Miss Lana likes her because she's from Charleston. She treats her like family."

"She's not family," I said, shocked. "But she does pay cash, and Miss Lana says that's sort of like being a distant cousin."

Dale snorted. "People pay cash so you can't trace them. Everybody knows that."

I nibbled a cookie. "Let's background check her. I'll call Skeeter."

"Good," Dale said, stuffing an extra cookie in his pocket. "Mo, we better get going." He looked at Harm. "This is because we're riding our bikes in pitch-dark and nobody's offered us a ride."

Harm grinned. "Hey, Gramps," he called. "Mo and Dale need a ride."

In the living room, something crashed. "Dog bite it," Mr. Red shouted.

"What's he doing?" Dale asked as Mr. Red opened the living room door. "It smells bad."

"Cupid attack," Harm said. "He says he's fixing the place for me and him—and he is. But he's hoping Miss Thornton will like it too. *Really* like it."

Mr. Red stomped into the kitchen, tool belt clacking. My eyes traveled from his paint-stained ratty sweater to the baggy britches cinched tight with an electric cord. Plaster dust covered him from his messy hair to his untied hunting boots. "Get in the truck," he said, and stomped out the door.

"So that's what Cupid looks like," Dale said. "I'd wondered."

That night I settled into bed and dialed. Skeeter picked up immediately. "Skeeter and Associates."

"Skeeter? It's Mo."

"Please hold, I'll see if she's available," she replied.

Brilliant. A faux assistant. I tucked the idea away for later.

Skeeter came back on: "Hi, Mo. What's up?"

"Can you handle a background check? Capers Dylan."

"I'm curious too," she admitted. "She looks familiar. The way she walks. . . . I don't know. Other people have mentioned it too." She hesitated. "Sal and I will each want not just *any* puppy, but pick-of-the-litter rights in exchange for our services."

I grinned. Dale would love it.

"Done," I said, and hung up the phone.

Dear Upstream Mother,
    Cupid's set up shop at Harm's house. The smell is repulsive.
    We're hosting Thanksgiving dinner at our personal home this year. You're invited.
    Miss Lana's invited Capers Dylan, from

Charleston. I'd like your take on her. Lately I'm having more questions than answers.

I'll set a place for you next to me, same as always. No need to RSVP.

Mo

PS: I hope you like collards.

Chapter 19
Consider It Done

The background check went through with blinding speed. "Desperados," Skeeter whispered as we zipped down the hall the next day. "In here."

She closed the office door behind us. "First a message from Miss Lana," she said. "Please pick up the inn's trash after school. The Colonel's on strike."

"Now the nitty-gritty," Sal said, perching on the desk and crossing her legs.

Skeeter slid a paper to us. "A hard copy of Capers Dylan's website." I squinted at a blurry photo of a redheaded woman with a big smile and a long list of publications.

"I called the editor of the *Greensboro Gazette*," Skeeter continued.

"Capers has written several articles that didn't make our paper, including an interview with Deputy Marla, who's volunteering in the prison kitchen while she awaits trial. Deputy Marla offered some pretty interesting quotes." She flipped to an article and read: "'I'm not surprised Macon's escaped,' Deputy Marla said. 'He's smart, he's fast. He was the brains of our operation. People underestimate him.'"

"Daddy?" Dale said, frowning. "Is Deputy Marla saying Daddy's the brains of her and Slate? Because Daddy's mostly drunk. He ain't even the brains of himself half the time."

True.

"But Capers checks out," Harm said, leaning forward.

"You decide. Here's her bio," she said, turning a page toward us. "She's vague about her age, but so is Miss Lana. Says she lives in Columbia, South Carolina. No family but a cat."

"She lives in *Columbia?* She told us she lives in Charleston," I said.

Skeeter shrugged. "The website's a few years old. She could have moved."

"And she told me she has a sister."

She stacked her papers and stapled them. "This is the South. People disown and reclaim relatives just to pass the time."

Harm reached for her information. Skeeter pulled it away and slid it to Dale. "There you go, one dog lover to another," she said. "Can we confirm pick of the litter?"

Dale blazed a look straight into Sal's eyes. "You would have been my first choice anyway. These puppies are family to me."

Sal gasped and knocked over Skeeter's pencil cup. "I won't let you down, Dale."

"I know," he said. And we headed for the door.

"Have a wonderful Thanksgiving!" Miss Retzyl shouted that afternoon as the bell rang and we stampeded the door.

Moments later we Desperados pedaled up the inn's drive.

"Back in a flash," I said, and ran inside. "Capers?" I shouted, flying through the front door. I pounded up the steps. Her trash bag sat outside her door. Outside the other doors—zip. Optimal. I bolted out and slung the bag into my bicycle basket. "We'll mine this for reporter notes later."

Then came the surprise du jour.

"Who's that?" Dale asked as someone revved an engine at the head of the drive.

"A motorcycle," Harm said. "Capers?"

The rider gunned the engine. As the bike hurtled up the path, Capers pulled her feet onto the seat beneath her and rose, her arms wide as bird wings. As the bike slowed, she dropped onto it and headed for the inn.

"Where did she learn to do that?" Dale asked.

"She learned when she was a girl," I said. "She told me. She broke her nose trying."

"She's a stunter," Harm said as she roared toward us.

"No wonder that parking lot crash didn't kill her."

The motorcycle coughed to a stop. "Fantastic," Harm said as we stepped from behind the cedars. "I didn't know you were a trick rider."

She jumped. "And I didn't know I had an audience." She took off her helmet. "It's an old bicycle trick. I've missed stretching my wings." She shook out her long red hair. "What are you Musketeers up to?"

"About four foot three," Dale said, standing a little taller.

"You must feel better," I said as she hopped off her bike.

She unbuckled her saddlebag. "I do. Guess I just had a sinus thing. I'm glad I ran into you all," she added, giving Harm a smile that would cripple a frail boy. "I have a question. What do you think about all these Tupelo crimes?"

"We think Daddy didn't do them," Dale said.

"Really?" she said, arching her eyebrows and looking at me.

I gulped. The Desperados had never really discussed Macon's guilt—not straight out. I wanted to support Dale and be a kind friend, but so far the clues didn't help. I turned the conversation in a safer direction. "What do *you* think?" I asked.

She studied us like we were a hand of cards. "I'm like

everybody who's playing the clues instead of their hearts," she said. "I think Macon's as guilty as they come. I also think he's smarter than people think. I've interviewed Slate and Marla. They don't seem that bright—especially Marla. But Macon? So far he's outsmarted us all."

She headed for the steps.

"Wait," I said, and she turned. "We saw you spying on us at Attila's."

She laughed, her red hair shimmering like sunset. "I wasn't spying on you, sweetie, I was trying to get my story. Maybe you'll invite me along next time. Oh, could you tell Lana I'll miss Thanksgiving dinner tomorrow? I have to go to Raleigh."

"To visit your sister?" I asked, but the door slapped shut behind her.

"I'm home," I shouted moments later, hurling my messenger bag and Capers's trash onto my desk and kicking off my sneakers.

"In the kitchen, Mo," Miss Lana called.

Miss Lana's true coppery hair glowed warm and soft as she worked on a bowl of stuffing, her sleeves rolled up to her elbows. "I love Thanksgiving," she said, smiling.

"Me too." We always back-and-forth with Miss Rose for Thanksgiving. Last year we ate at her card tables. This year we'll set up tables in our living room. People think we'd host in the café, but hosting there says work.

Hosting here says home.

"Capers says to tell you she can't come tomorrow," I said, washing my hands.

"Something else to be grateful for," the Colonel muttered. "The presence of the two of you in my life, and her absence. That woman gets on my nerves."

I looked at Miss Lana. "She's a trick bike rider. We saw her. And her website says she's from Columbia. Not Charleston."

Miss Lana floured the countertop and set out sugar and butter. "I know," she said, getting out a pie plate. "She mentioned her bike riding—remnants of a misspent youth. And nobody from Charleston makes the mistakes Capers makes. Rainbow *Road* instead of Rainbow *Row*? Really." She shook her head. "Don't hold it against her, sugar. Everybody has a past except me. And secretly, everybody wants to be from Charleston. Who wouldn't?"

Miss Lana's Go With the Flow has a generosity I admire.

The Colonel tumbled a bag of sweet potatoes into the sink and turned on the water. "I don't know about you, but I'd be more grateful for Thanksgiving if it meant less work," he said, and she laughed.

Miss Lana loves Thanksgiving because it's Thanksgiving. The Colonel loves it because Miss Lana loves it, and I love it because it's with them.

He tipped his head toward a knife. "KP duty, Soldier."

"Yes, sir," I said, slipping in beside him.

We settled into the kitchen, the three of us, slicing, dicing, roasting.

The round, rich scent of baking sweet potatoes and boiling collard greens, the tang of sage, the drowsy smell of rising bread. This is how family smells, I thought.

This is what it means to belong.

Chapter 20
Three Thanksgiving Shockers

Thanksgiving brought three shocking twists of fate—one good, one puzzling, one jaw-dropping bad.

As usual, I didn't see them coming.

Dale biked over early that morning. "Queen Elizabeth's snappy," he reported, shrugging out of his faded baseball jacket. "Mama says the puppies will come today or tomorrow. I'm getting on Liz's nerves, so I came to get on yours instead." He frowned. "That didn't come out right. How can I help?"

"Hey Desperado," I replied. "Ham biscuits in the kitchen."

Dale padded back with a biscuit in each hand.

"Glad you're here, Dale," the Colonel said. "I need reinforcements." He checked the To-Do List Miss Lana made for him the night before. "Not doing that one, not that one, not that one. Here's one. 'Get tables and chairs from the café.'"

He smiled at Dale. "Don't worry about Queen Elizabeth," he said. "She'll know how to handle the pups. She'll do fine."

Next to Lavender, the Colonel's the best father Dale's got.

By eleven o'clock, we'd smoothed white tablecloths over the café tables and set them with Miss Lana's good china. Miss Lana put out the place cards and leaf-and-pinecone centerpieces, and whirled away to change clothes.

"Mo," she called, "you've grown. If you'd like to try the Pilgrim outfit . . ."

"No, thanks. I'm going as a sixth grader from this century," I called. "So is Dale."

I found Dale in the kitchen, hovering over the ham biscuits. "Still hungry?"

"Just cleaning up," he said, loading the last of the biscuits onto a dinner plate. "I thought I'd put them out for the raccoons."

He's serving raccoons on Miss Lana's good china?

"Are you singing today?" I asked him.

"Me and Harm are. Miss Lana asked us. We're doing 'Over the River and Through the Woods,' and a new country tune I wrote: 'My Baby Said "Stuff This Turkey" and She Walked on Out the Door.' Newton likes it," he added as he plopped a dollop of jelly on the side of the plate.

Jelly? For raccoons?

He opened the biscuit and peppered the ham—same as Mr. Macon peppers his ham biscuits at the café. Then it hit me: "That food's for your daddy," I said.

He closed the biscuit. "Daddy eats early on holidays because Mama's usually thrown him out by dinnertime. It's a family tradition. You know that."

"But Dale, he's not here. They found his orange jump-suit . . ."

A scowl shuttled across his face. "What's the difference in me fixing a plate for a daddy who ain't coming and you setting a place for a mother who ain't coming?"

I gasped. The silence backed up between us like water behind a dam.

He turned to me. "I'm sorry, Mo. I don't know why I said that."

His sudden hug pressed into my heart like a child's hand into clay. He grabbed his plate and blasted for the door, one shoe string flapping.

Miss Lana swayed in, fastening a pearl earring. I sized up her almost-normal Girl Next Door outfit. Light blue pumps, neat skirt, trim sweater. "Doris Day? 1950s?" I guessed.

"Close enough." She smiled. "It's me, mostly. The Pilgrim outfit's available if you change your mind."

Outside, Dale ran to the old sycamore stump, put Mr.

Macon's plate at its center, and carefully draped a linen napkin over the top as Miss Lana went up on her toes to snag a bowl from a cabinet shelf. "This was my grandmother's, Mo. Let's use it for the cranberry sauce. I'd love to feel her sitting at our table today."

"Yes, ma'am," I said, watching Dale scamper back to us.

She gazed out the window. "A plate for Macon, like always," she murmured. She slipped an arm across my shoulders. "The comfort of the familiar, sugar. It's hard to let go of people, even when we know they're gone."

High Noon. Enter Shock Number One.

"Happy Thanksgiving," Miss Rose called. She pushed open the door, her face flushed. "Everybody, this is Bill Glasgow."

Her new boyfriend? And Dale didn't tell me he was coming?

The room froze: Me with a plate of deviled eggs in my hands. Harm holding one of Miss Lana's old-school vinyl albums over her record player. Grandmother Miss Lacy placing her coconut cake on the sideboard.

"Nice to meet you," Bill Glasgow said, smiling. He stood tall and thin, his neat dark hair combed to his scalp. He wore a trim brown suit and bolo tie, and boots that looked like they knew how to dance.

As second-string hostess, I stepped forward. "Welcome,"

I said, very poised. "Mo LoBeau. May I take your hat?"

"Thanks," he said, and handed me his Stetson.

A Stetson? Miss Rose lassoed a cowboy?

Miss Rose smiled. "Bill, these are my friends." Mr. Red ambled over to shake his hand, and the rest of the group followed. Miss Rose gave me a quick kiss. "I didn't think Bill would make it today," she whispered. "I'll find Lana in a minute and let her know I brought an extra guest. She won't mind."

Dale strolled in from the kitchen and screeched to a halt, the bowl of cranberry sauce quivering in his hands. "Hey Mama," he said. "Are the puppies here?"

"Not yet, baby."

"You must be Dale," Bill said, holding out his hand. "Bill Glasgow. Nice to meet you."

"Hey," Dale said, his eyes glazing over. "I'd shake hands, but I got cranberries." Bill let his hand fall to his side. Dale's been working on his social skills. Apparently he skipped the Meeting Mama's Boyfriend chapter. He took a deep breath. "I'm used to you on the telephone, but it's different in 3-D," he said.

"Yep," Bill said. "Without the phone I'm pretty solid."

Dale's bowl of cranberry sauce tipped. "I guess Mama told you I'm the man of the house now. Harm and me been working out."

"Message received," Bill said, grabbing the bowl. "I hear you're a musician. I play a little mandolin. Nothing like you and Harm, but . . ."

Music. Dale relaxed. They strolled away, Bill matching his long stride to Dale's short one.

I darted into the kitchen. Lavender looked up from the store-cut veggies he'd moved to Miss Lana's platter. Even holding cauliflower, Lavender's melt-down gorgeous. "Your mama's here with a boyfriend," I reported.

He swallowed so hard his tie bobbed. "Had to happen sooner or later, I guess," he said, glancing toward the living room. "Mama's smart and beautiful. And lonely. What do you think of him?"

Lavender wants my opinion on a matter of the heart?

"She could do worse. In fact she already has, once." I considered Bill Glasgow. "He looks at home behind his face."

"Good recommendation," he said. "Well, I hope he likes washed-up mechanics who can barely make the rent."

"You aren't washed-up anything, and I'll take down anybody that says you are," I said. He smiled, checked his reflection in the toaster, and smoothed his hair.

Could Lavender, who wears cool easy as he wears denim, be nervous?

He is! Lavender needs me.

I smiled the way Miss Lana smiles for me when my nerves skate too near a cliff. "You look handsome," I said. "Real handsome. If you'd give me half a chance, I'd snatch you up and marry you before sundown. That's no lie."

The nervous melted off his face.

"You? You're a baby," he said, and grinned his old grin. "Thanks, Mo," he said, and headed for the door.

At one o'clock, the Colonel and the turkey made their entrance.

The rest of us milled about looking for our names on the place cards. Harm grinned at me, looking rakish in Mr. Red's bow tie. Grandmother Miss Lacy settled between Harm and Mr. Red, her blue hair shimmering. Lavender sat by a twin.

"Bill," Miss Lana said, "you're right over . . ." She looked around the table. "I'm so sorry! In the excitement I forgot to set . . ."

I looked at Dale and took a deep breath. "No, you didn't. Bill's right here," I said, grabbing Upstream Mother's place card. "Miss Rose, you take my place and I'll take yours."

"Are you sure, sugar?" Miss Lana whispered.

The butterflies swirled in my stomach. What was I thinking? We'd always set a place for Upstream Mother at our Thanksgiving table. That scared place inside me folded in on itself, and I could barely breathe.

I looked up and caught Lavender's gaze, steady and sure as a lifeline. I walked toward him and my new place, by Dale.

Lavender caught my hand. "Hang on to that place card, Miss LoBeau," he said. "I'll jump up and set her a place the minute she walks through the door."

Nobody knows me like Lavender.

Shock Number Two got served up with the coconut cake and sweet potato pie.

Dale slumped beside me in a turkey-induced haze, his shirt dabbed with cranberry sauce. Miss Rose sat with her hand curled on the table, almost touching Bill's. Her talk flowed quicker and brighter than I ever heard, and Bill chimed in easy as second fiddle.

"Sweet potato pie, sugar?" Miss Lana said, slicing the cinnamon-colored pie.

"I can't," I groaned.

"I can," Dale said, sitting up. He looked at the window and jumped.

A shadow flitted by the window and Miss Rose, who sat with her back to it, shivered like somebody danced across her grave.

"Excuse us, Miss Lana," I said, leaping to my feet.

"Dale and me got to walk. Harm does too, before he cramps up," I added, very loud. Harm had just invited himself to stay at Grandmother Miss Lacy's until the fumes died at Mr. Red's.

"Thanks, Miss Thornton," he said, and followed us to the door. "What's wrong?" he asked as we stepped onto the porch.

"Somebody's out here," I said, surveying the backyard—Miss Lana's camellias, the Colonel's campfire pit, my old sandbox-turned-flowerbed.

Nobody.

Dale pointed to the sycamore stump. "Daddy's plate," he said. "I left the napkin on top. Now it's folded to one side." We thundered down the steps, to the stump.

"No footprints," Harm said, searching the ground.

"He left the biscuits," Dale said, and picked up the plate.

Bingo.

Beneath the plate, a pale blue paper. Harm picked it up and read:

NOT MACON.
THINK AGAIN.

"Same paper, same handwriting as before," I said. "But who left it?"

We quickly searched the side yards and the café parking lot. "Whoever it was, he's gone," Harm said as we circled back to the stump.

Dale plucked a biscuit from the plate and studied the note. "'Not Macon.' We already knew that." He nibbled the biscuit. "Daddy's innocent. That's our given. Right? Like in a word problem."

My stomach dropped.

Dale had never straight-out asked us about Mr. Macon before. But as far as I knew, the only person in town who thought Mr. Macon was innocent held a ham biscuit and wore cranberry sauce dribbled down his shirtfront.

Dale looked at us. *"Right?"*

Dale can outstare eternity.

Harm took a deep breath. His bow tie had gone crooked, but his dark eyes held steady. "It's hard to actually see that as a given, Dale. I mean, I say we keep searching, but so far all the clues lead to Macon."

"Because somebody's making it look that way," Dale said. "Tell him, Mo."

Right, or kind, or both? I went for both.

"I'm keeping an open mind, Desperado. But the truth is, all the clues *do* lead to Mr. Macon. And there ain't another suspect in sight. I mean that in the kindest possible way," I added.

Even to me it sounded lame.

The red started at Dale's collar and drifted up to his

ears. "I thought you two were with me," he said. "Lying to your best friend isn't kind."

"We *are* with you," Harm said, very fast.

Dale's stare diced my heart into slivers. "Do you believe me about the footprints being fakes?" he asked. I bit my lip. "No. About the wallet being planted? No. About Daddy being too professional to steal a collection plate from a church?" He shook his head. "You're thinking like an Azalea Woman, Mo. You're thinking like Attila."

I gasped.

"You take that back!" I shouted, and Harm grabbed my arm.

"I won't take it back," Dale said, his voice dead as the leaves under my feet. "You think Daddy's guilty because he's always been guilty. Just like the night you saw somebody outside Lavender's garage and said it was him. That isn't right. Right's bigger than Daddy. Right's bigger than you getting even."

Then came Shock Number Three, the jaw-dropper of my lifetime.

Dale slipped the note into his pocket. "You're my best friends and I love you," he said. "But you're fired."

Fired? From my own detective agency?

"This is my case now," Dale said, and he walked away without looking back.

*₊ * ₊ *

8 PM

Dear Upstream Mother,

Happy Thanksgiving.

Today Dale fired me from my own Detective Agency—which if you'd asked me if that was possible, I would have said no.

He owes me an apology and I'm waiting for his call.

Mo

PS: We missed you at lunch today.

9 PM

Dear Upstream Mother,

I have checked my phone and I <u>do</u> have a dial tone.

Mo

At 9:12 my phone rang—not that I sat clock watching. "Desperado Detective Agency, I accept your apology."

"Hey," Harm said. "I take it Dale hasn't called."

"No," I said, trying not to sound disappointed. "He's being stubborn."

"Right," Harm said. "There's a lot of that in Tupelo Landing." He sighed, and I could picture him leaning against the counter in Grandmother Miss Lacy's neat-as-a-pin old kitchen, his arms crossed and his dark curls glistening in the soft light. "Have you called him?" he asked.

Me call Dale? Is he mad?

"Dale owes *me* an apology, not the other way around."

"Well, I think I made a mistake," he said, "letting Dale think I agreed with him about something this important, when I didn't. I don't feel easy inside. And who knows? Maybe Dale's right. I mean, he usually is, isn't he? If it's not about school or girls."

He had a point. Dale's good at the Big Picture, it's the details that tangle him up.

"Plus, suppose life shifted sideways, so we stood in Dale's place and he stood in ours. What then?" He sighed. "Anyway, let me know if he calls, Mo. If he doesn't, I'll call him in the morning."

Dear Upstream Mother,

Sideways . . . Suppose I thought the Colonel was innocent, and Dale let me think he believed me when he didn't. Suppose I had to stand up for the Colonel alone. What would my heart say then?

Do you ever think sideways of me? It's trickier than it sounds.

Mo

₊₊*

That night I slept a roller-coaster sleep, plummeting into dreams, jerking up to wakefulness, free-falling into a different dream.

In my dream, Miss Retzyl taps her pointer against the blackboard. "You can't solve the problem without the right givens. Wrong givens, wrong answer."

I stare at the word problem on the board. *If the crime spree travels east at 200 miles an hour and Mr. Macon has twelve dollars in change but no nickels, how many guineas does it take to stop a crime wave if you aren't sure of the clues?*

Attila raises her hand. "Given: Mr. Macon's guilty. He always is. Everybody knows it. Even Mo-ron."

Dale looks at me. "You're the smart one, Mo. Think of something."

Harm pushes his hair from his eyes. "We get the good grades, Mo, but Dale's usually right about big things, isn't he?"

I sat up, my heart pounding. Sweat trickled down my back.

Maybe Dale *was* right. Maybe I'd grabbed the wrong given. Maybe Mr. Macon really *was* innocent. Maybe the Big Picture's different than the get-even landscape in my heart.

I grabbed my phone and dialed Dale's number, hoping Miss Rose wouldn't answer. "Dale. Desperados. 'Lo?" Dale whispered. Dale doesn't wake up good.

His phone clattered to the floor. Queen Elizabeth growled into the mouthpiece and the phone bounced back up the side of his bed. "Hello?" he said.

"Dale, it's Mo. I think I missed the Big Picture, and I'm sorry."

"Mo?" he said, his bed creaking. "Where are we?"

"Earth," I replied. "Dale, I was wrong to assume Mr. Macon's guilty. It's just he usually is guilty, and I hate him, and I'd like to get even. But you're right. It has to be somebody else because Mr. Macon's mean as a snake but he ain't that flat-out stupid."

"Yes," he said, his voice suddenly sharp. "That's what I've been saying in daytime without waking up friends."

Some people say things to make you feel guilty. Dale just says things. You do the guilt work yourself.

"I'm sorry I didn't see it sooner," I said. "And I'm sorry I didn't level with you before." I heard his bed springs squeak as he leaned to tap out a midnight snack of bugs for Newton.

"That's all right, Mo," he said. "You can't help it if you're slow."

Slow? I counted to ten.

"I want back on the case," I said. "We'll start over."

He rustled a potato chips bag. "I unfire you," he said. "Harm too."

Unfired.

The comfort of the familiar settled over me warm as Miss Lana's quilts. "Thanks, Desperado," I said as he crunched a chip.

"You're welcome," he said. "You and Harm can be lieutenants, but I'm still in charge of the case."

Dale's in charge? I'm a *lieutenant?*

The hair on the back of my neck stood up.

On the other hand, why not? We'd gone worse than nowhere with me calling the shots.

"I'll bring the evidence box to you tomorrow," I said.

"No," he said, very quick. "I forgive you, Mo, but my heart needs time."

And he hung up the phone.

Chapter 21
Friday Night Miracle

The next afternoon—Friday—I biked over to Grandmother Miss Lacy's. "Complimentary leftovers," I said, dangling a takeout bag.

"Right on time, LoBeau," Harm said, grinning. "We just finished moving my things over. I'll be a town kid for a while—until Gramps finishes renovating, anyway."

We settled in the kitchen with turkey sandwiches. "Good news," I said. "We're unfired."

"I know. I called Dale this morning, to apologize."

He clasped his hands behind his head and leaned back in his chair. He's easy to look at, in a city-boy way. "So, Dale's our new leader. Fascinating."

The boiler clunked and the guineas screamed past the window. Grandmother Miss Lacy closed her eyes. "Sometimes I wish I wore hearing aids just so I could turn them down," she said.

"Got any darkroom work I can help with?" Harm asked me.

"I got a ton of possible evidence photos to develop,"

I said. "Dale will want to see them. And I thought you'd never ask."

My phone rang at midnight—late for a kid, but not too late for a client in distress. "Desperado Detective Agency. Your tragedy is our delight. How may we help?"

"Puppies. Now," Dale said, and hung up.

The phone rang again. "Parking lot. Now." He hung up.

Puppies! At last!

I scribbled a note for Miss Lana, grabbed my camera, and flew out the door.

A few minutes later Grandmother Miss Lacy dropped Harm and me off at Dale's. "Take plenty of photos," she called, and roared away.

Me and Harm walked briskly up the steps, the cold nipping our faces.

In the distance, wild howls and high-pitched yips echoed along the edges of the dark forest.

"Coyotes," I said.

Harm gulped. "How many?"

I knocked. "That's the genius of their howl. You can't tell. You only know you're surrounded." Miss Rose swung the door open. "Congratulations on the pups," I said, stepping inside. "Blessed Event photos are a specialty of mine."

"Wonderful," she said. "But . . ."

A river of sound flowed from Dale's room. He strolled past the open doorway, his guitar strap over his shoulder, his hair tousled. The lamp's warm light glanced off his pale blue pajamas and red rubber boots.

Red rubber boots?

Harm cocked his head, listening. "That's Patsy Cline's slinked-up version of 'Won't You Come Home, Bill Bailey.' We've been working on it for parties."

Dale's crystal voice floated to us: "Won't you come home, Queen 'Lizabeth, won't you come home. I moan the whole night lonnnnnng . . ." He saw us and stopped playing, his last note hanging like a foot reaching for a drifting boat.

"Where's Liz?" I asked, uneasiness tiptoeing across my shoulders as we entered his room. "Where are the pups?"

"I didn't have a chance to tell them, baby," Miss Rose said. She put a gentle hand on my shoulder. "Queen Elizabeth is gone."

"Gone?" My stomach dropped like an anvil.

"We've searched everywhere," Dale said, his eyes filling with tears. "Barn, stable, smokehouse. . . ."

That explained the red boots.

Outside, the coyotes howled. They're hunting, I thought. They surround quiet as velvet, howl, and jump anything that moves.

Liz wouldn't stand a chance.

"She'll come home," Miss Rose said in the same fake-calm voice she used the day Dale and me went sledding off the stable roof.

I clicked into Head Detective Mode. "We'll search. Miss Rose, you pass out the flashlights and the puppy treats and get me some graph paper. I'll make a search grid. Harm, you call Skeeter and Sal. And Thes."

"Not Thes," Dale directed. Then he sagged. "Yes. Thes too. Everybody. Tell them to come."

In the distance the guineas chuttered like tree frogs.

"I'll need pencils, preferably number twos," I told Miss Rose, who, for some reason, had not budged. "All right everybody, chop-chop."

Dale, Harm, and me sprang into action.

"Freeze," Miss Rose barked.

We froze.

"Mo, we don't need to wake up all of Tupelo Landing. We need patience and common sense."

"But I don't have any patience," I replied. "I got to move."

"I appreciate your willingness to lead, Mo. But the first element of leadership is a sense of direction. Obviously Queen Elizabeth's doing a good job of hiding: *We* couldn't find her. But we do need a plan, in case the coyotes come near."

"Mama's right," Dale said. "I wish we had the shotgun to scare them away, but we don't." He frowned and tapped his chin. "Let's go to the kitchen."

A snack? Now?

"We can pass out the pots and pans," he added, looking at Miss Rose.

She started to shake her head and stopped, staring at her son. "Good idea. Between the four of us, we can make enough noise to keep those coyotes at bay."

"And I want to search again," he added, his voice stubborn.

A shadow of doubt crossed her face. "Coyotes hunt in packs, Dale. They rarely attack humans—but they have. I don't think—"

"This is Queen Elizabeth," he said. "This is family."

Before she could answer, the guineas charged by and something bumped at our feet. "What was that?"

Bump. Whimper.

Dale slung his guitar onto his back and dropped to his knees. "Liz?"

Queen Elizabeth gave a soft whine from beneath the house and thumped her tail against a floor joist.

"Thank heavens," Miss Rose whispered.

Dale sprinted to the front door. The reedy branches of the hydrangea rustled and his voice floated up through the floorboards. "Liz? Come out, girl."

Instead she bumped and thumped her way nearer the center of the house.

"Dale, you get in this house and leave her be," Miss Rose called, swishing to the front door. "If you worry her, she may move again."

"Call if you need me, Liz," Dale said, his voice soft. "I'm right here."

An hour later we settled in Dale's room, pots and pans by the doors and PB&Js hand-squished flat on our plates. Miss Rose had turned on every light in the house and opened every curtain to the night.

Like most thieves, coyotes hate light.

Harm stood by the window, watching. "There's no point standing guard against coyotes," I told him, sinking into the beanbag chair. "Coyotes are like ghost shadows. You won't see them coming."

Dale picked up his guitar. "Talk about something else," he said. "Let's sing something for Liz."

We went through every Patsy Cline song we knew, my voice off-key and wild, riffing like a lovesick hound, theirs winding like vines along an invisible trellis.

We finally wound down, and Miss Rose headed for bed. "I've been thinking about a new plan for the case," Dale said as he handed our covers around. "I say we give the last note we found to Starr, and get him to investigate."

"Good idea," Harm said, and I nodded.

"We got to think different to get different results," he said. "We got to shake up our clues and pour them out again, without thinking in advance where they'll fall."

He pursed his lips. "One more thing. I wanted to tell you Thanksgiving, but I fired you instead. I'd like you to be the pups' godparents."

A smile spread across Harm's face. "Yes. Thanks, Dale. It's an honor."

"Me too."

I settled into the beanbag chair and pulled Miss Rose's handmade quilt to my chin. And I—Miss Moses LoBeau, cofounder of Desperado Detective Agency, lieutenant to Dale and godmother to new pups—drifted off to sleep.

Creeeeeeeeeeak.

My eyes flew open. The glint of moonlight on a guitar, the aroma of earthworms.

Dale's room.

I squinted at his empty bed.

Harm curled in a sleeping bag, his eyes closed and his mouth half open. *"Snooooore."*

Where's Dale?

Step-step-step. The front porch!

I padded to the window just in time to see Dale slip

past, his flashlight sending a narrow cone of yellow light flitting across the yard. The hydrangea rustled and I heard a soft bump beneath the house. Then a chorus of whimpers.

The puppies!

I tiptoed to Harm. "The puppies are here," I whispered.

We settled on the rug and leaned against the side of the bed as Dale clunked and grunted his way beneath the house. His voice drifted up. "Liz? Where are you, girl?"

Queen Elizabeth stirred near the chimney and Dale crawled toward the sound. "Hey, Liz," he said, clunking forward. "Oh Liz," he whispered, his voice melting. "Six beautiful babies."

The puppies mewed. "Liz, they're so soft and warm . . . Here's a boy. And a girl—she has your nose." Queen Elizabeth whined and talked, her voice round and winding and full of love. Dale sang back so soft I almost didn't hear.

Harm's shoulder brushed mine. It felt good, being close and greeting new life.

"Are you hungry, Liz?" Dale murmured. "I'll get you some breakfast." He bumped toward the crawlspace. Harm jumped up and held out a hand. We tiptoed to the front door and into the cold. Morning's light just softened the sky.

"There he is," Harm said, pointing to a flashlight beam jabbing from the crawlspace. We scampered down the steps.

Dale rolled out, stood up, and slapped the dirt off his pajamas. Then he pulled the waist of his pants out from his thin belly and wiggled his hips, letting the dirt fall out of his pants and onto his sneakers.

"Hey, Desperado," I said. "That was nice, what you said to Queen Elizabeth."

Harm shivered. "Yeah, sweet. Manly," he added quickly, "but sweet."

Dale turned to us and flipped his light up into his face—not a good look. "Those are the ugliest puppies I ever seen in my life," he said. "What are we going to do?"

By breakfast time, Dale had dissolved into a full-blown funk. He sat at the table with his head on his place mat. Harm cracked eggs into Miss Rose's skillet as I set a plate of toast on the table.

"Even if the pups aren't quite cute, kids will want them," I said. Dale slid a hand toward the toast without lifting his head, like an octopus groping for fish.

Miss Rose stirred cream into her coffee. "And they'll

pretty up, baby," she told him as he snagged a piece of toast and pulled it toward him. "They need time to open their eyes and perk up their ears. That's all."

Someone rapped at the front door. "Who on earth?" Miss Rose murmured.

Dale slipped into Man of the House Mode. "I'll get it," he said, and padded down the hall.

Joe Starr strolled in smiling.

"Joe," Miss Rose said. "Have some breakfast?"

"Coffee would be great," he said, dropping a heavy plastic bag on the floor and swinging his laptop onto the counter. He grinned at Dale. "I hear you have puppies."

Starr's in a good mood? Odd.

"How did you know about the puppies?" Harm asked, pouring his coffee.

"Maybe he's psychic, like Liz," Dale said. "No, that's not right."

"Nope," Starr said. He's not bad-looking when he's happy. "Lana told me when I stopped by the café this morning. I have two things for you people." He opened the huge plastic bag, and the smell of old river seeped across the room. "Could you identify this jacket, Rose? It was in the patrol car."

She wrinkled her nose. "If you mean is it Macon's—I stitched his name inside."

Starr undid the top button, to show the label. "That's

his," she said, cupping her hand over her nose. "That thing stinks to high heaven. Get it out of my kitchen."

"A jacket doesn't prove anything," I said as he tossed it out the back door.

"Item two," he said, opening his laptop. "Surveillance video from a Florida gas station. We've found Macon."

Starr started the grainy video: Mr. Macon swaggering into a store, pulling out cash. Dropping something, shoving the cashier, walking out.

"It's hard to see his face," Harm said, squinting.

"Macon knows surveillance cameras," Starr said. "But you can catch enough glimpses from enough angles to match it to his mug shots."

"What's that he dropped?" Dale asked, watching again.

Starr smiled deep enough to show dimples. "That's the last nail in his coffin."

Dale gasped.

"Metaphor," Harm said quickly.

"Right," Starr said. "Sorry, Dale. It's a bloody dishcloth. From that drawer over there, I bet. From the day he trashed this kitchen."

I frowned. That was weeks ago. I plugged in our new given: Mr. Macon's innocent. "Why would he carry that around?"

"Who knows? We're running the DNA. But it's his."

For the first time since I've known Dale, I couldn't read a word on his freckled face.

"Joe," Miss Rose said, sitting up straighter. "When was this video made?"

"Thursday morning. Why?"

She took in a deep breath and let it go. Years fell from her face. "Then he's really gone." She put her hand on Dale's. "We can relax. You can think about boy things again—your schoolwork and those puppies. I can think about the farm."

"But we can't see his face," Dale said.

Starr snapped the computer closed. "The DNA will verify it, Dale. With Macon in Florida, I'm letting investigators there track him. And with the open cases here, I doubt Macon will be back," he said. "Sorry, Dale, I know you wanted a different outcome."

"We found another note," Dale said. "I'll get it. It said *Not Macon*."

Impatience flashed across Starr's face. "Sorry, Dale. Video doesn't lie."

That's the same thing he said about the footprints, I thought as Miss Rose walked Starr to the door.

"We're on our own," Dale said, his voice grim. "We better get this right."

˟˟*˟*

Lavender rumbled up just after breakfast and parked by the pecan tree. I walked to the porch to greet him.

"Morning, Mo. Check *that* out," he said, smiling and pointing behind me.

Liz trotted toward the steps, a fat puppy dangling from her gentle mouth. I hustled to get the door. Lavender and me followed her to Dale's room.

"I'll be back in a few, Desperados," Lavender said, peeping in as the Desperados trailed Liz to the closet. "I need to talk to Mama a minute."

Dale beamed as Liz brought her pups in one by one. "Good girl," Dale said as she settled each in the closet. "They're already cuter," he announced, relaxing.

He followed her out and took his post by the door.

"Jeez, they're funny-looking," Harm whispered, touching them. "Closed eyes, flat ears . . . They feel like warm velvet, though. Will they get cuter?"

"There's no such thing as an ugly puppy," I said, hoping I was right.

He stood. "Mo, Gramps needs our help tomorrow— if you have time."

"Help with what?" Dale asked, following Liz and the last puppy in. "Here, Liz," he said, offering her jerky from his bedside stash. "Extra-spicy, just the way you like it."

Harm's stomach rumbled. How are boys hungry all the time?

Liz gobbled the jerky down.

"Listen," Harm said, "I talked Gramps into repainting the living room, but pink's impossible to cover. It's just so . . . ruthlessly pink. We can get another coat on tonight. If you could help tomorrow . . ."

"A mission of mercy," I said. "What time?"

"After church. I'll fix lunch, and we can paint and plan the next step in the case." He looked at Dale. "If you want to."

"Yes," Dale said, looking up from the puppies.

"Great. I'll call Miss Thornton and see if I can get us a ride home."

Ride with Grandmother Miss Lacy when Lavender's around?

"I got a better idea," I said, and slipped down the hall.

I walked into the kitchen just as Miss Rose settled the black ceramic hat on her ceramic cash frog, and the back door slammed behind Lavender. "Where's he going?" I asked. "He hasn't seen the puppies."

"He'll see them later, Mo. He has something to do."

I watched Lavender stroll away easy as springtime. But when he rounded the pecan tree, and he thought no one could see, his face flushed red. His walk shifted into a skip-step, and he kicked the side of the GMC hard enough to set it rocking.

I gasped. "What's happened? Lavender loves that truck!"

"Nothing to worry about," she said, her voice firm. "I don't want you talking this around, Mo. What you see in my kitchen, stays in my kitchen."

Lavender slammed his truck door and roared onto the highway.

"Let's go see those puppies," she said. "Lavender will be fine."

Maybe so, I thought. But he didn't look fine to me.

Chapter 22
More Mystery than Clue

Unless St. Peter gives Show Up Credit, church was wasted on Dale and me the next day. Dale spent the hour basking in the glow of puppies he hadn't officially announced. I spent my time pondering Lavender.

Thes grabbed us as we headed out the door. "Dale, the things I said the other day. I was wrong. I forgive . . . whoever robbed the church. I hope you'll forgive me too."

Dale stuck out his hand. "Thanks, Thes. I already did."

"I'd like to have a puppy," Thes added, trailing us into the churchyard. "If Queen Elizabeth has enough, I mean."

Excellent. There's six puppies. Thes makes six first-rate puppy parents.

Dale picked up his bike. "I don't think so, Thes. You hurt me on purpose. I forgive you, but I take care of what's mine."

I take care of what's mine. Mr. Macon's words shivered me like ghost hands.

* * * * *

A few minutes later, we knocked on Harm's door.

"Before photos?" I offered, clutching my camera as we stepped inside. I scoped out the living room. The familiar baloney-colored sofa and crippled recliner skulked beneath paint-blotched sheets. The walls wore a streaky, pink-going-on-beige mess.

"It looks like Barbie threw up in here," Dale said, turning in a slow circle.

"Thanks, Dale. No before photos, then," Harm said, grinning. His smile faded as a red sports car cruised into the yard. "Here comes trouble," he muttered.

Flick Crenshaw. Proof that slime can stand up and walk.

"What's that son of a gun want?" Mr. Red asked, clomping in wearing his splotched painting clothes.

Flick swung the front door open without knocking. "Afternoon, Gramps," he said, ignoring the Desperados. "Thought you might like to do a little rabbit hunting."

Hunting? That would mean using Mr. Red's dogs to hunt Mr. Red's rabbits on Mr. Red's land. On Sunday—which is illegal.

"Nope," Mr. Red said.

Flick tossed Harm a thick manila envelope. "Brought these for you."

Harm peeked inside. "From Mom?" he said, smiling.

"I thought she'd given up writing to me . . . There's tons here. How long have you had them?"

Flick shrugged. "If you don't like the way I do it, find another delivery man."

"That's not what I meant," Harm said, placing the envelope on the sofa. "Mom's in Nashville," he told us. "Didn't have this address, I guess."

"Or didn't want to use it, afraid of someone's reaction," Flick said, glancing at Mr. Red. "Thought you might want them, even if she just wants cash." Mr. Red pried open a can of paint. "Speaking of cash, Gramps, I'm between jobs, and . . ."

So that's it, I thought. He's broke.

"Get a job," Mr. Red snapped. "Or sell that fancy sports car."

I looked out the window, embarrassed to see Harm's family inside out. Flick's car glittered in the sunlight, tickling something in my mind. *What?* Flick headed for the door. Whatever it was, it was about to drive away.

I grabbed my camera. "Nice car," I said. "Mind if I photograph it? Lavender would like to see it," I added— like Lavender would give a rodent's patoot.

Flick smiled like an oil slick. "Sure, Slow Mo. Show him what a real car looks like. How's he doing, anyway? I hear he's going under."

Lavender? Going under? My pulse jumped.

"If he gets any busier, he'll have to franchise himself," I said, strolling out and lining up my shot. *Click. Click.*

"Tell Lavender I'm ready to race whenever he is," Flick said, and he blasted out of the yard.

It's harder to tame pink than I expected.

We passed our painting time by chatting: puppies, school, the inn. "Miss Lana says an inn is like a newborn: It cries for something every three hours or so. She needs night help. And someone of *legal* working age," I said before Harm could ask for a job.

"Lavender came to see the puppies this morning," Dale reported.

Mr. Red rolled a streak of white on the ceiling. "How's he doing?"

"His racecar's great," Dale said. "The best he's ever had. He says she's his ticket to bigger races and better times. Except for that, his life's a disaster." Dale dabbed paint on a baseboard. "Lavender's work always fizzles when Daddy messes up," he said. "Then Daddy gets locked up in a day or two and business roars back."

Mr. Red nodded. "Sounds about right."

"So, with Mr. Macon gone, Lavender should be fine," Harm said.

Dale shook his head. "Daddy got away. Lavender says he's bleeding him dry. Mama had to help him with his rent this month. He never had to ask before."

So that's what I saw in the kitchen.

"Then that's one more reason to get this case right," I said.

Dale put his brush down. "I've been thinking. Now that I'm in charge, I want to cast a wide net. With a wider net you get sticks and trash—but you also get nice fish. Very nice fish."

Mr. Red froze, staring at him. Harm and me nodded.

"Let's brain-blizzard," Dale said. "Possible suspects—besides Daddy."

Brain-blizzard?

Harm finished off a windowsill. "You mean brainstorm."

Dale shot him his You're Fired Look.

"Not that a detail like that matters," Harm said, very quick. "Possible suspects. Flick tops my list. He needs cash for his race with Lavender, and he's broke. And he's not very honest."

Dale pointed to Mr. Red.

"The town's been eat up with strangers hunting Macon for the reward money," Mr. Red said. "Any one of them could be in on this."

Dale pointed to me.

"Wolf-Guy could be a suspect," I said. "The shadowy guy we saw talking to Capers. What did he say? *'It's too dangerous.'* Who is he, anyway?"

Dale pointed to himself. "Capers Dylan," he said. "She reminds me of something that used to leave a bad taste in my mouth. And she writes in code."

Mr. Red put his paint roller down. "Code?"

We explained the 2-6 code. "And there's this numbers thing she does," I said. I snagged my messenger bag. "I think I have one, from the day she crashed."

I perched on the sheet-covered sofa. "Here it is. A letter written in blue ink. And on top of the ink . . ." I held it up to the light. "Tan numbers and letters. Capers says it's a game, but I'm not so sure."

"What kind of numbers?" Mr. Red asked.

"Like 637A1. 100A10. 648B11."

"Could be another code," Dale said, his face thoughtful. "Sal will know."

Why didn't I think of that?

"Sal? The metaphor gal?" Mr. Red said, looking at Harm.

"Don't try to rhyme, Gramps," Harm said, grinning. "I told Gramps about the metaphor Sal wrote for you, Dale. Remember? 'Your smile walks barefoot across my lonely porch.' Gramps bought it from her for five bucks. It will knock Miss Thornton's support socks off. Hope you don't mind."

Dale shook his head. "I'm proud. Sal has a head for business good as Mama's."

"And Lacy will love it," Mr. Red said, his old eyes twinkling.

The room wore a handsome tan coat when Mr. Red finally walked us to the door. "Anything worth hiding is worth finding," he told Dale. "I'd investigate those codes."

Dale made an executive decision.

"I got Puppy Duties tomorrow," he said. "Mo, you line up Sal. Harm, keep an eye out for Wolf-Guy and think about where he fits in the big picture. I'll think about the strangers in town and about Flick."

He clapped his hands like he was playing football. "Hut!"

Maybe it was the paint fumes, but to me it sounded like a good plan.

We made the official puppy announcement the next day at school.

"Miss Retzyl," I said as we settled in. "Dale has extra credit news."

"The puppies are here," he said, and the class cheered.

"Is Little Agnes getting one?" Hannah asked. "For sure?"

Dale beamed. "The six pups go to Sal, Skeeter, Little Agnes with Hannah, Miss Retzyl, Susana, and . . ."

The Exum boys tucked their shirttails in. Thes gave Dale a hopeful smile.

". . . And one undecided," Dale said. "Puppy people may visit. Please bring a gift for Newton," he added. "He's sensitive to family dynamics."

Miss Retzyl frowned. "Isn't Newton an amphibian?"

I raised my hand. "Even a three-chambered heart can break."

She picked up her math book. "Thank you, Dale. Let's get started. Your homework was on rational numbers. Questions?"

Dale's hand waggled. "What happened to the irrational ones?"

Excellent! Dale, who hasn't asked a single classroom question since the jailbreak, is back! Harm cranked around in his seat and gave me a thumbs-up.

Miss Retzyl didn't miss a beat. "The irrational numbers are fine, Dale. Please open your books."

At lunchtime, I finally unfolded Capers's mysterious parking lot letter for Sal. "We need your help," I said as Harm slid into the seat across from me.

"Yeah. And thanks for selling Gramps that metaphor," he interrupted, smiling at Sal.

Sal swiveled to Dale. "I hope you don't mind. You didn't seem to get it at all. And Mr. Red's in the market for poetry about love and a house for Miss Thornton. I think it's sweet. Plus he paid me five dollars."

"Five dollars?" Jake barked. He and Jimmy looked up from their lunch. So did Hannah and six other kids.

"Does he need more?" Susana asked from the next table.

Sal shrugged. "Maybe. If you want to give me something to show him. . . ."

"Finally," Jake said, high-fiving his brother. "I know what metaphors are for."

Sal spent the rest of lunch period fielding metaphor questions. "Sorry, Mo," she said, sliding my paper back as the bell rang. "We'll talk later."

As the day crept by, kids scribbled, erased, scribbled again. At the end of the day Miss Retzyl sang out, "Language arts. Once again, we're working on—"

"Metaphors!" Sal cried, and the class whipped out their papers. She pointed to Hannah.

"A metaphor," Hannah said. "My heart sings beneath your window, a troubadour of my love."

Sal gave her a quick thumbs-up. Hands shot into the air.

"Jake?" Miss Retzyl said. *"You wrote a metaphor?"*

Jake picked up an erased-through paper. "My love is a fish camp by the river for you." Jimmy nudged him. "With a chain-link dog pen in back," he added.

Sal went thumbs down as Miss Retzyl staggered at her podium. "That *is* a metaphor," Miss Retzyl said, staring at Jake like he'd been beamed in by aliens.

The bell rang and we bustled out, placing our papers on Sal's desk. "I'll wait for you outside," I told her.

Moments later she leaned against the bike rack and set her beret at exactly the right angle. "Another code? I love codes."

"Come to the café," I said. "We can explore it over complimentary milkshakes."

She shook her head. "I have metaphor business." She whipped out her day planner. "Tomorrow morning's the best I can do. Eight-ish? Skeeter's office?"

"Great," I said, my heart sagging.

"The more samples you can show me, the merrier." She zipped her plush jacket and hurried away.

What could it hurt to wait one more day?

The Azalea Women clacked into the café around four. "Salads and ice waters all around," one called. "We're dieting."

I sighed. Dieters tip as skinny as they eat.

"I'll take them, sugar," Miss Lana said.

An Azalea Woman smiled at the Colonel. "I hear Macon's robbed a convenience store in Florida." Strangers looked up from their collard enchiladas.

"Unfounded rumor, as usual," the Colonel said, polishing the counter.

The Azalea Woman winked at me. "And how's our racecar driver, Mo?"

Word on the street is the Azalea Women took their cars to Jiffy Lube in Greenville for a tune-up this morning. I hate Azalea Women.

"Good," I said. "His new racecar's the best ever. He's a shoo-in at Daytona."

The Colonel tossed me my jacket. "Ride with me, Soldier," he murmured. "I need to check things at the inn."

"The inn?" Miss Lana said, loading ice waters on her tray. "Colonel?" she said, her voice nudging.

A sigh racked his frame. "And I'll pick up the trash while I'm there."

I followed him out. "Trash," he muttered as he settled behind the Underbird's steering wheel. "This is what my life's come to. Sometimes I long for the days when I had total amnesia."

"Yes sir," I replied, fastening my seat belt. I studied his rugged face. "Colonel, is Lavender going to be okay?"

He cranked the Underbird.

"I expect so," he said, heading for the inn. "But it may take time. Rose will be fine. Her farm tours begin again in the spring and she's developing markets outside Tupelo Landing. Business that's not so dependent on small-minded people who—"

"I think I might be small-minded too," I blurted. The whole ugly story fell out of me before I knew I wanted to tell it. "Now Dale's in charge of the case and Harm and me are lieutenants, which I'm not cut out for reduced rank." I dropped my bombshell: *"And Dale's doing a good job."*

He parked at the inn door and gave me a smile. "I'm not surprised Dale's a good leader. And I applaud your strategy. A smart leader knows when to step aside, and let others lead."

I love the Colonel. *Step aside* sounds so much better than *get fired.*

"You'll make a splendid lieutenant—temporarily, at least," he said. "A general's only as strong as his or her soldiers. Make Dale stronger, my dear. He deserves it.

"And I share your concern for Lavender," he added. "He's finishing a room for us here at the inn. But just so you know, it's the last work we'll have for a while. Sometimes you do what you can to help—and then what you can do is done."

Minutes later, I tapped at the door of guestroom #5. "Hey," I said. "Looks good in here."

"Thanks," Lavender said, smoothing putty in a joint on the new windowsill. He drummed up a smile, but his cheeks wore a red-gold stubble and his hair lay too flat.

He looked like a penny that had lost its shine.

The Colonel sat on a sawhorse. "Soldier, could you collect the trash for me?" he said, tossing me a skeleton key. "I have some things to discuss with Lavender."

Crud.

A heartbeat later I knocked on Capers's door. The key clicked and the door swung open on a room cluttered with clothes, shopping bags, papers. "What a pit," I muttered.

"Anything of interest?" Capers asked, exiting the bathroom with a towel wrapped around her head.

I jumped. "I knocked," I said, taming my runaway heart. "Just picking up the trash." I peeked at the papers on her desk. More tan numbers and letters. "How do you play this game?" I asked, snagging her trash bag. "I'd like to try."

"Another time," she replied, holding the door to the hall for me.

Smooth—but rude.

Her gaze followed me down the hall like cat follows mouse.

Moments later, the Colonel sprang the Underbird's trunk, which yawned open on a couple weeks' worth of trash bags. "I know, they go in the Dumpster. I'll get around to it," he muttered. He cut his eyes to me. "Lana doesn't need to know."

"You're a rebel, sir. I'll take care of this," I said, picturing the coded papers waiting in those bags. "One man's trash is a detective's treasure," I added. "Sir, about Lavender . . ."

"Lavender's losing heart," he said, his voice gentle. "We'll hope for the best. But a lost heart is a very hard thing to find."

That evening I set the Colonel's elegant 1940s fan on the floor of my flat and placed a trash can on its side a few feet away. I emptied the first trash bag between them and clicked on the fan, whirring the tissues and gum wrappers into the trash. Like panning for gold, I thought, grabbing a crumpled paper covered in the odd, ghostly letters. I snagged a 2-6-type code with the date-like key at the corner of the page torn off.

An hour later, I had a folder full of . . . what? More mystery than clue, I thought.

But Sal had said the more the merrier, and I'd see her first thing in the morning.

Chapter 23
Stakeout at Grandmother Miss Lacy's

"Where's Sal?" I asked the next morning, blasting into Skeeter's office.

"Sick," Skeeter said, marking her place in her law book. "She might be back tomorrow."

Tomorrow? Crud.

The day oozed by like a sloth on pain meds. Even Harm wilted as the morning slid into afternoon.

"Harm Crenshaw," Miss Retzyl said, clapping her hands. "Wake up!"

Harm lifted his head from his desk and gave her a sleepy smile. "The periodic table," he said. He blinked. "This *is* science, isn't it?"

Miss Retzyl went glacier. We'd finished science a half hour ago. "Harm," she said, "you've fallen asleep two days in a row. Why?"

Attila sneered. "I hear Mr. Red's building a still in his living room. Maybe the noise is keeping Harm up."

Harm stretched. "I'm sorry, Miss Retzyl," he said. "I

haven't been sleeping well. I'm Miss Thornton's house-guest and I haven't quite settled in." He gave her a sleepy smile. "I promise it won't happen again."

Harm corralled Dale and me on the way out of school. "You've stayed late at Miss Thornton's before," he said, looking at me. "Did you hear anything weird?"

"Weird?" I said. "You mean like guineas?"

He raked his fingers through his hair. "I mean like running water, or creaks and bumps? I don't want to seem lame, but . . ." He shrugged. "Maybe it *is* that old boiler. Or the house settling. Throw in those squawking guineas . . ."

"Squawking? At night? What's scaring them?" Dale demanded.

"How should I know?" Harm asked, exasperated. "But I thought we could check it out. You know. Pro bono her a stakeout."

"A luxury stakeout," I said. "Count me in. When?"

"Tonight."

"Come see the pups first," Dale said. "And I need to check on Newton."

I hopped on my bike. "Race you," I shouted.

"Hey girl," Dale said a few minutes later, rubbing Queen Elizabeth's ears. The puppies tumbled around her, mewing. The biggest rolled to his feet and tried to walk.

I laughed and scooped him up. He squirmed against

my chest, a warm armful of wiggle and mew. "He's like a little sumo wrestler."

Dale gently sorted the puppies. "That's Mary Queen of Scots—Miss Retzyl's pup. Sal picked little Ming. Skeeter wants King John. And Susana's taking Ferdinand I. Little Agnes wants this one," he said, picking up the only spotted pup in the litter. "She said, 'This one is different.' That's a kindergarten skill. She hasn't picked a name yet."

I strolled over to the terrarium. "Where's Newton?"

"Resting," Dale said, going shifty. He grabbed his guitar and sang: "How much is that puppy in the closet, the one with the cute little tail?"

Harm tromped back in. "Miss Rose says it's rude for us to go to Miss Thornton's hungry. She's warming up pizza for us."

"Pizza?" Dale gasped. "No!"

Miss Rose's scream pierced the air. "Dale Earnhardt Johnson III! You get in this kitchen right this minute!"

Dale dropped his guitar. "Mama," he cried, running to the door. "I can explain." Harm and I raced down the hall behind him.

Miss Rose stood at the open refrigerator. "What's the meaning of this?" she demanded, nudging a pizza box with a spatula. "What's Newton doing in my icebox, Dale? Did *you* put him in here?"

"Rhetorical?" he whispered, looking hopeful.

"Dale," Miss Rose said. "Why is your lizard . . ."

"He's not a lizard," Dale replied. "He's an amphibian. The difference—"

Miss Rose stomped her foot. When she spoke, her voice came out like canned cake frosting: unnaturally smooth and way too sweet. "Dale, there's a newt in my refrigerator. Explain."

"Newton's depressed. I think he's fallen off life's cycle, and he's my responsibility. Maybe he'll feel better if he hibernates."

Miss Rose stared at Dale like she was adding up to see if she could afford boarding school.

"I thought about putting him outside," Dale said, "but there's the possibility of cats. And coyotes. Still," he admitted, "the refrigerator may have been a mistake."

"Do you think so?" Harm asked, very innocent.

Newton lifted his head and blinked. "I'll take him to my room," Dale told Miss Rose. "Unless you want to keep him with you while we're on stakeout."

"Your room's fine," she said. "And Dale, *everything's* not your responsibility. You're eleven years old."

"Eleven and three-quarters. Can I borrow your electric blanket?" Dale asked. "Because Newton's—"

"No," she said.

"No," Dale echoed, heading down the hall. "I didn't think so."

⁺₊⁺₊⁺

"Newton? Depressed? Tragic," Grandmother Miss Lacy said a half hour later, placing a plate of cookies on the table. Her eyes traveled to the window, and Lavender's garage. "I'm afraid Newton's not alone," she murmured.

A vase of tulips graced the table by the window. A card lay beside it. I could just make out the word *troubadour.*

Hannah's metaphor. Harm's flower-of-choice.

Her eyes followed my gaze. "Red," she said, smiling. "It makes us young again." She strolled over to adjust the card. "Harm, I wish you'd told me you couldn't sleep."

"I'm a light sleeper," he said.

A total lie. I've seen him sleep through a fire drill.

"I just need to understand the sounds here," Harm said. "Like . . . I don't know. Water gurgling, things squeaking. I'll sleep better when I know what they are."

"We thought we'd pro bono you a stakeout," I said. "We brought our pj's."

"A sleepover! Wonderful," she said, flushing like a girl. "Having those sounds explained will be a bonus. Sometimes I feel like someone's staring at me—when I *know* nobody's here. And a chill slips right up my spine."

She shivered. "Why don't I cook some dinner? Liver and onions," she said, watching my face. "With rutabagas and wilted spinach . . ." She burst out laughing. "My word, your faces. Burgers and fries? I'll call the café."

Old people humor, I thought, shaking my head. I never see it coming.

After supper Grandmother Miss Lacy and me developed film. Harm helped Dale with his math homework. "But *why* would fractions even want to divide decimal numbers?" Dale demanded as I walked in from the darkroom. "It doesn't make sense."

"I don't know why," Harm said, his calm unraveling. "I just know it will be on the test. Try again."

Finally, we settled in. Dale and Harm upstairs in the guest room, Grandmother Miss Lacy in her room upstairs, me on the parlor sofa. I curled up with my pillow toward the door and my eyes on the window.

My eyes closed, closed, closed . . . *Bump.*

What was that? A man at the window?

The wind blew, sending a kaleidoscope of shadows across the window screen.

Just the wind.

I settled back and closed my eyes. A creak behind me, a sharp dance of prickles across my shoulders. Was someone behind me, in the doorway? I darted a glance.

Nobody.

I'd almost dissolved into sleep when . . . "Mo?"

"What?" I gasped, sitting up.

"It's Dale. Harm and me wondered if you'd been killed yet."

Yet?

Dale slipped into the room. "I mean, you're like a human sacrifice if there's a killer in here because you're the only one downstairs, so he'd get you first. We were just wondering if you were . . . you know."

"*Dead?*"

"Dale was wondering," Harm whispered. "I wasn't."

My eyes adjusted to the moonlight. They stood side by side in pale pajamas, the tall one slouching against the door frame, the short one shifting from foot to foot. "I'm okay, Desperados," I whispered. "Go back to bed."

I never could say for sure what woke me next.

Maybe it was the ragged tin-can squawk of Grandmother Miss Lacy's guineas. Or the clunk of the radiator. Or the flicker of flat orange light against the windowpanes.

I stumbled to the window half-asleep and tried to piece together the picture outside: Orange snake-tongues darting from the garage's eaves. Moonlight glinting off the curves of Lavender's truck. The sharp, greedy smell of smoke.

Fire.

"Fire!" I shouted. "Fire! The garage! Fire!"

Time slung me forward and shot me into the hall. I turned at the stairs. "Fire!" I screamed. "Fire!"

Upstairs, a door slammed.

The boiler thunked.

Footsteps thundered down the hall.

Then I heard it, faint and distant: "Help! Help me!"

Lavender!

Dale flew halfway down the steps and vaulted over the banister. "The garage!" I shouted as Harm pounded on Grandmother Miss Lacy's door.

"Hurry! It's Lavender! Fire!"

Chapter 24
Fire!

Dale and me sprinted for the garage. I yanked open the wide door and a tidal wave of heat and smoke slammed into us.

"Lavender!" Dale shouted, his scream more like a cat's than a boy's.

"Here!" Lavender shouted. "Dale! The jack slipped! Hurry!"

Flames scrabbled their fingers up the back wall and a thick black curtain of smoke pressed down from the ceiling.

We dashed to the heavy jack at the side of the car. "Turn the knob on the jack," Lavender shouted, struggling to squirm from beneath the car. "Hurry."

The lightbulb overhead exploded.

I fumbled with the small metal button on the side of the jack. The smoke grew heavier by the second, stifling me and clawing my eyes.

"Turn it, Mo!" Dale said. "Turn it!"

"*I can't.*" My world became a blur of smoke and tears. "Help!" I shouted as the fire crackled.

Dale's hand shoved mine away, his fingers rough and frantic in the heavy smoke.

The knob clicked.

"Mo, here," Dale gasped, grabbing the jack's handle. I threw my weight onto the blistering handle and together we jacked the car up up up.

Lavender skinnied from beneath the car. "Run," he gasped, staggering to his feet. "Get out. Now." He toppled sideways. We rushed to his sides—one beneath each arm—and half dragged him across the garage.

I slammed into Harm at the door. "I've got him, Mo," he said, scooting into my place. "Get away from the garage. Run."

Pop! Pow!

We ducked as small explosions rattled the building behind us.

Finally we collapsed, panting, on the cool lawn.

Grandmother Miss Lacy fell to her knees beside us. "Are you all right?" she asked, fumbling with Lavender's collar. "Breathe, child. Oh my word, breathe."

An explosion slammed against the ground and a wave of heat bowed us low.

"My car," Lavender said, turning to the garage. He closed his eyes. "My car."

The roof caved in, throwing a shower of sparks to the stars.

₊★₊★*

An hour later we sat in the parlor, watching the volunteer fire department rake coals and hose down charred rafters still glittering with embers. The ash-white skeleton of the number 32 car stood stark in the moonlight. Starr's men prowled the edge of the forest, searching.

The phone rang. "Mo," Grandmother Miss Lacy called. "It's Lana."

I hurried into the kitchen, suddenly starved for her voice. "Hey," I said, the tears crowding my eyes. "I'm sorry I didn't call sooner."

"Are you all right? We just heard."

"I'm fine," I said, very quick. "Me and Dale saved Lavender's life. Starr's taking our statement. Please don't make me come home. Lavender needs me. He almost died," I said, my voice wobbling.

Her silence hugged me tight. "All right, sugar. Tell Starr we're making free coffee and breakfasts for volunteers. Call me if you need me, Mo. Promise you will."

The phone rang just as I hung up. "Hey, Miss Rose," I said. "Dale and me just saved Lavender. Hang on." I covered the mouthpiece. "Dale," I shouted.

I strolled back into the parlor. "Miss Lana's making free breakfast for you all." Outside, neighbors stood in clumps. Capers talked to Sam, who'd tipped his volunteer fireman's hat back on his head—a movie-star look.

Dale stomped back in and glared at Lavender. "You

made Mama cry," he said, and hurled himself onto the sofa beside me.

"Tears of relief, I'm sure," Grandmother Miss Lacy said, letting the curtain fall. "We were lucky tonight."

Starr perched awkwardly on an old lady chair. "Any idea who hates you this much, Lavender? Jealous husband, jilted lover? Anybody?"

"I wish I knew," Lavender said, his voice cracking as he leaned forward to rest his forehead in his hands.

Starr tapped his pen against his pad. "Tell me again what happened."

Lavender coughed. "What I did was stupid."

"Understatement," Dale muttered, his face dark with anger.

Lavender gave him a tired smile. "Don't ever slide under a car without the jack stands in place."

"I already know that," Dale snapped. "You've said it a hundred times. *I* listened. Daddy said to watch your back. You aren't even trying to be careful."

Lavender closed his eyes. For one heartbeat, I thought he would cry.

"Dale, I made a mistake. I'm sorry. Let it go," he said. He turned to Starr. "Sam borrowed my jack stands this morning and I forgot. I couldn't sleep, so I came over to mess with my car. Tinkering settles me down."

He took a deep breath. "I wanted to check the muffler. I jacked her up, made *sure* the jack was set, slipped under, and . . . I heard footsteps."

I interrupted. "What kind of footsteps?"

"Good question," Starr said.

Lavender closed his eyes and rubbed his fingertips across his forehead. He cocked his head, like he could hear the footsteps all over again. "Light steps, like an athlete. I called hello, no one answered. I started to slide out and the jack fell. Something popped. Someone cursed, and I smelled smoke."

"A pop?" Harm said. "An accelerant, to speed up the fire." He gave us a sheepish grin. "I've been watching detective shows, trying to pick up some skills."

Harm's a self-starter, like me.

Lavender continued. "That's all. I called for help. Thank God, Mo heard me."

Grandmother Miss Lacy shook her head. "Flick Crenshaw's quick enough to set that fire and get out."

"It wasn't Flick," Starr said. "I've had an eye on him since the church robbery."

"Your stakeout," I said, thinking back. "So Flick robbed the church?"

Starr shrugged. "He volunteered to help search, which was out of character. Sometimes criminals return to the scene of the crime, to watch the investigation unfold. This wasn't Flick. I've checked." He stood. "Anything else?"

"I don't know who started that fire," Lavender said. "But I will never forget who ran into it to save me." His gaze found Dale's and mine. "Thank you," he said, his eyes filling with tears. "You are heroes to me."

My heart opened so wide I almost fell in.

Starr headed for the door. "It's three a.m. Get some sleep," he said. "Lavender, I'll send someone to watch your house soon as I can." For some reason, Starr pointed at me. "Stay away from the crime scene. In fact, stay inside. All of you."

"I'd better get going too," Lavender said, hugging Dale and then me.

He smelled like smoke and fear.

As the door closed, Dale leaned his forehead against the window's cool pane. "I can't believe Lavender went under there without the jack stands. He almost let that fire take him away," he said, watching Lavender climb into his truck.

Grandmother Miss Lacy touched his hair. "Lavender would never leave you, Dale—not if he could help it."

"Daddy did," he said, his voice flat.

Grandmother Miss Lacy studied him a slow Tupelo minute. "Lavender's not like Macon," she said. "If he were, he'd already be gone."

I'd never thought of it like that before.

From the look on Dale's face, I don't think he had either.

*. * . * . *

We Desperados sat in the parlor together for maybe an hour, trying to push the scared from our bones. Our talk dwindled, and the boys slumped in their wing chairs. Harm's snores and Dale's murmurs filled the silence.

I snuggled on the settee, waiting for a sleep too rattled to come.

Finally, I threw the covers back and slipped into the darkroom, to check my photos. They were almost dry . . . I squinted at my shot of Flick's car. What *is* it about that car?

I slid the negative back into the enlarger and cranked the enlarger up, casting the largest image I could. I focused. "Steering wheel, windshield wipers . . ."

Then I saw it: An air freshener dangled from Flick's mirror. A torn skull-and-crossbones.

"Gotcha," I muttered. I developed the photo and hung it up to dry. I'll tell the others in the morning, I thought. I tiptoed to my settee, and fell into a deep sweet sleep.

Thunk.

I woke up. Dale and Harm sat frozen in their chairs, their eyes wide.

Bump. The guineas squawked.

Not again, I thought, yawning.

Clunk.

I'll give Grandmother Miss Lacy my tips all year if she'll just get a new boiler.

Gurgle-gurgle-gurgle. Squeeeak.

"That ain't the heat system," I whispered. "Somebody's in the kitchen."

Harm crossed silent as nightfall to the fireplace tools. He grabbed the poker and handed the shovel to Dale. I plucked Beethoven's bust from the bookshelf. We slipped down the hall, to the kitchen.

Clunk.

Gurgle-gurgle-gurgle squeak.

I reached around the door casing. "We'll surprise him." They tightened their grips. "Now!" I whispered, flipping the light on and springing into the kitchen.

"Hyaaaa!" Dale shouted—the only thing he ever learned in karate.

"Nothing," Harm whispered, taking stock of the room.

A clatter behind us. We wheeled, weapons raised. Grandmother Miss Lacy gasped, her eyes round as saucers. "What on earth?" she said, stepping over the broom she'd knocked to the floor.

Another bump.

"Shhhh." Harm pointed to the floor. "Someone's under the house."

Under the house?

Every nerve in my body jumped, ready to run.

Grandmother Miss Lacy nudged her hairnet up. "OH MY WORD," she said, making her voice loud and clear like a first grader in a school play. "If you wanted a cookie, Mo LoBeau, why didn't you ask for one? And Dale, you scared me out of a year's growth with that terrifying karate scream."

Excellent. Old person cunning.

"SORRY," I said, very loud. "I DID NOT WISH TO WAKE YOU."

She stomped over to the refrigerator, opened it, and poured a glass of milk. She slammed the door closed. "Here is some milk. Now back to bed you go."

She lassoed her finger in the air like a cowboy signaling roundup, and pointed to the door. We crept to the parlor, quiet as shadows. "What now?" she whispered.

Good question.

"Well, I *would* call Joe Starr," I said, "but the phone's in the kitchen and Starr's in the woods looking for clues. We're on our own."

Dale nodded. "That's what I think too."

Harm gulped. "I'm in."

"I'll get the flashlights," she said. "You get the coats. And be silent, my lambs."

"Aren't lambs sacrificials?" Dale asked, his voice cracking.

"No," I lied. "And don't worry. I have a plan."

* * *

We slipped out the front door and crept to the back of the house. The guineas scattered, shrieking to the stars.

For the first time in my life, I hoped Starr would show up.

Grandmother Miss Lacy, armed with a brass-tipped walking cane, bounced into me. "What's the plan, dear?"

"She doesn't have one," Dale said. "She hardly ever does, and if she makes one up, you won't want to do it."

Sometimes I think detective work has made Dale old before his time. Other times I think it's made him smarter.

"Of course I have a plan," I lied, scoping the shrubberies and the brick work beneath the house. "Is that the only way underneath?" I whispered, pointing to a tiny wooden door. She nodded. "Good. We'll flush him out and make a citizen's arrest."

"What if it's a girl?" Dale whispered.

Pronouns? Now? Really?

"Then we'll flush *her* out."

"How?" Grandmother Miss Lacy whispered, gripping her cane.

I studied her. Grandmother Miss Lacy has the heart of a warrior, but she couldn't stun a rabbit with that walking stick. "You tap on the door and we'll jump him. Or her."

Dale nodded. "You're old. If he kills you, it won't be as sad. No," he said quickly, "that's not right. Pretend I didn't say that."

She nodded.

"Everybody settle down," Harm said. "I'll knock. You all do . . . whatever detectives do and I'll help."

Grandmother Miss Lacy raised her walking stick. Dale raised his fireplace shovel. I hoisted Beethoven over my head.

A man's voice rang out behind us: "Are you insane?"

"Rhetorical!" Dale screamed. Grandmother Miss Lacy whirled, slamming her walking stick across the man's arm. It bounced off.

"Give me that!" Joe Starr shouted, yanking the cane from her hands. "I told you people to stay inside!"

"There's a murderer under the house," I replied, very cool as I lowered Beethoven. "We have him surrounded. Arrest him."

Starr ran his light along the crawlspace door. "Under the house? What kind of lunatic . . ." He pulled his gun. "Come out," Starr demanded.

"We have you surrounded," I shouted.

"Don't make me come under there," Grandmother Miss Lacy warbled.

Nothing.

Starr studied the closed door and gave us a wink. "I'll

call for the canine unit," he said, very loud. "A couple of dogs will flush this maniac out in no time."

A rustle. A clunk. The sound of something being dragged.

The door popped open. A man stuck his head out through the crawlspace and blinked into the lights.

"Daddy?" Dale said. "What are you doing here?"

Chapter 25
One Thing for Him

"Hands on your head," Starr said, snatching Mr. Macon to his feet and shoving him against the wall. He patted him down and cuffed him. "Macon Johnson, you're under arrest for breaking and entering, arson, and the attempted murder of Lavender Johnson. And that's just for starters."

"Wait," Dale said, grabbing Starr's arm. "Daddy's being framed."

Mr. Macon did a double take. "Who told you? *You* didn't figure it out."

I'd forgotten how much I hated Mr. Macon.

"For your information," I said, "Dale's the one who *did* figure it out. And the one who's been standing up for you."

"What are you doing under my house?" Grandmother Miss Lacy demanded.

"Staying warm next to your old boiler and watching Lavender's back. You got this wrong," he told Starr. "I didn't set that fire."

"Yeah? Then who did?"

"Same guy who slit that tire. He ran out the back as Mo and Dale ran in. Slight, fast, wears a hat. I ran in, fixed the jack, and got out. I didn't set the fire."

"You fixed the jack?" I gasped.

I flashed back to hands pushing mine from the jack. Rough, strong hands. "I thought that was you," I told Dale, and he shook his head.

"I couldn't see," Dale said. "I thought it was you. The smoke was so thick. . . ."

Starr's stare darted past us, into the woods. "If Macon didn't start that fire, whoever *did* is still out there. Harm, get the door. Everybody inside. Now."

Starr shoved Dale's daddy into a kitchen chair. Even dirty and unshaven, Mr. Macon glinted like a knife. "I'm being framed. I swear it on his mama's grave," he said, jabbing his cuffed hands at Dale.

"Wow," Harm muttered.

Vintage Mr. Macon.

"Listen," he told Starr. "Somebody's trying to kill Lavender, but it ain't me. Why would I kill him? Why would I bust out of jail, for that matter? The Colonel had set up a deal for me."

"Really? Why would he do *that?*" Starr demanded.

"Because he's my friend," Dale said, very soft.

Mr. Macon continued. "I went in to change. I heard

a thud. I found Earl on the floor—holster empty, keys at his side. I knew I'd be blamed and I ran. I took my brother Austin's car. I knew he'd keep quiet. He knew I'd leave it someplace easy."

"We saw it on the side of the road," Dale said.

Mr. Macon's eyes glittered like glass. "The smart question is, why would I run when I had a plea bargain?" he coached.

"All right," Harm said. "Why?"

"Because bad news travels in prison. I knew somebody planned to kill Lavender. I didn't know who, only that it involved his car. Nobody takes what's mine. Lavender's been mine since the day he was born."

Mr. Macon leaned toward Starr. "I didn't take a car, I didn't rob a bank, the only house I broke into was mine. And somebody else had already kicked in the door and trashed the back part of the house before I got home."

"You don't live there anymore," Dale said. "That's Mama's home. And mine."

Mr. Macon kept his eyes on Starr. "I did not set that fire."

"No? Then who did?" Lavender demanded, walking in from the hall. His voice downshifted to a fury I never heard in him before. "What the heck do you think you're doing, Macon?"

"Sit down and find out," Mr. Macon said, kicking a chair toward him.

Lavender exploded like dynamite.

He blasted across the room, grabbed the front of Mr. Macon's filthy jacket, and dragged him to the center of the kitchen. "You almost killed me!" he shouted, his voice breaking like a little boy's. "Me, Dale, Mo!" He slammed him against the wall. "What's wrong with you?"

"Lavender!" Dale cried. "Stop."

Lavender's fist slammed against Mr. Macon's jaw, snapping his head back. He raised his fist again and Mr. Macon quartered away, shielding his face.

Starr pushed between them. Before I even thought about moving I flew to Lavender and grabbed his raised arm with both hands.

"Let me go!" He jerked his arm free, spinning me into a cabinet.

The room tilted. Lavender whirled and grabbed for my shoulders as I slid toward the floor.

"Oh God," he said, coming back into his eyes. "I'm sorry, I'm sorry, I'm sorry, Mo. Are you all right?"

Am I all right?

"No," I shouted. "I am not all right! Stop it. All of you. Now."

"Everybody calm down," Starr said as Harm bulldozed

Mr. Macon into a chair. "You." He grabbed Lavender's arm. "Cool off or get out."

Lavender threw himself into a chair and closed his eyes. The rage rolled off of him and his breath came and went like a bellows, slowing, slowing.

Mr. Macon wiped his bloody lip on the back of his hand, but his voice came calm as a razor swipe. "I saved your life tonight, you ungrateful buzzard," he said, staring at Lavender. "If you'd waited for these little dips to crank that jack, you'd all be dead. This is the thanks I get? I should have let you burn."

Grandmother Miss Lacy gasped. "Macon!"

Dale watched his father, his face still as clay.

Harm leaned toward Mr. Macon and sniffed. "He stinks. But I do smell smoke."

Starr shrugged. "Saving Lavender looks good unless you set the fire in the first place, Macon. Which I, for one, think you did."

Mr. Macon snarled. "Bull. Whoever slashed that tire set it. I put the note in your toolbox," he said. "Wrote it left-handed. The one under the plate too."

Grandmother Miss Lacy strolled over to put her teakettle on. It's the small things, she says, that keep us civilized. "If Macon wasn't staying to help Lavender, why *is* he here?" she murmured.

Starr tapped his pen against his pad. "Because he's

robbing us blind?" he said. "Because he wanted to kill Rose's son to get even with her for leaving him? Because he's hiding and doesn't want to do hard time?"

"All of the above," Lavender muttered.

"But the surveillance video and the prison jumpsuit," Harm said.

"Uncle Austin," Dale said. "Throwing all of us off the trail, keeping us from searching for Daddy. It worked too."

Harm studied Mr. Macon. "The patrol car?"

Mr. Macon's handcuffs glistened in the lamplight. "Found it in the woods, the keys inside. Slept in it a few times, left prints." He shrugged. "Send me a bill. But steal a black-and-white? Please."

Grandmother Miss Lacy shook her head as she lined up cups. "Under my house. Listening to my every move."

"Your fault," he said. "I told you last time I fixed that boiler to replace it. Good for me you didn't. Its clunking and bumping made perfect cover." He glared at Starr. "Arrest me if you want to, but whoever wants to kill Lavender is still out there."

Starr pulled him to his feet. "Thanks," he said. "I believe I will."

"Good riddance," Lavender muttered.

Dale jumped up. "Wait," he said. "Daddy's hateful, but he's only partway guilty. He's being framed, and the Desperados will prove it."

He gave Harm and me a smile. "Don't worry," he said. "I have a plan."

Mr. Macon snorted. "He's too addled to have a plan. But he's right about one thing: I'm not guilty."

"Dale isn't addled and he does too have a plan," I snapped. I shifted into ad-lib overdrive. "In fact, the Desperado case is borderline ready," I told Starr. Harm looked at me like I'd just sprouted an extra head. "We'll lay our evidence out for you as soon as humanly possible."

"Or sooner," Dale added.

Ad-libbing is like dreaming you're flying. As long as you believe it yourself, you sail on. "In the meantime," I said, "throw the book at him if you want to, but don't tell a soul you nabbed his sorry hide."

"Right," Harm said. "Especially don't tell Capers Dylan. We don't want this in the paper. We don't want to tip off our prey."

"Prey," Dale said. "Good."

I finished our pitch: "I'll notify you when we're ready for our Big Reveal."

It sounded good. Darned good.

Starr shook his head. "Sorry, kids."

Kids?

Grandmother Miss Lacy put her hand on Starr's arm. "Really, dear. The Desperados have given you Macon. Why not give them a chance? What can you lose?"

Being old is like being bulletproof. Not even Joe Starr fires back.

I looked at the clock over Grandmother Miss Lacy's stove. "It's five o'clock in the morning," I said, trying to figure how much time we'd need.

"Longest night of my life," Harm muttered.

Starr pushed Mr. Macon toward the door. "I'll give you until five p.m. tomorrow, but that's it," he said.

Five p.m. tomorrow? Is he mad?

That's just a day and a half, and we don't know squat! And most of that would be gobbled up by sleep and school. Plus puppies, homework . . . We needed more time!

Dale gave Starr a quick nod. "We could do it faster, but as lead detective I accept," he said.

Crud.

"One condition," I added, glancing at Lavender, who sat simmering like one of the Colonel's pots. Lavender Shade Johnson, who sang to Dale and me when we were little even though he can't sing, who's taken us to the speedway to time laps, who's listened to our problems and driven us around like he felt proud to know us.

I stared into Starr's eyes. "Mr. Macon ain't worth spit, but if he *did* watch over Lavender and help us in that fire, that's one thing for him. With him in custody, you better protect Lavender. I mean it. Because if Mr. Macon didn't set that fire, Lavender's still in danger. And if anything happens to him, you have me to deal with. Forever."

A hint of Lavender's old smile flitted across his face.

"Believe me, sir," Harm told Starr. "You don't want that. Forever is a very long time."

Even the moon looked sleepy as Starr carted Mr. Macon away.

Grandmother Miss Lacy and me walked Lavender to the door. "I've been thinking," she said. "The old store on the way to the inn's empty, and it happens to belong to me."

It's amazing how many things happen to belong to her.

"Buildings are like people: Nothing destroys them like emptiness. That store would make a wonderful garage, and I'd love to have a tenant," she said. "Or a partner. Why don't you see what you think?"

"Thanks," he said. "I'll look, but all my tools were in that garage. My car. I just don't know if . . ." His voice fell away like ashes.

He turned to me. "Mo, I'm sorry," he said.

"I'm okay," I said, very quick. "I just never seen you like that before."

"And you never will again," he said. "Not if I can help it."

He walked away like a soldier who'd just lost his war.

"He'll be okay, Mo," Grandmother Miss Lacy said as his truck roared into the darkness. "He needs time. And time . . . takes time."

Grandmother Miss Lacy took her tea upstairs, hoping for one last wink of sleep. We settled around the kitchen table with cereal.

"Okay," I said to Dale as he dug in. "You told Starr you had a plan. What is it?"

"I don't have one," he said, milk running down his chin. "I just said I did. I learned that from you. I see how it works now. Very nice."

"Great," Harm muttered. "Thirty-six hours and no plan."

"Thirty-five hours," I corrected. "Well, I can get us started," I said, hopping up. I scurried to the darkroom and grabbed my enlargement of Flick's car. "While you were sleeping, I figured out who took the patrol car from the courthouse." I tossed the photo in the center of the table. "See this? A torn skull-and-crossbones air freshener."

"Like the patrol car," they said together.

"I think Flick tore them both when he opened the pack."

Harm sighed. "Two-fers. Flick never was that bright. He's not smart enough to have done it all, though. He needs a boss. Besides, Starr was keeping an eye on him—part of the time, anyway."

"Then who?" Dale asked, his voice soft. "We got a thread from the church windowsill, a photo of an extra set of tire tracks heading away from my house the day it was robbed, a torn air freshener, and a bunch of stupid letters we can't read."

He eyed us like a general surveying his troops. I waited, fighting back an urge to tell him he'd buttoned his pajama top wrong.

"We need Sal," he said. "The clock is ticking down."

Chapter 26
And the Clock Ticks Down

At school that morning, we caught a double break: First, Sal was well enough to make it back to class, putting our decoding operation on Go. Second, Miss Retzyl sent us to the school library to scrounge up books for book reports.

I found Sal at a reading table.

"This is fascinating," she said, closing her book. *The Enigma Machine—How Math Shaped World War II.* She gasped. "You look terrible, Mo. What happened?"

"The usual," I said, very cool. "Dale and me saved Lavender from a burning building and got in a fight and I've had maybe two hours sleep," I told her, opening my messenger bag. "I got something to show you."

I slid my file of letters to her. "Coded messages—like the one we showed you earlier—from Capers's trash. I tried the 2-6 code, where you start with the second word and read every sixth word, but . . ."

She flipped through the letters. "Each one probably has a different key. But the keys are all torn off the corner of the papers," she said, her voice thoughtful. "Probably to keep trash thieves like you from decoding them."

Sal picked up the last page—the page of numbers I found in the parking lot the day Capers came to town—tan numbers and letters over a letter written in blue ink. She held the page to the light as Harm and Dale slid into seats across from us. "Is this the only one like this?"

I slid the second file to her.

Jimmy drifted by. "Lemon juice," he said, glancing at the paper. "You got to heat it to make it look old. You still won't get extra credit, not even for the Pilgrims' Thanksgiving menu."

Lemon juice?

"Really?" Harm said. "What's it like before you heat it?"

"Nothing," Jimmy replied.

"Invisible?" Harm murmured. "Brilliant." He laughed. "That's why Capers wanted an iron. She didn't want to iron her clothes. She wanted to iron out her messages." He turned to Sal. "Can you decode these?"

The bell rang. "Maybe. I'll review them during class," she said.

"Excellent," Dale told her. He slid one Lemon Juice Message to me. "My detail division will help you, Sal. But hurry."

I glanced at the clock. "It's ten a.m.," I said. "Time's flying by."

₊₊₊₊*

I pretended to listen to Miss Retzyl and stared at my Lemon Juice Message, trying to find a pattern. Sal peered at hers and worked a calculator beneath her desk.

Nothing.

I refocused just in time to hear Attila say, "It's just that I'm so sagacious."

Dale, who had his head on his desk, opened his eyes. "She's *what,* Mo?"

"Mo? Dale? Question?" Miss Retzyl asked.

"No, ma'am," I said. "We were just thinking there's maybe a less show-offy word that would work there. I'm guessing *obnoxious,* but I'm not sure."

"Try the dictionary," she said, nodding to the faded book on our shelf. Miss Retzyl is old-school. Blue dictionaries, white chalk, black-and-white composition books.

She likes technology, but she wants us smart if our batteries die.

Dale and I dragged ourselves over and I plopped the dictionary on the windowsill. Dale yawned and thumbed through the pages . . . "I'm too sleepy for this," he muttered. "Emergency, mushy, saddle . . . Here," he said. "Page 541."

I ran my finger down the column of words. "*Saddler, safe, saffron* . . . Here it is, *sagacious.* Second column, fourth word. '*Quick and shrewd . . .*'"

I gasped. "*What* did I just say?"

"Quick and shrewd," he whispered. "I don't think it sounds right either."

"Not that, the other: Page 541. Second column. Fourth word . . . That's it!" I shouted, snapping the dictionary closed. The class rustled behind me. "I mean, thank you, Miss Retzyl. May I take the dictionary to my seat for further reading pleasure?"

"You may not. Please sit down."

I lowered my voice. "Dale, I think I just cracked the Lemon Juice Code. What's the best way to get out of here?"

Dale practices school exit strategies like Houdini practiced rope tricks. He recited: "Forge a note, set off an alarm, fake a throw-up . . ."

I clamped my hand over his mouth. His nostrils flared. "Stand back!" I shouted.

"Mmfff," Dale said, struggling against my hand.

"Dale's sick! Sal, where's his medicine? We need your help!" Sal grabbed her things and mine. The class leaned away from us, clearing a path to the door.

"They're faking!" Attila cried, jumping to her feet.

I looked at Miss Retzyl. "Dale could go projectile any minute. Your call."

Miss Retzyl froze, caught between the probability of a bald-faced lie and the possibility of projectile vomiting. "Go!" she commanded.

Harm jumped up. "I'll help," he said. "Everybody stay calm."

We led Dale into the schoolyard.

"My place," I said, wiping Dale's breath off my hand. "I think I broke the Lemon Juice Code. Hurry." Sal hopped on Dale's handlebars. We took off like a fleet of bats, dumping our bikes in the café parking lot and sprinting for my flat.

I opened my dictionary—a dead ringer for Capers's. "First blob of numbers, any message," I said.

"420A25," Sal read.

I ferreted out the word: "Page 420. *A* means first column. 25 means the twenty-fifth word. Doubt."

We went through the message word by word. Finally I read it out: "Doubt clears your debt to me. The odds of getting even are in our favor. Shell."

"Brilliant," Harm murmured.

True. I tried to look modest.

"No, it was mostly dumb luck from trying to use a dictionary while sleepy," Dale said. "Usually we don't have to pay much attention to finding words."

My glory moment keeled over dead.

"Who's Shell?" he asked.

"Shell. Short for Shelly?" Harm guessed. "Michelle? But whoever Shell is, why would she write in code?"

Dale frowned. "Capers interviewed Slate and Deputy

Marla. They're in prison. Maybe Shell is too. Letters get guard-read going in and out. I know because of . . ."

"Family reunions," Harm guessed, and Dale nodded.

Sal studied her fingernails. "Dale, if you'd like my help with the rest of these letters, I'd trade my fee for a consulting credit on this case. That would free you up to handle other clues. But if there's any *reward money* . . ."

"An even split. A fourth is yours," Dale said.

Now he learns fractions?

"Deal," she said. "Don't worry, Desperados. Sal's on the case."

"Where to?" Dale asked as we grabbed our bikes.

The café door swung open. "Message for you, sugar," Miss Lana shouted, holding up a note. "From Thes. He has a clue. He wants a meeting at four thirty, at the church." She winked at Dale. "Glad you're feeling better, Dale," she said.

I plucked the message from her fingertips. At least *Thes* has a clue, I thought. "Thanks," I said, glancing through the window. "Is Capers in there?"

"She'll be back tomorrow morning. Why?"

I pictured that last note sitting on her desk. "I still have the Colonel's skeleton key. We'll pick up her trash for you," I said, and we zoomed away.

As we crossed Fool's Bridge, my chain slipped and my pedals went into free spin.

"Not again," I muttered, coasting over to the old store. I hopped off and bulldogged the bike to the ground.

"I got the back," Harm said.

I fed the chain around the big sprocket, and rocked the pedal. The chain clunked on. "Come on, Dale," I called, wiping grease on my jeans.

"No," Dale replied.

He stood by the door, his fingers thick with webs. "Smell these. I thought they smelled bad when I got them in my hair the day we lost the patrol car. They're fake."

Fake cobwebs?

He pointed to a faint trail in the dirt. "Bicycle tire tracks."

Harm knelt. "Perfect tread," he muttered, studying the track.

My heart jumped. Only Attila possesses perfect tread. The rest of us ride on the slick memory of new tires. "Attila's show bike," I said. "From the break-in."

We followed the tracks around the building to a small, lop-sided back door. A hammock of webs covered its lock. Dale sniffed. "Also fake," he said.

Harm went up on his toes, ran his fingers along the top of the casing, and flashed a tiny key. "Score."

The lock clicked and the door scraped open ... Slowly my eyes adjusted to the dim light. "Nobody's here," I said. We stepped inside. In the corner sat a pile of pale shadows. "What's that?"

The door slammed and the room went dark.

The lock clicked shut behind us.

"Not good," Dale whispered.

"Hey!" I shouted, wheeling to the door. "Let us out right this minute!"

Footsteps pounded around the side of the building. Please, I thought, don't let me smell smoke. "We got to get out."

I stumbled to a crooked door outlined in light and rattled the knob.

"We need a plan, now," Dale said, his voice tinged in panic.

"I got one. Move," Harm gasped. He lowered his shoulder and charged the door. "Jeez," he said, ricocheting into Dale and then into me. "That hurt more than it looks like on television."

He backed up and charged again. The door splintered and he tumbled out, Dale and me on his heels. Tires screamed against the blacktop.

"Fast car," Dale murmured, listening.

I knew we were all thinking the same thing: Flick.

Dale plucked something from the grass at his feet. "Attila's turkey earring," he said. "It's ugly, but they wouldn't throw it on the ground, not on purpose. Somebody's moving the loot. Another rookie move."

"They know Lavender's coming to look at the building," I said.

He hopped on his bike. "We need to talk to Lavender. Now."

Lavender straddled a kitchen chair as we settled on his worn sofa and chair. I glanced at his NASCAR clock. 1:15 p.m. Our time was melting away.

"I'm glad Starr's got a man watching you," I said, nodding at the car outside.

"Me too," he admitted. "And to answer your question—sure. I told people I was thinking about the old store for a garage."

Lavender's fall-apart gorgeous, even in a torn T-shirt and tired jeans. "I told Sam and the Colonel and a twin or two," he said, hopping up and padding to the kitchen. "Let me get you guys something to eat. It's way past noon."

I strolled to the window and peeped across the street, at the twins' House of Hair. Four cars and a golf cart sat outside. "If you told the twins, you told the town," I said.

"The old store will be a good garage," Dale said as Lavender handed Pepsis and Nabs around.

Lavender sank onto his chair. "I wanted to talk to you about that, little brother. I was going to tell you later, but . . . I've been thinking. That blessed fire took most of my tools. I might try to find work in a garage that has its own tools. Someplace close—Greenville or Kinston, maybe. But not here. Not in Tupelo Landing."

My world wobbled.

Dale shook his head. "No," he said. "That would be what? Twenty miles? You'd have to drive back and forth . . ."

"Maybe not," Lavender said, opening his Nabs. He watched Dale's face. "Maybe it would make sense for me to live somewhere else. For a while."

Tupelo Landing without Lavender? The sky without blue would make better sense.

"You can't live somewhere else because this is where we live," Dale explained.

Lavender leaned toward him. "Dale, no matter what I do in this town, I'll never be more than Macon's son. I want to be more than that."

Dale's soft frown crinkled his brow. "You're already more than that," he said. "You're my brother. You're Mama's son."

And you're my date in just seven more years, I thought.

The room went so quiet, I could hear Dale breathe.

Dale tossed his Nabs on the sofa. "I see. Desperados, mount up," he said, his voice hard. He walked out, grabbed his bike, and flew across the yard.

"I better catch him," Harm said, and dashed out the door.

The NASCAR clock on the wall ticked the time away. Lavender raked his fingers through his hair. "Mo, every tool I own burned in that fire. My ride out of here went up in smoke. If I don't get out now, I'll wind up as bitter and twisted as Macon one day. You understand that, don't you?"

I crossed the room, *right* and *kind* fighting inside me like bobcats.

I turned at the door. "I ain't making the same mistake with you that I made with Dale," I said. I took a deep breath. "I think you're feeling sorry for yourself, and you want to run away. I got news for you. You're going to be Macon Johnson's son no matter how far you go. The Azalea Women don't decide who we are and what we think and do. *We* do."

He jumped like I'd pinched him. "Feeling sorry for myself?"

"There's other tools in this town and other cars and Grandmother Miss Lacy will back you in a garage. She already said so." I put my hands on my hips and took the biggest risk of my life so far. "If you leave Dale now, I got just one thing to say to you."

I gazed into eyes so blue I could float away in them.

"I *won't* go out with you in just seven more years," I said, my voice wobbling. "Go get yourself a big-haired twin, Lavender Shade Johnson. Because our wedding's off."

I slammed the door and pedaled away in a blur of tears.

"Are you all right?" Harm asked as I skidded up beside him. Dale had gone pale as a ghost boy on a faded Schwinn.

I nodded—a total lie.

"Whoever locked us in the old store went toward the inn," I said, trying to focus on the case. "Capers is still our best lead. I say we go there," I said, and pushed off on my bike.

"No," Dale said, clamping my handlebar tight. "To capture a Capers, think like a Capers. In her mind, where's the safest hiding place? A place that's already been searched. Where did she make us search?"

"The old fish camp," Harm and I said at the same time.

"She's loop-brained," Dale said, nodding. "We were straight-line thinking the day we lost the patrol car and she was already looping back to make a Plan B. She's smart, but she's never run over the Desperados before."

Somehow it seemed like bad luck to let that one go.

"You mean *run up against* the Desperados," I said. "And you're right. Let's ride."

Twenty minutes later, we rumbled through the forest, past the old marl pit, to the fish camp at the edge of the river. We held our breath as the shack door swung open.

"Ba-ba-bing," Dale said as we stared at the loot from the break-ins. "They moved everything from the store to here. Sad for them, good for us."

We checked the stash: the collection plate, Attila's bike, a sack of jewelry, Mr. Macon's shoes. "If they didn't need these shoes to fake footprints, they'd have thrown them out," Dale said.

I wrapped the collection plate in my jacket as the coyotes howled in the distance. "Starr can pick up the rest."

"Right," Dale said. "We're meeting Thes a quarter past a while ago at the church," he added. "We better hurry."

I was out of breath as I read the clock in the church office. "We got just twenty-four hours left," I said as I dialed the phone. I left a message on Miss Retzyl's answering machine: "The loot's at the old fish camp shack. Please ask Starr to pick it up—pronto."

Thes strolled in. "Hey," he said, smiling. "How's that last puppy?"

Miss Lana says people like pets like themselves. "The

puppy is unreasonably optimistic and has a round head," I said. "Sorry we're late. Miss Lana says you have a clue for us."

"An excellent one," he told us, leading us to a bathroom at the back of the church. "Daddy pays me to tidy up. Last night I found *this* in that vase." He grabbed a ceramic Garden of Eden vase on a table by a small window, and emptied out a red-brown button.

"The thief came in here," Harm said, examining the window. He squinted at a thread dangling from the button. "I bet this matches our windowsill thread."

"It's off a hunting jacket," Thes said. "I *could* have given it to Starr."

Come on, Dale, I thought. Give him a puppy.

"Thanks, Thes," Dale said, and headed for the front door.

Thes hurried to catch up. "About that puppy . . ."

We stepped into the twilight and froze.

A coyote slipped like a ghost-dog from the cemetery—thin, hungry, razor-eyed. It shadowed the edge of the churchyard as another slipped from the tombstones, and another from the brush at the edge of the field. Another, and another.

"They're hunting," Dale whispered.

In the center of the churchyard, a twitch of orange.

Spitz!

Spitz looked at us, his orange fur puffed, his eyes electric with fear.

The coyotes howled like creatures possessed.

"No!" Thes screamed, and hurled himself from the porch. He dashed for Spitz, his legs pumping as the coyotes charged. "Spitz!" Thes shrieked, grabbing the cat and snatching him to his chest. The coyotes skidded to a halt, eyes glinting.

Before I could think, I'd leaped off the porch with Harm and Dale and run to Thes, shouting and waving my arms as we ran. "Get out of here! We ain't scared! Get!"

We surrounded Thes, facing the coyotes. "Get!"

The lead coyote stared at us thin and ragged as winter's wind.

He took a slow step back and faded into the graveyard. The others followed, melting among tombstones, slipping into the brush and trees along the river.

We turned to Thes. He gasped for breath, his green eyes round as Spitz's.

"That was brave, what you did," Dale told him.

"Right," Thes said, his voice shaking. "I don't know what came over me."

Chapter 27
Lavender's Leaving

By the time the Supper Rush rolled around, I'd gone bone tired and Lavender's news had swept the town. "Lavender's leaving?" an Azalea Woman said. "The nerve! Who will take care of our cars?"

Sometimes I say I'd like to give the Azalea Women a piece of my mind. The Colonel says they wouldn't know what to do with it.

I polished off my collard bisque. "Lavender's being recruited by All-Star Repair Teams in Greenville and Kinston," I said. "You can push a car that far if you work together."

"Mo," Little Agnes called from her place with Hannah. "Thanks for the books."

Miss Lana waltzed over. "I lent her your oldies, sugar. *Cinderella, Alice in Wonderland, The Little Prince.*"

"Happy reading, Little Agnes," I said as Sal bustled in.

"Mo," Sal said, her eyes sparkling, "we need to talk." The Azalea Women's ears perked up. "We'd better take this to your flat," she whispered.

The Colonel smiled. "Go ahead, Soldier. You need some rest."

"Is Dale here?" Sal asked, her voice hopeful.

"We'll call him," I said. "Come on."

By the time Harm and Dale arrived, Sal had the evidence stretched out in long neat chains along the length of my bed. Our letters now sported sticky notes and paper clips.

"I could use a laser pointer if you have a spare, Mo."

A laser pointer? Do people own those?

"Mine's temporarily unavailable due to the fact that I don't have one," I said.

"That's okay, Mo." She took a sip of water. "These 2-6 style messages are from Capers," she said, pointing to the first row of notes. "You can see her working out the words. These are her rough drafts. I believe she mailed the final versions. I worked out the messages—here, on the pink sticky notes."

"Very nice," Dale murmured, and Sal blushed.

"The second row holds letters from Shell—the Lemon Juice Code." She gazed into Dale's eyes. "According to my research, World War II spies used book codes. Any book works if both people have the *exact* same book. Like Mo and Capers have the same dictionary, which is why we could crack these. I put Shell's messages on the blue sticky notes. I'll read you the most important ones."

I am in. I will wait on you.
Babe

Doubt clears your debt to me. The odds of getting even are in our favor.
Shell

Flick is too stupid, need better help.
Babe

No one to send, improvise.
Shell

Everything done but murder. Bank shot no good, pattern broken. Advise.
Babe

Lavender's heart rules everyone. Try him again. Fire?
Shell

I gasped. "Fire! That's an order to set the garage fire." Sal's eyes filled with tears. "I'm afraid so."

"But why? Who's Shell?" Dale asked, his voice shaking.

"The *why's* in the message," Harm said. "Lavender's heart rules everyone—all of you. Because you love him so much. Hurting him would hurt every single one of you. But what did you ever do to Shell and Capers?" he asked, staring at me.

Sal plucked a last paper from her file—the parking lot letter from Capers's first day in town. "I think this holds your answer."

She placed the paper, with its orange sticky note, on my bed.

> Find those who put me in this cage. Create the doubt
> that sets your sister free. Revenge is icing on the cake.
> Shell

"Sets your *sister* free?" I gasped, grabbing the note. "Shell is Capers's *sister*?"

"Deputy Marla Everette is the only girl we've put in a cage," Dale said. "We put her in jail. And *marl* is ancient shell, like in the marl pit on the way to the fish camp. Remember?" he asked Harm. "I taught you that."

"Shell. Marl. Marla," Sal said, slipping her hand into Dale's. "Oh Dale, you're a genius, only disguised as . . . you."

He squeezed her hand. "Thanks, Salamander. You're smart too."

Harm studied the notes. "You're both terrifyingly bright. But is this proof? We may need more than this to tie Capers to Marla."

"DNA proves kinship," I said, heading for my reject trash from Capers's room and dumping it on my desk.

"Ick," Sal muttered as I pawed through the garbage.

"Here." Harm plucked strands of red hair from the litter. He held it up to the light. "Red hair with . . . black roots. Perfect."

Sal took a new envelope from her satchel and held it open. "The prison will have Marla's DNA on file. Skeeter and I can *try* to rush an analysis through." She bit her lip as she glanced at my clock: eight p.m. "It will be costly, Desperados, if it's even possible."

"Done," Dale said. He slipped up beside me and whispered: "We don't want to look cheap."

I sighed. If we didn't solve this case soon, Sal would own the agency.

Dear Upstream Mother,

    I clued the Colonel and Miss Lana in tonight after Sal left.

    "Capers will be back tomorrow," the Colonel said. "I'll keep an eye on her."

    The Big Reveal is tomorrow at 5. You're invited.

    I'd hoped to get us out of school, but Miss Retzyl says if we're truant again, we're academic toast.

With sleep tonight and school tomorrow, we have lots of details to tie up and not much time.

Fingers crossed on the DNA evidence.

Mo

PS: Lavender's leaving Tupelo Landing. A lost heart is a very hard thing to find.

Chapter 28
The Big Reveal

The next morning we settled into our desks, exhausted from the last two days of investigation, and nervous about the Big Reveal ahead. I raised my hand.

"Excuse me, Miss Retzyl," I said, "the Desperados adore classwork, but we feel like the town's safety maybe tops our love of math. I hope you're civic-minded enough to give us a day off to prepare our five p.m. Big Reveal at the café for your boyfriend, because—"

"There are no days off in sixth grade, Mo," she said, her voice icy. She looked at Dale. "And I am *so* glad you're feeling better after yesterday's stomach upset, Dale."

Sarcasm. We were doomed.

"Thank you," Dale said, and gently burped.

"Please take out your spelling books," she said.

I raised my hand. "Excuse me. I left a message at your house, but I haven't heard from Joe Starr yet."

She closed her eyes. "Joe's working. I'm sure he'll be at your Reveal. Spelling books. Now."

We whipped out our books and set up shop.

Behind his spelling book, Dale worked on his remarks for the Big Reveal.

Harm, who'd stayed up late worrying about our iffy evidence, stared straight ahead, but from the rasp of his breathing, I knew he was dead asleep.

As for me, I reviewed our evidence and hoped Skeeter would pop in to say Starr had called about the Fish Camp Loot, or the lab had called with good news on our DNA.

She didn't.

The lunch bell rang and I shot to the door. "Hurry, Desperados," I said. "Skeeter's office, now. Time's running out."

Dale unwrapped his sandwich as Skeeter slid her phone to me. "I'm sorry, Desperados. Our lab says four days to confirm sibling DNA. They're searching for a faster lab now and they'll call if they find one. If their call comes, it will be at the end of the day. Feel free to use the phone."

I dialed. "911? This is Mo LoBeau with an emergency. Tell Joe Starr to bring Mr. Macon's hunting jacket *and* the Fish Camp Loot to the Big Reveal this afternoon . . . Sure, you're invited too. Bring your friends. Five p.m. at the café."

I hung up and looked at Harm. "Did you call Flick?"

"Yes, but I'll remind him." He dialed. "Flick, don't forget. Gramps has some cash for you . . . I don't want you to miss out. Five o'clock. Be there or lose out . . . big."

"Now we got everybody but Capers," I said. "She should be back by now."

Dale nibbled his sandwich. "A story would be good Capers bait," he suggested.

I made one last call.

"Café, Lana speaking," Miss Lana said.

"Miss Lana, it's Mo. I'm strictly ad-lib, so work with me."

"Fine," she said. "Go ahead with your order."

"Is Capers back yet?"

"Yes," she said. "We have that. But it's selling out fast."

Selling out fast?

"Leaving town?" I gasped. "Don't let her go. Tell her we have Mr. Macon in custody and can prove he did every single crime. She can have an exclusive interview after the Big Reveal. But watch your back, Miss Lana. She's dangerous."

"Thank you," she said, and hung up.

"I would enjoy making a call," Dale said. "To the Azalea Women."

The Azalea Women?

I handed him the phone. "Hello, this is Dale," he said. "We've captured Daddy and he's in jail for all the town's crimes plus more. . . . That's right. I turned him in for the reward money because that's the kind of boy I am. We'll explain everything at five p.m. at the café, and I knew you'd want a good seat."

Excellent.

The news will be all over town in two minutes flat.

Finally the end-of-day bell rang, and we sprinted for our bikes.

We pushed into the café at four p.m., straight up. Just one hour to go.

Capers sat at a window table, the Colonel watching her like a hawk watches a rabbit. "Thank heavens *she's* here," Harm said, putting our evidence crate on a table. "I just wish Starr would let us know about the loot. Or that the lab would call." He shook his head. "And where's Flick?"

The Azalea Women bustled in and pushed their tables together.

Outside, Lavender pulled up in the GMC.

Tupelo Landing without Lavender, I thought. My heart fell like a stone.

Lavender strolled in holding a large cardboard box, Queen Elizabeth on his heels. "I invited Queen Elizabeth and the pups," Dale explained, heading for his brother. "It's good for the pups to meet everybody. And they can see us in action."

Hannah and Little Agnes grabbed seats at our evidence table.

"Lavender," an Azalea Woman called, "I hear you're leaving us. What a pity."

Lavender stared at her just long enough to wilt her smile. "You hear all kinds of things," he said. "Doesn't mean they're true. Where you want the pups, little brother?"

"Over here," Dale said, slapping an OUT OF ORDER sign on the jukebox. Lavender gently placed the box by the old Wurlitzer and Liz stepped in, one careful foot at a time.

Skeeter and Sal bustled in together. "Did the lab call?" I asked.

Sal shook her head. "We tried," she whispered, turning her back to Capers. "I asked them to call me here if they learn anything, but don't count on it."

Crud.

Lavender sauntered over, smiling his old smile. "Mo," he said, "do you have a minute?"

At least he has his shine back, I thought.

Used to, I always had a minute for Lavender. But used to, I would be going out with him in just seven more years.

"Sorry," I said. "I got a Big Reveal to set up."

Harm grabbed the photo folder. "Shoot," he muttered. "We left half our photos in your filing cabinet."

"I got it," I said, and pounded out the door.

I blasted through the crowded parking lot and pelted into my flat. I grabbed the forgotten file and darted out.

Lavender stood waiting on the porch. "Mo, I need to talk to you," he said, falling in beside me. "I wanted you to be the first to know. Well, the second really. I just told Dale. I've decided to buy Miss Thornton's old store—a little at a time."

I skidded to a halt. "You're staying?"

He nodded. "Mo, I've tried all my life to be better than Macon. The other night at Miss Thornton's I just . . . wasn't. And you're right," he said. "I *was* running—from the shadow of Macon left inside me. It takes a good friend to tell you the truth, Mo. Thank you for being that friend for me."

Me. A friend to Lavender.

I smiled. "The Desperados can help you whip that old store into a garage. I'll send over the painting division."

He laughed. "You're on, Miss LoBeau. The Colonel tells me Miss Lana needs a night clerk at the inn—until I get the garage going. I think I'll be fine."

The Colonel and Miss Lana never let me down.

A dark blue Volvo wheeled into the parking lot and parked by the Underbird. Bill Glasgow jumped out and popped his Stetson on. He reached into the back-seat and pulled out a pet carrier.

A kitten? A hamster? Interesting.

Miss Rose slipped out the passenger side wearing a bright red coat.

A red coat? What happened to her sensible gray coat?

"Miss Rose got a date coat," I said. "She looks good."

"Darned good," Lavender said.

"I better get inside," I told him. I hesitated. "I'm glad you're staying. I'll PR the grand opening of your garage, if you want me to. When it's time, I mean."

He grinned. "Once again, you're on."

Then I said what I've said maybe a million times before. "Give me half a chance and I'd snatch you up and marry you before sundown, Lavender. That's no lie."

The words felt sweet to me, like a half-forgotten voice singing a lullaby.

He grinned his old grin. "Me? Marry you? You're a baby," he said. He messed up my hair and headed for Miss Rose.

Lavender always settles my heart, even when he's walking away.

By the time I strolled into the café, the place was packed. Bill Glasgow was working his way through the clump of kids gathered around the puppies.

"Clear the way for Miss Rose's boyfriend," I shouted. "Step aside."

"Thanks, Mo. Hey, Dale," Bill said. "How are the pups?"

"Cute," Dale said.

Bill handed Dale the carrying case. "Dale, meet Madame Curie. Your mama and I thought she might keep Newton from being lonely. Like her?"

Does Dale like a hideously unattractive newt whose skin oozes toxins like Attila oozes mean? Of course he likes her.

"Thanks," Dale said. "I never thought of Newton feeling lonely."

Bill Glasgow smiled. "You know, I've been thinking about Newton's terrarium. Newts are awfully sensitive to pH—acidity. I was thinking . . ."

I walked away. Miss Lana says it's best not to know the end of some sentences. This sounded like one of them.

I hurried to our files. Capers placed her hands on her table as she watched Harm and me deal our photos around. "Nice gloves," I told her, glancing over. "Are they new?"

She placed her hands back in her lap. "Got them in Raleigh."

Odd, I thought, fluffy purple gloves in a warm café.

Little Agnes settled in by my photos. "This one's different," she said, pointing. Her kindergarten skill.

Miss Lana says to be grateful. Little Agnes makes me grateful I'm an only child.

Flick swaggered in at three minutes 'til five, Joe Starr on his heels. Starr dropped a large evidence bag on the floor.

"Finally," Harm muttered.

An Azalea Woman oozed a sympathy look at Dale. "Good for you, for turning Macon in. I can't wait to hear the details."

Capers smiled. "So Macon really is behind bars? Great job. I'll want a quote."

We need that DNA report, I thought, looking at Sal. Sal shook her head no.

Five p.m. Miss Lana sashayed over as Grandmother Miss Lacy and Mr. Red walked in arm in arm. "Showtime, sugar," Miss Lana whispered. "People are standing in the parking lot, waiting for your news."

I gulped. If this worked, it would work big. If we failed . . .

Live by the footlights, die by the footlights, Miss Lana always says.

"Colonel, could you cover the kitchen door?" I asked. "I don't want our suspects slipping out. Harm's got the main door."

"Ten-four, Soldier."

I stepped onto my Pepsi crate. Dale cleared his throat and tapped his index cards on his table.

Message received.

"Welcome to Desperado Detective Agency's Big Reveal," I said. "At this time I'd like to introduce Dale, the lead investigator on our case. If Tupelo Landing's safe today—and it is—you can thank Dale."

The room applauded—all except Capers. Odd.

Dale took center stage. "Thank you for coming," he said. "I'm a big-picture person and Mo's detail, and that's one reason we're so good. Together with Harm, the newest Desperado, we got Daddy back in jail for the crimes he did."

"Hear, hear! Well done!" the mayor said, and the café applauded.

Dale continued. "Lavender's Garage opens in a few weeks, with Sam opening a franchise branch in Greenville. And now, the Colonel says a good leader delegates, so I'm lobbing back to Mo for the details of our case, which ain't what you're thinking. When you start with the right given, you get the right answer. Miss Retzyl taught me that. Thank you."

Miss Retzyl smiled at him. To me, she looked worried.

The crowd swiveled back to me. "Thanks to Dale, the Desperados have found the loot from the bank heist *and* the break-ins. Detective Starr?" I said, hoping I wasn't bluffing. "I believe it's all in evidence?"

"It is," Starr said. Capers went pale.

I faux-smiled at Attila and her parents, who sat by a

window like a family of glossy mannequins. "This loot includes Attila's show bike. Mrs. Simpson, thank you for that two-thousand-dollar reward, which we hope you'll cough up before you leave. Small bills work best for us."

Jimmy Exum raised a grubby hand. "What about our party?"

Crud. I'd forgotten I promised cash for a class party. Would there be *anything* left for the Desperados?

"Naturally, a chunk of the reward will go into the sixth-grade party fund," I said, and the sixth grade cheered.

Harm stepped near and whispered, "Present the clues we know for sure first. Without that DNA, this thing is a whole lot of Show and See What Happens."

"Right."

He strolled to the front door and crossed his arms. The Colonel moved to the kitchen door. I took a deep breath.

"Mr. Macon's guilty of a lot of crimes," I said. "But he ain't guilty of everything. Dale, who would probably be a genius in another dimension, knew that from the start."

Mayor Little's mother hooked a finger at me. "Get on with it. Stop putting on airs."

Lavender held up ten fingers. I counted them down.

"Thank you for mentioning air, Mrs. Little. That reminds me of air fresheners." I strolled over and picked up the photo of Flick's car. "Exhibit A," I said. "An excellent photo of the air freshener dangling from Flick Crenshaw's rearview mirror."

"Lovely darkroom skills," Grandmother Miss Lacy murmured.

Flick's beady eyes glinted. "I hate a stale-smelling car. So what?"

I handed the photo to Starr. "See anything unusual about this air freshener?"

He shrugged. "It's a skull-and-crossbones, torn across one corner." I opened our evidence file and lifted out the air freshener from the patrol car. "And is it an exact match for this one? From the stolen patrol car?"

"An exact match." He did a double take. "From the *patrol car?*"

"Two-fers," Harm said, pointing at his brother. "Sad proof that Flick drove the patrol car from the courthouse."

Flick scowled. "I did not."

Dale stood, holding little Mary Queen of Scots. "Flick knocked the guard out and put the keys where Daddy would see them. Only Daddy's too smart to swipe a black-and-white. He ran instead."

"I didn't," Flick said, looking around the room.

I walked away from him, every eye following me. "Flick drove the stolen patrol car to Miss Rose's. He kicked in the door, and took things to make it look like Mr. Macon did it."

Dale shook his head. "Squash," he muttered. "Daddy won't eat squash."

I pressed on. "Flick waited until dark and hid the patrol car in the woods."

"It's a lie," Flick said. He whipped a look toward the door. Mr. Red walked over to stand by Harm. "I can explain this," Flick said. He pointed at Capers. "She—"

"Don't listen to him. He hates me," Capers interrupted.

Excellent, I thought. Flick's already turning on Capers.

Capers smiled around the café. The café smiled back. "Flick asked me out," she said. "Of course I said no. He tried to push me around and . . . Mo and Dale *saw* me slap him. Ask them. Flick will say anything to get even with me."

The café glared at Flick.

She's smart, I thought. But not smart enough.

"After Flick left Miss Rose's house, *Mr. Macon* drove up in his brother's old car." I grabbed my crime scene photo of the two sets of tracks—one leading to Dale's stable. "Exhibit B. Two sets of tracks."

"Circumstantial," Flick muttered, crossing his arms.

"Then there's the break-in at the church," I said. "Harm?"

Harm looked at Starr. "Did you bring Mr. Macon's

hunting jacket from the patrol car? Is it missing a button?"

Starr opened the bag, holding it away from him. He peeked in. "The buttons are all here."

I opened our evidence file. "This thread came from the windowsill where the robber slithered into the church. Is it a match for Mr. Macon's jacket?"

He held it to the jacket. "No," he said, looking puzzled.

"How about this button?" Harm asked. "Thes found it in the church, beneath the window that was the point of entry." Harm winked at me. TV detective lingo. Good.

Starr shook his head. "That's not from Macon's jacket either. So what?"

"So Mr. Macon's jacket didn't skinny through the church window when it was robbed, but another hunting jacket did," Harm said.

I hesitated. Flick or Capers?

I'd never once seen Capers wear brown. And if *she* lost a button, she'd be smart enough to find it—or replace it. Like the Colonel says, sometimes you just got to take your best shot. I went for it.

"Flick hunts," I said. "If you search his place, you'll find the jacket that wants this button—and Miss Rose's shotgun too."

"Bull. It was her," Flick said, pointing at Capers. "Search her place."

"Why don't I search both places?" Starr suggested, and Flick went red with anger.

"Then there's the loot from the Simpson break-in," I said. "Anna's bike and jewelry. . . ."

"That was definitely Macon," Mrs. Simpson said. "We have his footprint."

"Dale found Mr. Macon's shoes at the old fish camp with the rest of the loot—the shoes used to *plant* prints at your break-in," I said. "The church break-in too."

Capers snorted. "Plant footprints? I say Macon was wearing those shoes."

Dale shook his head. "Why would Daddy wear slick-soled toe-pinchers when he could wear his brogans?"

Grandmother Miss Lacy raised her hand. "Brogans, dear?"

"Prison boots," Dale explained.

"Very penitentiary chic," the mayor said, nodding.

"She's wrong," Capers said. "Those shoes *tie* Macon to the break-ins. Ask Starr."

"No, Mo's not wrong," Dale snapped. "Nobody walks with their feet totally flat. Nobody steps in just the clear spots or leaves just one footprint. And only a rookie wears the same shoes to two robberies in a row. Do that, and you tie the crimes together for any chucklehead to see."

I gave Starr a smile. "We mean *chucklehead* in the best way," I said.

Little Agnes grabbed my arm. "Mo, this picture is different," she said again.

She placed a pudgy finger on my photo. "Capers is different. She's smiling."

I looked at the photo and my stomach dropped like an anchor. Why hadn't I noticed that?

"Exactly, Little Agnes," I said, very smooth. I walked away, pulling the café's attention like a magnet draws iron. "Detective Starr, perhaps you will tell us why criminals return to the scene of the crime," I said.

He shifted. "To watch investigations of their crimes unfold. Why?"

"Correct," I said. "And who kept showing up at *our* crime scenes? Capers Dylan."

Capers looked at the ocean of shocked faces. "I'm a reporter. It's my job."

"Or your cover," the Colonel said.

I held up a photo like show-and-tell. "I took this at the river, the day Starr pulled the patrol car out of the water. We thought Mr. Macon was in that car. Every face in this photo looks sick with dread—except one. Capers is smiling."

The room gasped.

"Different," Little Agnes said, shaking her head.

I handed a stack of photos to Hannah. "Pass these around. You'll be surprised how often Capers shows up at crime scenes. You won't want to miss the one where she's spying on us through binoculars as we investigate the Simpson break-in."

"I haven't done anything wrong," Capers said. "You people know me."

"Do we?" I asked. "We know you crashed in our parking lot the day of the trial."

"Dreadful," Mayor Little said. "Run off the road."

"No. Capers fell down all by herself," Little Agnes said. "Nobody pushed her."

"Thank you for that eyewitness account, Little Agnes—the only person in the café who saw the crash." I whipped to Capers. "That crash made us want to take you in. Even a Desperado was smitten by you," I said, my voice like steel. Harm shrugged.

"She isn't even really from Charleston," Miss Lana said, her voice hushed.

"Then we caught you trick-riding on your motorcycle. You're good. Good enough to fake-crash along the only clear pathway in the parking lot that day."

"*What?*" the mayor cried.

Capers nudged her saddlebag forward with her foot and leaned to open it. She winced as she raked her notebook off the table and into the bag.

Why the wince?

I looked at her soft new gloves. My blood ran cold.

Of course.

"But what about motive?" I said.

"Good question," Starr said, eyeing Capers.

"Who would benefit most from the Tupelo Landing crime spree? At this time, I'd like to introduce Desperado Detective Agency's consultant Sally Amanda Jones. Sal?"

Sal stood and smoothed her skirt. "I'm pleased to announce I've deciphered Capers's coded messages."

"Coded messages?" Starr said, leaning forward. "What are you talking about?"

"Messages between Capers and her sister—Deputy Marla Everette," she said.

The crowd roared. "Deputy Marla? But she's in jail!"

"Her *sister?* I knew Capers looked familiar," Miss Retzyl cried.

Sal adjusted her beret and waited for the crowd to settle down. "The notes were taken from Capers's trash."

"My notes are protected by the First Amendment," Capers snapped.

Attila flounced her hair. "At least you got the amendment right this time."

"Shut up, you mealy-mouthed little cretin," Capers snarled.

"Hey!" I shouted. "Attila is *my* enemy. Leave her alone."

"You're all crazy," Capers said, jumping up. "I don't have to listen to this."

"I think you do," Starr said, rising. "Sit down."

Capers slammed back into her seat and Sal waited for our eyes to find her. "Dale?" she said. "My easel, please."

Dale darted into the kitchen and staggered out with an easel. Sal's notes hung on the board in two neat rows. "These messages between Capers and Deputy Marla lay out their plan, beginning to end," she said, whipping out her laser pointer.

"Their plan? To *re-create* the pattern of Deputy Marla's crimes." She walked briskly to the easel, her Mary Janes clicking on the tiles. "Capers and Flick framed Mr. Macon for a long list of crimes."

"You're nuts. It was her," Flick said again, pointing at Capers.

"Dale?" Sal said, and Dale rose.

"This is a Big Picture issue," he said. "It came to me when I was trying to think about science. Look at the Big Picture of what Slate and Marla have been charged with," he told the café. "With killing a man and sending his body floating down the river. Robbing a bank and shooting a guard. Breaking and entering. Kidnapping."

The café nodded. So did Harm and me.

"Now look at the Big Picture pattern in Tupelo Landing. No murder," he said. "But everything else matches.

Bank job, shots fired, breaking and entering, evidence placed in the river."

"So?" Starr said, but he'd opened his clue pad.

"Retro-framing," Dale said. "First they framed Daddy for the crimes here in Tupelo Landing. Then they could retro-frame him for the crimes they already did before. They made the crimes match up. And they used a new given to make the whole thing go. They tried to make it look like Daddy was mastermind of their group."

The café chuckled.

"Retro-framing?" Harm muttered. "Dale, you *are* a genius."

Dale beamed at Sal. "You tell why they did it," he said, and she blushed.

Sal tapped the easel. "To create *reasonable doubt* for her sister, Deputy Marla. Because if there was even a *suspicion* that Macon could have done Deputy Marla's crimes, Marla would get off."

The Colonel poured himself a cup of coffee. "Brilliant plan," he said, studying Capers.

"Flick and Capers even attempted murder," I said, pointing to them. "Once with a slit tire at the racetrack, once with the guard's gun at the bank, once in the fire at Lavender's garage."

"The crimes got bolder and bolder," Harm said. "Adrenaline is an addiction."

"Hold it," Flick said. "I didn't try to kill anybody. This was all Capers."

The café turned toward him.

"She hired me to knock out the guard and make it look like Macon robbed Rose's house. She paid cash—fine. I needed the work. She hired me to rob the church. Fine again, nobody got hurt. *Then* she fired me for trying to join Starr's search, said I was too stupid to ad-lib her jobs. But I didn't try to kill *anybody*. I left the guard's pistol with her. *She* used it to rob that bank."

Gotcha, I thought.

"He's lying," Capers shouted over the hubbub. "*He's* your man, Starr. Who else knows how to slit a tire so it blows after a few laps?"

Flick jumped to his feet, his face red with fury. "Liar. I refused that job. She slit that tire herself. And she called me yesterday, and said if I didn't move the loot from the store to the fish camp, she'd turn me in for stealing all of it. I'm telling the truth. Check with my phone company. You'll see."

I looked at Harm. He winked.

"Flick's telling the truth, for once." I reached into the evidence box. "Here's Attila's hideously ugly turkey earring, stolen from her home and recovered by Dale at the old store."

I reached back into the box and hoisted the collection

plate over my head. "And we found this at the old fish camp, with the rest of the loot."

The café swiveled to Capers, their stares accusing, as Thes walked in and whisked off his cap.

"Sorry I'm late," he said, and Capers sneezed.

I waited for Little Agnes to sneeze. She didn't. Odd. Little Agnes has been faux-catching everything going around. "This woman isn't even really Capers Dylan," I continued. "The *real* Capers Dylan has a cat—and no family. It's in her bio. *This* Capers is allergic to cats and has a sister in Raleigh."

Dale raised his hand. Another brilliant Big Picture connection? Excellent.

"Our head investigator has something important to add," I announced.

"No," he said. "I'm just wondering about that Wolf-Guy we saw Capers with, that night at the inn. How does he fit in?"

I went dizzy. I had no idea how Wolf-Guy fit in.

Dale kills me.

"Actually," Harm said, "I'm glad you brought that up. Wolf-Guy was just a courier. A go-between delivery guy, so Miss Lana wouldn't see letters from the women's prison coming to the inn. The same way Flick gets mail Mom sends to me, so the return address doesn't upset Gramps—who doesn't like Mom singing in Nashville. That night at the inn, I suspect you and Dale heard him refuse to join Capers's spree because it was too dangerous. But that's just a guess."

"Right," Dale said. "That's what I think too. Go ahead, Mo."

"*Wolf-Guy?*" Capers said. "Secret codes translated by little girls in berets? You think *Deputy Marla's* my sister? Please. You have no evidence. This is . . . drivel."

Once again, she stood up. Starr put his hand on his pistol.

We needed that DNA evidence—now.

I looked at Starr. "About the DNA hooking all of this together," I said.

Skeeter cut in. "Mo?" she said, snapping her briefcase open. "I forgot to give you this DNA report." She plucked a folded paper from her briefcase.

What? The DNA report?

My heart turned handsprings.

I unfolded the paper and blinked at the page: Skeeter's geography test on Africa. Over the map, she'd written *DNA REPORT, JUST IN CASE.*

Crud.

"Excellent," I said, trying not to retch. Ad-lib talents, don't fail me now, I thought.

"DNA does not lie," I said. "Footprints may lie. Video can lie, as you'll soon see. DNA does *not* lie. This DNA test report absolutely confirms our theory. Capers Dylan *is* Deputy Marla's sister!"

The crowd gasped.

"So what?" Capers shouted. "Big flipping deal! I have a sister. You people will hear from my attorney. I'm out of here." She grabbed her saddlebag—and again she winced.

Poor, murderous Capers Dylan.

"Let me help you," I said. I reached for the saddlebag, and at the last second swerved to grab her gloved hand. I squeezed—hard.

Capers wailed and doubled over.

"Our final piece of proof," I said. I pointed to Lavender. "What did you hear the night of the fire?"

"The pop of an accelerant, a muffled curse, and light footsteps," he said.

"Capers burned her hands on the accelerant as she set that garage on fire—with Lavender in it. A murder she planned to blame on the brainless Flick Crenshaw."

"Hey," Flick said.

"We have an eyewitness who saw her running from the burning garage, dressed in men's clothes, her long hair stuffed beneath a hat."

"Who?" Dale whispered.

"Your daddy," I whispered back, and he nodded.

Starr took out his handcuffs.

"A murder would not only complete the crime pattern," I said. "But it was *Dale and me* that captured Deputy Marla, and the sisters wanted revenge. Nothing could hurt us more than losing Lavender." I looked around the hushed room. "Dale?" I said. "Take it away."

Dale pointed at Capers. "Book her," he said, and the café cheered.

Chapter 29
Tough Interviews

Joe Starr took Capers and Flick to jail. Everybody else stayed for supper.

Dale set Starr's laptop on the counter and ran his surveillance video for the crowd—twice. "It seems like Daddy," he explained again. "But you never get a real good look at his face. That's Uncle Austin, driving down in his ratty old car and dropping DNA evidence. Daddy put him up to it, to throw Starr off his trail. Same as he sent him to throw out the broke camp stove and his orange prison jumpsuit."

"Enough," Miss Rose said, shutting the laptop. "Go check on your puppies."

"Rose," an Azalea Woman said, "I'd like to order collards and sweet potatoes for this week."

"Sorry," Miss Rose said. "I'm only supplying fine restaurants from now on. You'll have to grow your own."

Grandmother Miss Lacy laughed as Miss Rose strolled away.

A gaggle of dog-lovers followed Dale to the puppies.

He lifted them one by one into waiting arms. Little Ming to Sal. Mary Queen of Scots to Miss Retzyl. King John to Skeeter. Ferdinand I to Susana.

Across the room an Azalea Woman sneezed. Little Agnes didn't. "What's up with Little Agnes?" I whispered to Hannah.

She stepped nearer. "She stopped catching every disease in town when I started reading her your old kiddie books instead of my medical books."

"Thank heavens," Miss Lana murmured.

"I picked a doggy name," Little Agnes told Dale, petting the spotted pup.

"It needs to be a royal name," Dale said, very stern.

She opened her thin arms. "The Little Prince."

"She loves that book," Hannah said. "And it *is* royal."

"She's only five," I added, and Dale sighed. He lowered The Little Prince into her arms and the pup licked her face. Little Agnes giggled. Good match.

"Fifteen minutes with the pups," Dale called, "and then back to Queen Elizabeth."

He scooped up the last fat puppy and cradled him in his arms. Jake and Jimmy tucked in their shirts and stepped forward. Thes stood, his cap in his hands.

Dale gave the Exums a smile. "I'm sorry, Exums," he said, "but coyotes do the toughest interview I've ever seen, and Thes aced it."

He placed the puppy in Thes's arms. "Name?"

"King Solomon," Thes said, his voice quaking. "Thanks, Dale. I'll take good care of him."

"I know you will," Dale said. "I've seen you in action."

Dale smiled easy as rain. "The puppies are all settled. They'll all be safe in this world."

Later that evening, I found Dale in the backyard sitting by the water, the twilight dancing across dark currents. "What you doing?" I asked, settling in next to him.

"Watching the river watch me," he said, pulling his knees to his chin.

Queen Elizabeth stirred in the box beside him, and the puppies muttered and whined. "I want to go see Daddy before he goes to trial," he said. "I want to thank him for the things he taught me, and I want to say goodbye."

He looked at me, his blue eyes serious. "You wanted to get even with him," he said, and I nodded. "I used to think I'd get even with him one day too. But there ain't no getting even, Mo. The only even you ever get is inside yourself—when you don't need to get even anymore."

"Maybe," I said, tossing a rock. "But I still enjoy trying."

"When Daddy goes to court again, I'll testify," he said. "He did a lot of bad. But he watched over Lavender and ran into that fire same as we did." He reached into the box to smooth Queen Elizabeth's ears. "If you don't stand up for the glimmer of good left in somebody, how will it ever be more?" He side-armed a stone across the water. "Rhetorical," he said.

We sat by the river and waited for stars.

A week later I settled down with the *Piggly Wiggly Chronicles*.

Dear Upstream Mother,

    Today Lavender drove Dale, Harm, and me to county lockup to see Mr. Macon, whose trial was this afternoon. He sat in the cafeteria, like always, his face chiseled and hard, his hands folded on the table.

    "Hey Daddy," Dale said, sitting down.

    "Nice outfit," I told Mr. Macon as Harm and me sat down. "Not many people can wear orange good as you."

    "I came to thank you," Dale said.

    Surprise flickered like lightning in Mr. Macon's eyes.

    "I want to thank you for listening to yourself when nobody else did, for risking extra jail time to help Lavender, for watching over him and running into that fire to save him. You could have been long gone instead of sticking with him, and I appreciate that about you." He took a deep breath and looked into his father's eyes. "But if they call my name in court, I'll testify."

I went tense, waiting for him to ask for pre-forgiveness but he surprised me. He stood up. "Good luck to you, Daddy," he said.

Then Dale walked away, calm as strolling into Sunday school. Harm and me hurried to catch up.

We'd just reached the door when Mr. Macon spoke. "Dale," he said. "Stick with Lavender and the Colonel. You might make a decent man."

"Understatement," Harm and I said at the same time, and we headed for Lavender's truck.

Mr. Macon's trial took less than two hours. He got ten years hard time. "You can thank the Desperado Detective Agency for that brief sentence," the judge said. "Without their work, I'd have put you away forever and been glad to see you go."

Mr. Macon turned and gave Dale a quick nod, and walked out the door.

That was that.

Mr. Macon and Lavender.

A glimmer of good in a bad man; a shadow of

bad in a good man. I wonder if there's a whisper
of you in me.

    Love,

    Mo

PS: Harm's hosting a housewarming party for their
upgraded living room next week. Miss Lana says
you should always bring a housewarming gift. I'm
bringing tulips.

PPS: Send us some cases if you got some,
Desperado Detective Agency is open for business.

Acknowledgments

Thank you to the many people who helped create this book.

As always, thanks to Rodney L. Beasley, first reader and fellow traveler, for your love, support, and unerring sense of direction—both in life and in airports. Thanks to my family—Allison & Johnny, Michael & Susan, Lauren & Elvis, Haven & Nick; Karen, Alan, Vivian, Julian and Lillian. Thanks also to my many cousins, especially librarian Mary Jo Floyd.

To my friend and writing teacher, novelist Patsy Baker O'Leary—and to my fellow students in her creative writing seminar at Pitt Community College—thanks for your help! You all are brilliant.

Thanks also to Claire, Mamie, and Catherine.

My gratitude to Eileen LaGreca for the great maps in *all* of the Mo & Dale Mysteries, and for your friendship and support.

Thanks, Gilbert Ford, for the knock-out cover art.

Thanks to Karen T. Boyd of Turnage Boyd Law, PLLC for your ready info and constant support. Thanks also to Stacy Byous of Any Lab Test Now in Charlotte, NC, and to Detective Kenneth Ross of the Pitt County Sheriff's Department. Joe Starr tips his hat to all of you.

Many people at Penguin Young Readers Group and Kathy Dawson Books poured time and talent into this book. Thanks, Don Weisberg, Lauri Hornik, Jasmin Rubero, and Regina Castillo; Doni Kay and the other amazing sales reps; publicists Marisa Russell and Tara Shanahan; school and library wizards Carmela Iaria, Venessa Carson, and Alexis Watts. Thanks also to Dale's friend the intrepid Claire Evans. Mo and Dale say hey!

Thanks to Scottie Bowditch, Laura Antonacci, and Melissa Jeglinski.

To my agent, Margaret Riley King at William Morris Endeavor—thanks for your excitement for this book and those to come.

A special thanks to all the librarians and teachers who have welcomed me into your libraries and schools, and to all of Mo and Dale's reading friends. You amaze me.

Last but certainly not least, thank you to my very talented editor/publisher, Kathy Dawson, for loving Mo and Dale as much as I do. The good folks of Tupelo Landing couldn't live and breathe without you.

Join Mo on the riskest, scariest,
and possibly richest case of her life:
the Case of her Upstream Mother!

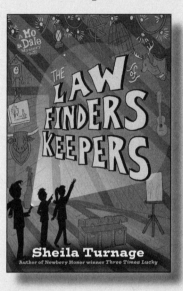

And don't miss out on ANY of
Mo & Dale's adventures!

The Law of
Finders Keepers

Chapter One
The Odds-and-Ends Drawer

The Desperado Detective Agency's biggest case ever crept up on tiny Tupelo Landing in the dead of winter, and kicked off on the rarest of days. Unlike most of our borderline famous cases, it started with two things found.

One thing found by me, Miss Moses LoBeau—ace detective, yellow belt karate student, and a sixth grader in her prime.

One thing found by a stranger.

Before all was said and done, it plunged me and my fellow Desperados—my best friends, Dale Earnhardt Johnson III and Harm Crenshaw, the agency's newest detective—into a blood-thirsty chapter of our town's history, and an unspoken chapter of Harm's past. It put our lives in peril, tested our courage, and sent us racing for treasures of the world and treasures of the heart.

As for me, Mo LoBeau, it bent my rivers and scattered my stars.

As usual, I didn't see it coming.

In fact, I was dead asleep in the wee hours of January 11,

when my vintage phone jangled. I clicked on my Elvis in Vegas lamp. "Desperado Detective Agency, Mo LoBeau speaking. Your disaster is our delight. How may we be of service?"

I squinted at my alarm clock. Five thirty a.m.

The voice came through scratchy and worried. "Mo? It's Thes." Crud. Fellow sixth grader Thessalonian Thompson, a weather freak desperate to take me to a movie.

I yawned. "No movie."

"It's not that, Mo. I'm over you," Thes said. "It's going to SNOW. I'm giving a few special friends a heads-up."

SNOW? We haven't had *real* snow in Tupelo Landing since third grade!

"Really?" I said, kicking off my covers. "Is school out? Is this a snow day?"

"That's the problem. School's *not* out. Miss Retzyl makes that call, and she doesn't know my forecast because she's not answering her phone."

Our teacher, Priscilla Retzyl—tall, willowy, able to do math in her head—is the most normal person in my shy-of-normal life. I adore her. Secretly she likes me too, but ever since she got Caller ID she's been slow to pick up sixth graders' calls.

"Mo, will you go to her house with me?" Thes asked. "I'm an introvert and you're not."

True.

The gardenia outside my window shimmied in the moon-light. *What in the blue blazes?* Dale's face popped into view, his mama's flowered scarf pulled tight over his blond hair and knotted beneath his chin. Not a good look. "Mo," Dale whispered. "Wake up. Thes says it's going to snow."

"I know," I said, tapping on the glass. "Come to the door."

"Which door?" Thes asked.

"Not you," I replied into the phone as Dale crashed to the ground. I made an Executive Decision. "Thes, call Harm. Ask him to meet us at Miss Retzyl's house in twenty minutes for an Ensemble Beg. But you better be right about the snow."

I smoothed my T-shirt and karate pants as I strolled the length of my narrow, window-lined flat. I swung the door open and Dale bolted inside with his mongrel dog, Queen Elizabeth II, at his heels. "Hey," I said. "We got a snow mission. I'll be ready in three shakes."

"Sorry about the gardenia," he said. "I didn't want to knock, and wake up . . . anybody."

Anybody would be Miss Lana, who wakes up slow. Also the Colonel, who's moody thanks to an eleven-year brush with amnesia. The Colonel and Miss Lana are my family of choice and I am theirs. The Colonel saved me from a hurri-cane flood the day I was born. Together, we operate the café at the edge of town.

Dale unzipped his oversized jacket—a castoff from his

daddy, who won't need it for seven to ten years unless he gets time off for good behavior, which he won't. "Hurry, Mo. I'm sweltering to death," Dale said. "Mama made me layover."

"You mean *layer*," I said, sliding my jeans over my karate pants.

Dale, a co-founder of the Desperado Detective Agency, ain't a dead-ahead thinker, but he thinks sideways better than anybody I know.

I pulled on my red sweater and combed my unruly hair. I opened my filing cabinet, shoved aside unanswered Desperado Detective Agency letters, and snagged my orange socks.

"Get gloves too," Dale instructed as someone swished across the living room.

"Morning, Miss Lana," I called. "Dale and Queen Elizabeth are here. Can I borrow some gloves? It's going to snow."

"Snow? Really?" she said, peeking in. Miss Lana, a former child star of the Charleston community theater and a fan of Old Hollywood, gave me a wide, sleepy smile—the real one, not the one she keeps in her pocket for pain-in-the-neck customers at the café. "I love snow!"

She leaned against my doorframe, her *Gone with the Wind* bed jacket over her pink nightgown, her short coppery hair glistening in the lamplight.

"Hey, Miss Lana," Dale said, whipping his mama's flow-ered scarf off his head. "I hope you slept good. The scarf wasn't my idea. Mama said wear it or my ears would freeze off."

Dale's a Mama's Boy from the soles of his red snow boots to his scandalous good hair—a family trait. Because I'm a possible orphan, my family traits remain a mystery.

I tossed Dale my bomber cap and laced my plaid sneakers.

"Help yourself to my gloves, sugar," Miss Lana said. "They're in my odds-and-ends drawer." As she stumbled toward the smell of coffee, we raced to her room. I zipped to the curvy white chest of drawers. Her top drawer erupted in elastic and lace.

"*All* her drawers are odds-and-ends drawers," I muttered, opening them one by one and plucking a pair of blue driving gloves from the bottom drawer.

"Mo!" Miss Lana shrieked from the kitchen. "Don't open my bottom drawer!"

"Too late," I shouted as a note drifted to the floor. *For Mo When She's Ready.*

"Ready for what?" I murmured, uncovering a large white box. I touched a sticky spot where the note used to be as Miss Lana skidded through the door. The Colonel eased in behind her, his bottle-brush gray hair dented on one side, the plaid robe I gave him in first grade cinched at his thin waist.

"What's in here?" I asked, hoisting the box. "Can I open it? I feel ready."

"No," Miss Lana said, grabbing it. She looked at the Colonel and gave him a soft nod. He nodded back. "Tonight, sugar. When we have time to talk," she said, her voice going tinny.

Weird. Miss Lana's a theater professional. Her voice never goes tinny.

"But it has my name on it *now*."

"It's waited almost twelve years," the Colonel said. "It can wait until the end of something as rare as a snow day."

Our snow day!

"Come on," Dale said, pounding for the door.

We grabbed our bikes and blasted down the blacktop, into tiny Tupelo Landing. But with every pump of my pedals, my curiosity tapped at the lid of that mysterious box.

What's *in* it, *in* it, *in* it?

Chapter Two
A Second Thing Found

Dale and me zipped across Miss Retzyl's yard and thundered up the steps to Harm, who sat on the porch rail, one black loafer flat on the floor, the other on the bottom rail. Lately Harm practices looking good sitting on different things, in case the big-haired twins are watching. At nineteen, the twins ain't looking his way.

Harm flipped his scarf over his shoulder and nudged his dark hair from his eyes. "Hey LoBeau," he said, very cool. "What's cooking?"

Dale snickered. "Café humor. Smooth."

"Café humor, *lame*," I said as Thes's dad, a preacher, pulled to the curb in his faded old sedan. Reverend Thompson says if Jesus rode a donkey, he's not driving a new car.

Thes hurried toward us. "What's our plan?" he asked as the porch light clicked on.

"Ad-lib," I whispered.

Miss Retzyl opened the door. "Why are you on my porch?" she asked.

"Because you don't answer your phone," I replied, very

polite. "Thank you for taking our meeting. I'm glad to see you in warm pajamas on a snow day but just between us, I always thought you'd wear a gown. I yield the floor to Thes."

Thes stepped forward. "My forecast today: five inches of snow in Tupelo Landing."

Harm leaned close. He smelled like Old Spice. Lately, he pretends to shave, in case girls like that. "Won't the town's snowplows handle that?" he whispered.

Like I said, Harm's new. The Tupelo Landing learning curve starts at the edge of town. "We don't have a snowplow because it never snows," I said. "Sometimes Tinks Williams cleans a lane with his tractor, but only if he wants to go somewhere."

I smiled at Miss Retzyl. "After declaring an Official Snow Day, please drop by the café for complimentary snow cream. Detective Starr too, if he ain't busy with traffic accidents, which he will be. Nobody in Tupelo Landing can drive in snow, but we still try."

Miss Retzyl's boyfriend, Detective Joe Starr, is the Desperados' main competition. She looked into our first flurry and smiled. "Thanks, Thes. I'll call the mayor and cancel."

"Really?" Harm said. "But it just started. In Greensboro it snowed all the time. We used to . . . Never mind," he added, shoving his hands in his pockets and grinning—a good look.

Not that I care.

"Enjoy your snow day," she said as winter breathed a curtain of snow across the sunrise. "And Mo, tell Lana I'll take her up on that snow cream."

Like I said, secretly Miss Retzyl likes me.